SHAKY CITY WELCOMES THE WORLD

Shaky City Welcomes the World

A NOVEL BY
PETER ADUM

Dedication

To those wonderful people in the historic preservation community. Endangered buildings can't advocate on their own behalf. They require an army of idealistic and persistent humans to champion their cause. Sometimes, even millions of dollars can't force an unnecessary demolition. Occasionally, beauty, fine architecture, and historical significance win the day. But this only happens when good people stand up and say "Hell no!"

Shaky City Welcomes the World

Tuesday
July 17

⬤◆ About a month ago, I started having the same dream every few days. This dream wasn't exactly a nightmare, so I found the ordeal more annoying than troubling. It was like scanning the TV channels and only finding the same one episode of *The Twilight Zone* playing on each and every channel. Come to think of it, that could qualify as a nightmare, having a stone-faced Rod Serling announcing: "Submitted for your approval..." or "Picture if you will..."

Fortunately, this wasn't my dream. I wasn't *that* messed up. Instead, my dream had to do with an event from February 1971. That was more than thirteen years ago, while I was still in high school. After a couple of weeks, this dream started to bug me.

As I researched the matter, I discovered the experts were divided into two opposing groups. One theory claimed my dream didn't matter much; it was just some random brain impulses passing through my unconscious mind. While the other theory declared my dream was meaningful, a sign of deep psychological distress. In other words, the experts either believed my dream was significant, or it didn't mean shit. So much for getting an "expert opinion." I could have just flipped a coin. "Heads it's serious, tails it's not," or "Heads you're sane, tails you're crazy."

Anyway, that evening, I once again reexperienced this dream of mine. Here it is, you can decide for yourself:

I'm asleep in my bedroom in San Pedro, California, and it's six o'clock in the morning. My father was up early, like he always was back then. He realized a light bulb had burned out in the living room's ceiling fixture. So, he decides to replace it. He's up on a chair removing the old bulb, when an earthquake begins to shake our home. Even though my eyes have opened, I'm still half asleep. Now, my dad is practically in the dark, up on a chair, and the whole place is beginning to sway and roll. Fortunately, my dad was a commercial fisherman, so he was used to things swaying and rolling beneath him. But for some reason, he thinks I'm the one causing this shaking, that I'm out of bed and somehow creating this ruckus.

"Niko, what are you doing? Stop it."

"Dad," I yelled. "It's not me, we're having an earthquake."

"I think you're right," he said, quickly stepping down from the chair.

When the shaking finally stopped, my mom and I both joined dad in the living room, where he turned on the TV news. As the reports came in, we learned the earthquake had been centered in the city of Sylmar in the San Fernando Valley, and had registered a 6.5 on the Richter Scale. We discovered sixty-five people had died. Two Hospitals, Olive View, and the Veterans Administration, had been destroyed. Several freeways were also affected, the Golden State, the Antelope Valley, and the Foothill Freeway had roads that collapsed. We also learned that thirty area schools had been damaged, including Richard Henry Dana Junior High, which I'd attended only one year earlier.

This all happened back in 1971, and fortunately, we hadn't experienced another major earthquake since then. But the next big one was inevitable; we just didn't know when.

As I awoke from my dream, the wall calendar reminded me it was still 1984, and not somehow 1971. I noticed it was July 17th and a Tuesday. I realized I had the day off from work. This made me very happy.

Even though it was morning, I could already smell the Korean cooking wafting up from my neighbor's apartment below. I'd lived in Koreatown for five years, and I still hadn't gotten use to all the different smells. For any Korean-American, I'm sure the smells were ordinary. But to my white boy nostrils, the fragrances were exotic and unique. When I first moved here, the area was still known as Wilshire Center, but that began to change as more Korean families moved in. My neighborhood, like the city itself, was always changing and evolving, like a living thing.

Originally, I'd gotten this apartment because it was close to the Fourth Street Studio, where I'd been taking acting classes. Sidney Mordecai, my acting coach, liked my organizational skills a lot more than he liked my acting, so he asked me to be his stage manager for a play he was about to direct. That play got me started, and before long I was a working stage manager. It paid the bills, but I had bigger dreams. My problem was I was almost thirty now, and I decided years ago I would re-evaluate my life when I reached the big "3-0." I guess you could say, I had something of a plan.

While having my coffee, I noticed the *Los Angeles Times* was covered with articles and photographs about the upcoming Olympic Games, which were arriving here in a week. I found this all very exciting, and a once in a lifetime event. Since I had the day off, I thought I would go see the preparations for myself. After finishing a bowl of cereal, I grabbed my silver Raleigh 12-speed bicycle and carried it down to my apartment building's front entrance. My landlord, Mr. Lee, was just coming in and held the door for me. Mr. Lee was a short Korean man with dark hair and eyes. He owned several other apartment buildings in the area and also a liquor store in South Central L. A.

"Hello, Mr. Niko," he said. "You pay rent?"

"Yeah. I gave Mrs. Trask my check." Mrs. Trask was the elderly tenant who acted as his manager. "And my last name's Petrovich, remember? Niko's my first name."

"No problem, Mr. Niko," he said. "You pay rent, no problem."

Mr. Lee wasn't a great landlord, but he wasn't terrible. I remember the first time I met him. He was showing me the one-bedroom apartment he had for rent. I'd been looking for days and hadn't found anything decent I could afford.

As I inspected his empty unit, I noticed the shag carpet was worn, and the ceiling resembled cottage cheese. But the place was clean, and it had a fresh coat of white paint. Out on the small balcony, I could actually see the Hollywood Sign in the distance. From one direction, I heard classical music being played on a piano, and from another direction, I could hear a man singing Italian opera.

"It only $300 a month," said Mr. Lee.

"$300 is more than I can afford."

"It rent control," he sneered. "Rent barely go up."

I knew I could do a lot worse, and probably no better, so I wrote Mr. Lee a check right there on the spot. That was five years ago.

As Mr. Lee now stepped inside, I wheeled the Raleigh to the sidewalk, then looked back at the apartment building. The dingy white stucco resembled frosting on a stale cake. On the building's face, black cursive letters had once spelled out the apartment's name, "Villa Serrano." But somehow the letter "V" had flipped upside down. Now it looked more like "Nilla Serrano," which I thought sounded more like an ice cream flavor at Baskin Robbins.

I hopped on my bike and started the four-and-a-half mile ride to Exposition Park. I'd always been interested in local history, and that only intensified when I moved to Koreatown. I found the city's history so rich I could eat it with a spoon. The more I learned about my new city the more I wanted to learn.

These past few months, I was fortunate to have been a part of the Olympic Arts Festival, which was just now winding down. The festival had been 10-weeks long, with 146 different theater, dance, and music companies, representing 18 different countries.

For my contribution, I stage managed an irreverent film-noir type comedy titled *Sam Sphincter Private Eye Proctologist,* which was set during L.A.'s first Olympics, the 1932 Summer Games. Our play was a crazy mash-up of Raymond Chandler meets Saturday Night Live. It was produced by a local improvisational comedy group called the Drama Geeks.

They'd put out the word they needed a stage manager who was polished and professional. Instead, they decided to hire me. Actually, it was a good match. I brought just enough structure to their zaniness but not enough to stifle their creativity.

This show was so different from my usual stage managing work. After years of working in small 99-seat theaters, I was finally hired at the Mark Taper Forum, the city's main regional theater. Working at the Taper had been my goal since high school. Theater kids in New York dreamed of Broadway; I dreamed of working at the Mark Taper Forum.

A few months ago, I stage managed a play at Taper, Too, the theater's second space. They'd hired Len Sebastian, the famous *Avant Garde* director from New York to come and develop a new play. I'd been warned about how difficult Sebastian could be prior to my accepting the assignment. I'd been told he was egotistical and narcissistic, and those were his good traits. But since I never had problems working with anyone, I agreed to work with him. It turned out to be a truly unpleasant experience, but our little show somehow became a hit, and it was now being considered for a main stage production. Working with Sebastian again wouldn't be much fun, but I could certainly use the money.

The third play I was involved with was an adaptation I'd written myself based on the 1930s novel, *Sonora Town*. The late author, Carlos Cruz, was a long-forgotten L.A. novelist, who'd just recently been rediscovered. I brought the Taper's Literary Cabaret the idea of doing a reader's theater version of Cruz's novel. They liked the book and hired me to write an adaptation for the play. While stage managing at night, I was writing during the day. I'd already finished several screenplays, and just as many stage plays. My rejection letters could have filled a file cabinet. Instead, I just tossed them all into the round file.

I never really set out to be a writer, it just happened, like any natural disaster. Seriously, I wish I'd prepared myself better in school. Instead, I just had to learn by doing.

Now, amazingly, the Taper had produced my first show. The reviews were good, and every performance had sold out. It finally looked like my writing career was moving in the right direction.

∞ ∞ ∞

As I rolled along on my bike, I remembered my ex-girlfriend, Carol, was getting married that Saturday. Carol was six years older than me and already out of school when we first started dating. At that time, she was a promising young architect, while I was still fumbling my way through college. Her blonde hair and shapely figure reminded me of the actress Lee Remick, who had the most amazing blue eyes. We were both deeply in love and thought we'd found our soulmates. Sadly, the relationship didn't last. Maybe it was because of our age difference, or the different places we were in our lives. She was just coming into her own, while I was still a long way from finding myself.

Carol and her fiance, Douglas, worked for the same architectural firm which specialized in historic restorations. I didn't even know Douglas, but he didn't like me for some reason. Carol said he actually took scissors and cut me out of every photograph she had of the two of us together. This really bothered me, because those photos were the only proof of our time together. Without them, it was like our relationship never existed. Maybe that was his plan after all. Carol invited me to have lunch with her one last time before they tied the knot.

As I pedaled my bike through the Pico-Union area, I dropped down to a lower gear for quicker acceleration. When riding through inner-city neighborhoods, you had to keep your eyes and ears open. I'd had several close calls. In fact, I was shot at once on this very block. The shot came from a moving car and shattered the windshield of a parked car that I was passing. That brush with death shook me up at the time, but I quickly got over it.

As I continued down Union Street, I noticed several young Latino men hanging out on a street corner. They all wore white t-shirts and chinos, their arms covered with tattoos. One of them noticed me.

"Hey, man," he shouted, moving toward me. "What time is it?"

"Time for me to get the hell out of here," I answered, quickly speeding away.

Instead of chasing after me, they all busted up laughing. Maybe they thought I was a naïve University of Southern California undergrad who had foolishly wandered away from campus. The fact was, I had gone to USC, but that was six years ago. I was hardly an undergrad anymore.

At Jefferson, I crossed the street and entered the USC campus at Trousdale Parkway. The brightly colored flags and Stars-in-Motion logo of the Olympic Games were everywhere. Besides hosting one of the venues, the school's dorms also served as one of the two Olympic Villages, the UCLA dorms across town being the other.

At Alumni Park, I stopped for a moment to admire the stately Doheny Library, which I'd spent many hours in as a student. I don't know how it happened, but I somehow developed a genuine love of libraries. Not just the Doheny, which was grand and marvelous, but any library, no matter how plain or common. Lately, I'd been spending long hours at the Central Library downtown, a wonderful old building.

Just past the football practice field on McClintock Avenue was the new McDonald's Swim Stadium. The stadium was actually just an Olympic sized pool surrounded by large temporary bleachers, the type they'd set up every year for the Rose Parade. This pool, and the 7–11 Cycling Velodrome at California State Dominguez Hills, were the only two new structures built for these Olympics. All the other events were to be held in existing facilities. These were to be "Spartan Games," privately funded, and financed within a tight budget.

Even the decorations, beautiful as they were, were temporary and ephemeral. Metal scaffolding, that you'd see set up at a construction site, was re-purposed and decorated with bright and colorful fabric. The dominant color was magenta, and the color palate included aqua, yellow, orange, and lavender. In the *Los Angeles Times*, one designer referred to this look as "festive federalism."

Across the street, in Exposition Park, colorful banners flapped in the breeze and brightly colored flags waved. White stars on aqua and yellow bands rimmed the edge of the Los Angeles Memorial Coliseum, adding color to this mostly gray structure. Built in 1923, and later expanded in 1932, to host the Games of the 10th Olympiad, the Memorial Coliseum was once again the centerpiece of these 1984 Olympic Games.

∞ ∞ ∞

After satisfying my Olympic Games curiosity, I started for home. It was lunchtime, so I stopped at Langer's Deli on Seventh and Alvarado and bought a pastrami sandwich and a Coke. MacArthur Park, which was across the street, had become pretty trashy. The area was populated mostly by refugees from South and Central America. The people were poor, and a few of them made money selling illegal drugs. Some of the nearby residents were also addicts, and I'd seen plenty of used hypodermic needles discarded on the park's sidewalk or pathways. The park was also contested turf for some of the city's street gangs, who fought over it nightly. Langer's had recently cut back to only daytime hours to avoid the violence that occurred at night.

I used the pedestrian tunnel and crossed under Wilshire Boulevard to the other half of the divided MacArthur Park. Many years ago, Wilshire Boulevard was lined with the mansions of the rich and powerful. Large, beautiful homes once lined both sides of this wide concourse. Harrison Gray Otis, the influential publisher of the *Los Angeles Times*, had his home, the "Bivouac," right across from the park. In 1916, he donated the home to the city and it became the Otis Art Institute. In the 1950's, his home was torn down and new buildings were constructed for the school.

My friend, Danny Sanchez, had earned a scholarship there in the 1970s. He and a small group of local muralists were recently commissioned by the Olympic Arts Festival to paint murals alongside the area freeways. Danny had his home and studio over in the Angelino Heights section of town, a wonderful old neighborhood of beautifully restored Victorian homes, the last vestige of Victorian Los Angeles.

As I ate my pastrami sandwich there on the grass, I thought back to when I first discovered Carlos Cruz's novel *Sonora Town*. I was attending a lecture at the Central Library, and the speaker was discussing Los Angeles as the topic for literature. He first mentioned several writers I was already familiar with. Then, he mentioned Carlos Cruz's novel *Sonora Town*. I was surprised I'd never heard of the book or its author. Within days, I bought a used copy and brought it here to MacArthur Park to read. The book was a revelation. Cruz's novel portrayed a Los Angeles, once so alive, but now only a faded memory.

After reading *Sonora Town*, I was inspired to submit a proposal to the Mark Taper Forum's Literary Cabaret to honor the late author. This was the cabaret's mission, and to me Cruz was a natural choice. The land the Mark Taper Forum was built on was only blocks from the Sonora Town that Cruz had so eloquently written about.

After I finished my lunch, I headed home on busy Wilshire Boulevard. Office buildings and stores had long ago replaced the mansions. Until recently, the original Brown Derby Restaurant stood right across the street from the Ambassador Hotel. Built in the shape of a derby hat, the Brown Derby was probably the most famous example of programmatic architecture. Now, all that remained of this once famous restaurant was a dirt lot and the decapitated dome of the old derby. The dome was to be incorporated into a new strip-mall. Just what the city needed, another strip mall. Back in 1980, when I first moved to Koreatown, I joined the Los Angeles

Conservancy, a historic preservation group. We waged a campaign to save the Brown Derby, but after a long battle we ultimately lost the war.

Before it was torn down in the 1960s, the Chapman Park Hotel once occupied the entire block just west of the Derby. The hotel served as the women's Olympic Village for the 1932 Olympic Games.

While we were fighting to save The Brown Derby, I was stage managing a play for Sidney Mordecai at the Fourth Street Studio. One day, after rehearsals, Sidney and I took a walk and ended up by the Wiltern Theatre on the corner of Wilshire Boulevard and Western Avenue. Built in 1931, the Wiltern was an Art Deco palace, modeled after Radio City Music Hall in New York. But at that moment, the building was a flurry of activity with construction workers hurriedly removing fixtures and seats from the historic structure. Since I knew the building had been designated as a historical landmark, I immediately called the Conservancy offices and informed them of the situation. The Conservancy's lawyers moved quickly and handed a cease and desist order to the building's owners. Not being able to demolish it as they'd planned, the owners reluctantly agreed to sell. Fortunately, a perfect buyer was found who gladly agreed to renovate and restore the once magnificent structure. My former girlfriend, Carol, and her fiancé, Douglas, were associates of the architectural firm that was supervising the restoration. In the battles over historic preservation, these types of victories are few and far between.

∽ ∽ ∽

Once home, I set my bike aside and grabbed some cold water. A couple of weeks ago, I went to see the movie, *Stop Making Sense,* and afterwards stopped on Melrose to buy a new Talking Heads CD. I haven't stopped playing it, and I wanted to play it right now. I set down my water, and went into the living room. That's when I discovered my CD player was somehow missing. All that remained on that shelf was dust. I quickly realized all of my stereo components were now gone. "Shit!" I shouted. "I've been robbed!" For some reason, my TV had not been taken, and my two large stereo speakers remained there on the floor. Lying beside one of the speakers was the empty CD case for the Talking Heads *Speaking in Tongues,* the album that had been inside the CD player.

For a moment, I just stood there stunned. Then, I began to look to see what else had been taken. In the hall closet, I found my entire set of soft-sided luggage was missing. I figured the burglars could have used those bags to carry out my electronics. I went into my bedroom and glanced over at my small writing desk. My typewriter was gone. "You bastards!" I shouted. That typewriter was probably the one thing I couldn't live without.

Besides anger, I also felt violated and helpless because there was nothing I could do. I didn't even have renter's insurance, so I was completely screwed.

"How dare they come into my home!" I thought. Why didn't they go to Windsor Square or Hancock Park? Those two neighborhoods were only a few blocks away, and the people who lived there had lots of money and good insurance. Hell, even the Chandler family lived there. If the burglars had asked me for help, I would gladly have given them a grand tour of those neighborhoods, pointing out the many fine homes they could have robbed. But no, these idiots chose my little Koreatown apartment instead- the dumb bastards.

After I found their number in the phone book, I called the Los Angeles Police Department's Wilshire Division. They said they'd send some officers to take a report. While I waited, I decided to ask my neighbors if they had seen or heard anything. I knocked on the Cho family's door across the hall. The Cho's were a young family visiting from South Korea. Sung-ho, the father, was here attending a graduate program at UCLA. When I told him about the burglary, he admitted he hadn't seen or heard anything. His young wife, Hyun-sook, joined him at the door. The Cho family spoke good English and were always friendly. That wasn't the case with most of my other Korean neighbors, who tended to keep to themselves. Hyun-sook was also an excellent cook, and she'd often bring over plates of delicious Korean food. Their children, Min-ho, the boy, and Eun-ju, the girl, were funny, well-behaved kids.

Vidor, a black male about my age, lived in the apartment directly below the Cho family. Vidor was born in Panama but lived for most of his life in New York City. He was gay and wildly flamboyant. When Vidor spoke, he used grand gestures like a silent movie star. His mother named him Vidor after the great film director King Vidor. Vidor once told me his mother was white and Hungarian, while his father, whom he hardly knew, was black and Panamanian. Vidor's accent was a unique combination of Hungarian and Spanish.

"My father," Vidor would say, "was a black bastard who screwed my mother and then left."

Vidor was the neighbor who played classical music on his piano. He was funny, and I always enjoyed talking to him.

"Niko, my friend," he smiled. "How are you?"

"Not so good, Vidor," I said. "Someone broke into my apartment."

"Oh, how terrible. Did they take anything?"

"Yeah, quite a bit."

"Probably heroin addicts," he raged. "Those hoodlums would steal from their own mothers."

"You're probably right."

"If the police gave these criminals free heroin, the burglaries would stop just like that," he snapped his fingers.

Somehow, I didn't see the LAPD providing junkies with free drugs. They'd much rather allow them to steal our things, then try to arrest them afterwards. Job security, I assumed.

"Did you see anything unusual this morning?" I asked.

"Oh my God," he realized. "I think I did."

"What did you see?"

"There were three men in the building. But I figured they were here to take someone to the airport."

"Why the airport?"

"They had suitcases," he said, frowning. "But you should have seen their bags, old and cheap," he cringed. "No sense of style or flair."

"Those suitcases were mine," I said, "and they probably had all my electronics inside."

"Niko, I'm so sorry," he said. "I must sound like a bitchier version of Mr. Blackwell, if such a thing is possible."

"What did these three guys look like?"

Vidor thought for a moment. "One was white, one was an Asian, and one was black."

"Well," I said. "At least it was a diverse group of burglars."

Vidor laughed.

"The worst part about it is they took my typewriter. I've been trying to do some writing."

Vidor thought for a moment. "Wait here," he said, then headed back into his apartment.

I peeked into his apartment and noticed his baby grand piano sitting in the center of his living room. Vidor returned carrying a portable typewriter in its case.

"Here," he said, handing it to me. "Now, you have no excuse not to write."

"Are you serious?"

"Keep it as long as you like."

"Thanks, Vidor." I said, accepting the typewriter.

"You're welcome," he smiled. "Now go and write a great soup opera or something."

"I think you mean, a soap opera."

"Yes, soap opera, soup opera, what's the difference? Just go write something good."

∞ ∞ ∞

Vidor's typewriter was an electric Smith Corona, and it looked great sitting there on my desk. I plugged it in and it gave off a gentle hum. Just as I was rolling in a sheet of paper, the doorbell rang.

When I opened the door, I wasn't surprised to find two uniformed police officers, but I was surprised one of them was my old friend from high school, Randy Ferlinghetti.

"Oh, shit," Randy said, smiling broadly. "Niko fucking Petrovich."

Randy's crew cut had replaced his long brown hair, making him look quite different. But his squinting blue eyes looked exactly the same.

"Hi Randy," I said, shaking my head. "I can't believe you're a cop."

Randy and I lost touch over the years. I'd gone off to college, and he stayed in town. Back in high school, Randy was a lot of fun. But he was always getting himself into trouble. If anything was ever found missing, Randy was always the main suspect, and usually the actual culprit. He also liked to pull pranks to get attention. He once organized a nude streaking of our girl's Catholic high school. Those girls got an eye-full. I'm sure Randy had some sort of criminal record by now, so I had no idea how he was able to become a police officer. His brother-in-law Matt was also in the LAPD, and I'd heard he'd recently become a commander.

"This is Officer Watkins," Randy said, pointing to the black officer standing beside him.

"Hi," I said, shaking Officer Watkins's hand.

"Man," Watkins said, referring to Randy. "You know this fool?"

"Yeah," I said, "from high school. He was always a little crazy."

"Niko," Randy said. "I'm a good Pedro boy, so why do they give me a spook for a partner?"

"Who you calling a spook, asshole?" Watkins asked, glaring at Randy.

I explained to both of them what had happened and exactly what was missing. Officer Watkins examined the living room, while I showed Randy the bedroom. Randy immediately noticed the typewriter on my desk.

"I thought you said they stole your typewriter?" he asked.

"They did," I said. "My gay neighbor downstairs lent me this one."

Randy's eyebrows raised as he gave me a strange look.

"Oh, I understand," he said. "You start doing theater, and the next thing you know, you become a homo."

"Very funny."

"No, I get it," he smiled. "Dump the bitch, make the switch."

"Your partner is right," I said. "You are an asshole."

"This fag does you a favor," he said, wrapping his hand around an imaginary penis that he brings to his mouth, "and you do him a sexual favor." He pretends to put the imaginary penis into his mouth, pushing his tongue against the inside of his cheek.

"You do that well." I said. "Obviously, you've had some practice."

"How do you think I got this job?" he laughed.

The three of us sat at the kitchen table while they completed their paperwork. I told them about the three men Vidor had seen leaving.

"How did you ever become a cop?" I asked Randy.

"My brother-in-law, Matt, helped me out," he said. "Most of the things I'd gotten busted for were when I was still a minor."

"So, they weren't on your adult record?"

"That's right."

"How about your drug use?"

"I just told them I never used drugs."

Randy was a year behind me in high school, but I'd heard during his senior year, he'd gotten involved with all types of drugs. His grades suffered, and for the first time in school, he didn't do well.

"So," I asked, "you lied?"

"Niko," Randy frowned. "You're such a boy scout."

Randy went on to tell me about some of his experiences on the streets. Some of his stories were funny, while others were violent and dangerous. Seeing Randy now made me realize I'd actually missed having him around. He was fun, impulsive, and completely unpredictable. We exchanged phone numbers and said we'd try to get together.

∽ ∽ ∽

Jules Herbert and his wife Betty Gidman owned a single-family home directly behind my apartment on Oxford Avenue. Jules was about forty, with red hair, and a well-manicured mustache. I'd met him early on when he was walking his two rottweilers, Mimi and Rudolfo, on Fourth Street. For some reason, our personalities just clicked, and we became friends. I also learned Jules was the person I'd heard singing Italian opera.

Jules' family was originally from France, but they eventually came over and settled in Philadelphia where he trained to be an opera singer. He imagined himself becoming the next Pavarotti, but that never happened.

He took his small inheritance and moved to Los Angeles where he bought the home on Oxford, then leased a small building in Larchmont Village, where he opened a French restaurant he called Le Petit Mustache. He met Betty, who was blonde and about his same age, when she applied for a waitress job. Betty was an aspiring actress who'd done some plays and had a few small roles on TV. Jules liked her immediately and hired her. They quickly began seeing each other, and just a year later, they got married. They were a great couple, and seemed very much in love. Jules had hoped for a partner to help him run the restaurant, but Betty was far more interested in her acting career. She worked at the restaurant only when it suited her, and as time went on, it rarely suited her.

One evening, Jules was there at his restaurant, being the gracious host, when he began to softly sing "Nessun Dorma" from the opera *Turandot* by Puccini. At first, he was just singing it to himself, but then he slowly raised his voice and began singing out loud. Although still no Pavarotti, Jules mesmerized the crowd with his strong operatic voice. After he finished the aria, the crowd gave him a standing ovation. He's been singing in the restaurant ever since. He also enlisted his opera friends, who now came to sing for their supper. The food at Le Petit Mustache was good, but the opera was magnificent. I went there for the French Onion Soup and French bread. Sometimes Jules would drop off a French pastry to my table.

After the police left my apartment, I went over to Jules's and Betty's home and told them all about the burglary. We sat outside on their small patio with my apartment's balcony visible just over the fence.

"That's too bad," said Betty. "I hope the police catch them."

"That's why we have two dogs," said Jules. "They're our security system, and they're trained to go for the crotch."

"The burglars would arrive here as baritones," said Betty, "and leave as sopranos."

"That would serve them right," I said.

"It wouldn't be the end of the world for them," said Jules. "They could always sing with the Vienna Boys Choir."

I liked the image of the burglars reduced to singing in a boys' choir.

"I'm going to the gym," said Betty, getting up from her chair. "I'll see you at the restaurant."

"See you there," said Jules, watching her go with a suspicious glare.

Betty had recently gone on a diet, joined a gym, and dropped a few pounds. She even went out and bought a whole new wardrobe. Betty, now, always seemed to have a smile on her face. Jules, for some reason, seemed to be smiling less.

❧ ❧ ❧

After one of the first performances of *Sonora Town*, I was approached by a literary agent named Natalie Slesinger. Natalie liked my play and told me she might be able to "market me." She recently asked me for a few copies of *Sonora*

Town, so she could send them around to various theaters. The place where I usually had copies made was called Charlie Chan's Printing. It was in an old converted house on Wilshire Boulevard near Wilton. The house had once belonged to Academy Award winning film director Frank Borzage, a veteran of more than a hundred Hollywood movies.

I liked the name Charlie Chan's Printing even though I wasn't a big fan of the old Charlie Chan detective films. I never understood why a white actor always played the title role. It didn't seem fair to the Asian actors, since any one of them could have done a better job.

While I was placing my order for copies of *Sonora Town,* I could hear the conversation going on at the next cash register between the Asian clerk and a customer.

"I can't wait that long," the customer complained. "I need it today."

"Sir, this is a very large order," the clerk said. "It'll take some time."

"That's completely unacceptable," he said. "I need it now."

"I'm sorry," said the clerk. "But that's the best we can do."

For a moment they were at a standoff, then the customer finally spoke.

"Look, I happen to know Mr. Chan, the owner, and I've seen all of his movies."

Everyone in the shop stopped to listen to their conversation.

"You and Charlie Chan are friends?" asked the clerk, with a broad smile.

"Yes," he said. "And I've seen all of his films."

It was obvious to everyone this guy was full of shit.

"Sir," said the clerk. "My father, Charlie Chan, owns this printing business and he's never been an actor, and he has no relation to the fictional movie character who goes around quoting Confucius, the Chinese philosopher."

I suddenly felt compelled to quote some fake Confucius myself. I guess I was just another white guy trying to play Charlie Chan. I turned to the customer and managed to get his attention.

"Confucius say, man who farts in church, sits in his own pew."

After a moment, the man grabbed his papers and stomped out.

໐ ໐ ໐

On Ingraham Street, directly behind Charlie Chan's printing was another old house that had also been converted into a business. For the last sixty years, this old craftsman bungalow had served as the Hartgrove Photography Studio. Over the years, many fledgling companies had hired Beryl Hartgrove to document their growth as they grew from small companies into major corporations. Beryl, sometimes known as B. K., was probably the best-known commercial photographer in the city and one of the very few women in the business. Her photographs had documented almost everything that occurred in our region over the last six decades. She had also been the official photographer for the 1932 Los Angeles Olympics, and with the 1984 Games arriving next week, her old images were once again in demand.

Beryl was a cranky old gal, and a heavy smoker. She had a deep, husky voice, which over the phone could easily be mistaken for a male voice. She used that misconception, and her initials', B. K., so that prospective clients wouldn't discriminate against her for being a female. As a young woman, Beryl had been married twice, but neither marriage lasted very long, or produced any children. Since then, Beryl told me, she'd been married to her work.

Beryl didn't like many people, but for some reason, she liked me. She also provided me with some great photos for the slideshow introduction to my play *Sonora Town*. The other photo archives in town asked exorbitant fees to use their pictures, but Beryl's fees had been reasonable. Before each performance of the play, her images of 1930s L. A. were shown to the audience, accompanied by a melancholy clarinet. That introduction helped transport the audience back to that era, setting the mood for the play they were about to see. I hadn't spoken to Beryl since the play opened, and I'd never properly thanked her for her contributions. This would be a good time to finally do that.

When I pulled my bike up to her studio, I noticed the front door was boarded up and there was a handmade sign, which read "Out of business." On the front lawn, there was another sign, which read "Nina Levenson Estate Sales." A date and time were listed for the sale. Nina Levenson was the wife of Sidney Mordecai, my acting coach. Nina had once been an accomplished actress, but now she made her living organizing estate sales. She catered to the Windsor Square and Hancock Park neighborhoods where they lived.

I was concerned about my friend, Beryl, but I was also concerned about her photo collection, which I considered an irreplaceable archive of the city's history.

I rode my bicycle west on Wilshire to Irving Street. Sidney and Nina purchased their 1923 Mediterranean style home as a fixer-upper back in the 1970s. For a very short time, Windsor Square and Hancock Park had become a bargain. The original families were dying off, and the prospective home buyers saw these aging homes as passé and antiquated. Anyone with real money wanted to live in Beverly Hills and Bel Aire. The lack of buyers made these wonderful old homes suddenly affordable. That's when Sidney and Nina pooled their resources and bought their home.

In the late 1940s, wealthy oil baron, J. Paul Getty, purchased this entire block with the purpose of demolishing everything and building an office complex. If the nearby homeowners hadn't protested so vigorously, he would have gotten his way. As it was, he was still able to tear down the one house facing Wilshire on Irving. That house had been the actual movie location of Norma Desmond's Renaissance-style mansion in the film *Sunset Boulevard*. In 1957, the house was torn down to make way for Getty's white marble office building that housed his oil company, Tidewater Petroleum.

I pulled into Sidney and Nina's driveway and stopped at the home's service entrance. Sidney Mordecai answered the door. The dried paint spots on his shirt told me he'd been doing some house painting. Sidney was a handsome man of about fifty, with a stock of dark hair that was graying at the temples. He wore horn rim glasses, which gave him a professorial air.

"Hello, Niko," Sidney said. "We weren't expecting you."

"Sorry, Sid." I said. "Is this a bad time?"

"Who the hell is it?" shouted a female voice from inside the house. "It's not one of your goddamn children, is it?"

"No, Nina," Sid shouted back. "It's Niko Petrovich."

"Oh," she said, calmly. "What does he want?"

Sidney looked at me, waiting for my answer.

"Nina is doing an estate sale. I have some questions about it."

"The photographer?" asked Sidney.

"Yeah."

Sidney turned back toward the inside of his home. "Your estate sale," Sid yelled. "Niko's here because of your estate sale."

"Well, bring him inside," Nina shouted. "Don't leave him there like some fucking delivery man."

"Come on in," he offered, sheepishly.

I stepped into the small entry way. To my right was a tiny bedroom that had once been considered the maid's quarters. Straight ahead was a small bathroom, and to our left, the newly remodeled kitchen, which we then stepped into.

"Everything looks great," I said, admiring the care that had gone into their renovation.

"Thanks. We're pleased with how well everything has turned out."

As a young man, Sidney had been a working Broadway stage actor with some early success. After things dried up for him, he moved to Los Angeles where he appeared in a number of guest rolls in various television series. He never got that one TV series or movie that would have made him a household name. Sid was a wonderful acting coach though, maybe not a Stella Adler or a Lee Strasburg, but extremely well respected. Gordon Davidson, the Taper's artistic director, often spoke highly of Sid, and was always trying to find something for him to direct.

"I'll get you a paint brush," Sidney smiled. "You can help."

"Sure, Sid," I replied, smiling. "What are you two working on now?"

"The sitting room."

Sidney led me into the home's main entryway. We passed the formal dining room on our left, and the grand staircase to our right. The living room was just past that. Since I'd last seen the living room, it's restoration had been completed and it was also newly furnished. Many of the furniture pieces, artwork, and rugs had been acquired by Nina through her estate sale business. She always managed to keep the finest pieces for herself.

Just past the living room was the home's sitting room. Tarps were spread out and a step ladder was set up. Nina Levenson stood in the center of the room. Like Sidney, she was also dressed for painting. A scarf covered her sandy colored hair, which she wore short. Nina was small in size but fierce in nature. Where Sidney was calm and measured, Nina was quick-tempered and volatile. This was the second marriage for both, and they each had two grown children from their first marriages.

"Well, hi, Niko," she said, warmly.

"Hi, Nina," I said. "The kitchen and the living room both look great."

"Thank you," she smiled. "We just booted both of Sidney's kids today. I thought maybe it was one of them at the door, pleading to be allowed back in."

"David and Debra?" I asked, surprised to hear the news.

"Yes," she said. "David admitted to us that he was queer. Do you believe that, a goddamn faggot?"

"Gay is what he called himself," said Sidney. "I believe that's the term he used."

"I don't give a shit," she shouted. "I don't care if he's calling himself Queen fucking Elizabeth."

"So, Debra's gone too?" I asked.

"Yes," she said. "Today was her eighteenth birthday. I told the little bird it was time to leave the nest."

"Some birthday present," said Sid, under his breath.

"Did you say something, Sidney?" she asked, threateningly. "You weren't complaining, were you?"

"I didn't think your timing was very good."

"Who cares about my timing?" she said. "They're both so spoiled."

"But on her eighteenth birthday?" he asked. "It couldn't have waited?"

"Why? So, she can make you feel sorry for her?"

"Feel sorry for her?" he replied. "It's her birthday."

"So, buy her a fucking cake."

Sidney just shook his head in disgust. Nina looked over to me.

"I told little Miss Debra it was time for her to fly on her own. I left home when I was eighteen, and she could do the same. She's a big girl now."

Nina had always been a doting mother to her own two children, but to Sidney's children she was awful. She was a true evil stepmother. The kind everyone assumed was just a myth. Nina was no myth. What saddened me, was how Sidney seemed to put up with it. When I worked with him as a director, he was completely in charge of everything and totally in command, but with Nina, not so much.

"Your estate sale sign was posted at Hartgrove's Studio." I said. "What happened to Beryl?"

"She had a stroke about a week ago," she replied. "She's at Cedars-Sinai, and from what I hear, she's doing better. Her sister's family is selling the house and everything in it to pay for her medical bills."

"What about her photo collection?" I asked.

"I'll be selling that too," she said.

Nina always tried to get the most money for her clients, and of course, a healthy commission for herself. She'd recently acquired her real estate license, which also allowed her to sell her clients' homes as well.

"Why are you interested?" she asked, smiling. "You have a million dollars lying around?"

"No, of course not. I'm just concerned about Beryl and her photographs."

Nina looked at me for a moment, then she set her paint scraper on the stepladder.

"Have you ever been upstairs?" she asked.

"No," I replied.

"Sidney," she said. "I'll be right back; I'm going to show Niko something."

Nina motioned for me to follow her as she led me back out to the main entry way and up the grand staircase.

"Did you know this house was built during prohibition?" she asked.

"Yes. Sid told me it was built in 1923."

"That's right and Prohibition had started in 1920."

We stopped at the first door at the top of the stairs.

"What do you think this room might be?" she asked, with a grin.

At first, I thought it was a silly question because it had to be a bedroom. But then I realized a bedroom was too obvious of an answer.

"I don't know," I admitted. "Maybe it's a library or a den."

"No," she said, opening the door and inviting me inside.

To my surprise, the room was a completely preserved 1920s home bar, with the look and feel of a speakeasy. Everything seemed to be from that era. On the far wall, long curtains were parted to reveal French doors that opened onto a large balcony.

"So, this is how they partied back in the 1920s," I said. "It's wonderful."

"During that time, the home was owned by a silent movie star. That era was nothing but drinking and debauchery. They never had to learn any lines, so they would party all night. When talking pictures arrived, it changed everything. Actors had to go home and learn their lines for the next day's shooting. For the most part, the fun was over."

She stepped over to what looked like a large cabinet with two doors.

"Look at this," she said, swinging the doors wide open.

Inside was a closet sized room with a narrow staircase that led down.

"What's this?" I asked.

"An escape route. In case the police ever raided the place. As you know, alcohol was illegal during Prohibition. Each home in this neighborhood had something similar."

"So, Prohibition didn't really apply to rich people."

"F. Scott Fitzgerald was around here during that time, and always said: 'The rich are different from you and me.'"

"Yeah," I said. "For one thing, they always have escape routes."

ↂ ↂ ↂ

Nina wouldn't share her plan for selling Beryl's photographs, and that worried me. I knew I needed to visit Beryl at the hospital. Hopefully, she was well enough to see visitors. I made it to Cedars-Sinai in only a few minutes. On the border of Beverly Hills, Cedars had an excellent reputation as a hospital. Although, I'd once heard someone run off a long list of all the famous people who'd croaked there, like the closing credits at the end of a movie. "It's a great hospital," he boasted. "Even Jack Warner died there." I thought that was a strange testimonial for a hospital.

After I got Beryl's room number, I took the elevator up to the third floor. When I got to her room, she was sitting up in bed reading a newspaper. Her gray, pageboy hairdo needed combing. When she saw me, her blue eyes brightened behind her thick reading glasses.

"Well, look what the cat dragged in," said Beryl, putting down her newspaper and removing her glasses. I noticed she still had her large emerald ring on her finger. I assumed the hospital would have asked her to remove her jewelry, but nobody makes Beryl do anything she doesn't want to do.

"Hi, Beryl," I said. "You look pretty good for a gal who just had a stroke."

"I'm doing better," she said. "As long as they're not pulling a sheet over my head, I'm okay."

Beryl never had the sunniest disposition. She loved her cats, but she could be ornery with people. A Los Angeles native, Beryl grew up in the area just south of USC, where she eventually attended college. Back then, the area was a white, working-class neighborhood; this changed over time. When Beryl started her photography studio, the university became one of her first clients. She told me it was only because they could get away with paying a woman less than a man. But that opportunity got her on her feet. Her fledgling studio was well situated to take advantage of the region's dramatic population growth, and the business boom of the 1920s.

"I saw your boarded up studio," I said, "and I was worried about you."

"My sister is 'helping me' get rid of things," she sighed.

Beryl said "helping" as if that was the last thing her sister was doing.

"I know the woman running the estate sale," I said. "She'll make sure you get top dollar."

"That's all my sister cares about," she complained. "I wish she cared more about preserving my photos."

Beryl had shared many of those photographs with me during my visits. She was meticulous, and kept everything stored in a huge vault, which she'd rescued from a failed bank during the depression. Her photographs spanned the early 1920s all the way until today. Beryl had shown me pictures of the construction of L.A.'s City Hall, DC3 airplanes rolling off the assembly line in Santa Monica, and the Griffith Park Observatory taking shape up on its hilltop. Almost everything that occurred during those years was documented in her collection.

"What's going to happen to all your photos?" I asked.

"I don't know," she said. "But I'd really like the pictures to remain together."

I remembered some of the great pictures she'd shown me from the 1932 L. A. Olympics. "How did you ever get to photograph the '32 Olympic Games?" I asked.

"I was working for Billy Garland at the time doing commercial photography. Garland made his money in real estate, just like Harry Chandler. That's why the two became such good business partners. It made sense for Billy to have me photograph the Olympics, along with everything else I was photographing for him."

Billy Garland was head of L.A.'s Olympic Committee and the driving force behind bringing the 1932 Games to Los Angeles. Harry Chandler was the publisher of the *Los Angeles Times*, having taken over from his father-in-law, Harrison Gray Otis. Chandler was probably the largest land owner in the region, but his wheeling and dealing remained secretive. No one really knew just how much of the area he actually owned. During the 1920s, men like Garland and Chandler built an astonishing 32,000 new subdivisions. The two men were also the main proponents for bringing the Olympics to Los Angeles. Chandler's motto was: "Sell the sunshine."

"You took some wonderful pictures of those Games," I said.

"Maybe you're referring to those photos at the Olympic Swim Stadium," she smiled, adjusting the emerald ring on her finger. "Those young women were very special."

"Oh, yeah?" I asked. "Bathing beauties?"

"No," she corrected me. "They were athletes first, they just happened to also be attractive. Those Olympics were really the first time women were given a chance to prove themselves, and prove themselves they did."

I really didn't know that much about the athletic competition during the 1932 Olympics. It was so long ago, the fifty-two years seemed more like a hundred.

"It sounds like the women did well?" I asked.

"Before those 1932 Olympics, most sportswriters didn't even believe women belonged in competitive sports. One year earlier, there was serious talk of ending women's participation in the Olympics altogether. Fortunately, that didn't happen, and after they proved their worth, the sportswriters changed their tune. It became a brave new world."

I knew that the female Olympians stayed at the Chapman Park Hotel on Wilshire, but not much else.

"Who was their big star?" I asked.

"Babe Didrikson was the best known, and she was fun to cover because she never stopped telling everybody how good she was. She was cocky and self-assured. The press loved her, but her competition not so much."

"She sounds like a female Mohamed Ali."

"The sportswriters invited her to a round of golf at the Brentwood Country Club, knowing she'd only played golf a couple of times. But she played just as well as they did earning even more of their respect. She eventually became a professional golfer, the greatest female golfer of her era."

"Huh," I replied, amazed at how little I knew.

Beryl and I talked about the need to preserve her photographs, and how we could keep the collection intact. We knew her sister wouldn't be much help because she was mostly concerned with making Beryl some money. Even though I already had a lot on my plate, I agreed to help Beryl. I told her I'd be back soon, and we'd continue our conversation.

കൗ കൗ കൗ

While riding back to Koreatown, I tried to think of a solution to Beryl's problem, but nothing came to mind. Her sister wanted to make all the money she could, and Nina Levenson was ready to help. Working together, I was hoping Beryl and I could come up with a way to preserve her photo collection. It would be a shame if the collection was broken up and sold off in pieces to private collectors.

Once in my apartment, I noticed the flashing red light on my answering machine. I played the new message:

"Hi Niko. This is Tom Williams. I just wanted to remind you we have a basketball game tonight, seven o'clock at the Echo Park Recreation Center. If you could remind your friend, Hank Pilsner, that would be great. Oh, and you said you might have another player in mind. We're a little thin at the moment, so bring him tonight if you can. See you then."

Tom was the Taper's production manager and my boss. He was also the captain of the

Taper's basketball team. Tom didn't know it, but the player I was hoping to bring to tonight's game wasn't a "him," the player was a "her," and if she came, she would easily be the best player on the court.

I called my friend, Hank Pilsner, but I was only able to leave him a message. Like Randy Ferlinghetti, I'd known Hank since high school, and we'd played a lot of basketball together over the years. Although Hank looked more like a football player, he was a surprisingly good at basketball. We also enjoyed watching sports together, and were fans of all the local teams.

As baseball fans, we even shared part of a Dodger season ticket package, and because of the Olympics, we'd received tickets for the Olympic baseball games, which were to be played at Dodger Stadium.

Hank worked as an auto transport driver for Tinsel Town Picture Vehicles, which provided unique cars for television shows and movies. He'd gotten this job through another old friend, Jake Polanski, who managed the large fleet of vehicles for the company's owner. Once Hank trucked the vehicles to the filming locations, he could just sit around and enjoy the catered meals and small talk. When the filming was completed, Hank would load the vehicles back onto his truck and return them to the storage yard. While sitting around with the cast and crew, Hank often scored cocaine. Always a big drinker, cocaine now seemed to dominate his life. The entire entertainment community seemed to be under its powdery spell. Fortunately for me, I couldn't afford a cocaine habit, the benefits of being poor.

The player I was hoping to bring to tonight's basketball game was our friend Bobby Jefferson's sister, Wanda. Wanda was an unbelievably good player. She was black, six feet tall, and as fast as a jungle cat. She'd been too young to compete in the 1976 Summer Games in Montreal, the first Olympics that included women's basketball. But a few years later, Wanda was a college All American and destined to be the star on the 1980 USA women's basketball team. Unfortunately for her, the United States boycotted the Moscow games, and Wanda lost her opportunity to play.

Thankfully, a new women's basketball league, the WPBL was formed, and they invited Wanda to join. She played a year for the team in Dallas before the whole league suddenly folded. Since then, she's been playing professionally in Europe. With her season now over, Wanda returned home to support her brother Bobby who was coaching some of the female sprinters on the U.S. Olympic track team.

I played quite a few pick-up basketball games with Wanda and Bobby. Whenever Wanda challenged either of us to a one-on-one game she would easily kick our butts. Sometimes, she'd bet us our basketball shoes she could beat us, and of course she'd always win. More than once, Bobby and I had to walk home in our socks.

In college, Wanda was so much fun to watch, and the first woman I'd ever seen dunk a basketball. She was a little bit like Cheryl Miller over at USC, who was now the star of women's basketball and the leader of the 1984 USA Olympic Team. But Wanda was pretty amazing too, she was Cheryl Miller before there was a Cheryl Miller.

"Sure, Niko, why not," Wanda told me over the phone.

"Great," I replied. "I was hoping you'd want to play."

"A girl's gotta stay in shape," she laughed. "I just can't sit around eating jelly donuts."

"Speaking of jelly donuts, do you remember Hank Pilsner?"

"You mean, 'the round mound of rebound?' Is he still playing?"

"Yeah, and he's on our team."

"Good. He could really post up, and he also had a mean jump shot."

"He's still got it, and he'll be happy to see you."

"I'll be there," she said, taking down the information.

Wanda told me she was staying in West Hollywood with one of her former WPBL teammates. I wondered if she was a girlfriend or just a friend.

I told Wanda to say hi to her father, Solomon, whom I'd known for years.

Before I headed over to Echo Park, I stopped at the Shell station to get some gas. My olive-green, 1967 Pontiac Firebird was always thirsty. Having grown up in the California car culture of the 1960s and 1970s, I was still trapped in the past. I couldn't get these old muscle cars out of my system. But because of the gas crisis of the mid '70s, and the current high gas prices, these cars weren't as popular as they once were. In fact, I'd picked mine up cheap. While driving up Western Avenue, Steely Dan's song, "Babylon Sisters," played over my stereo.

Hank Pilsner and I arrived at the Echo Park Recreation Center at about the same time. We were both wearing our team's black jersey with the graphic of "El Pachuco," from the play *Zoot Suit,* which had premiered at the Taper just a few years earlier. I told Hank that Wanda Jefferson was going to be joining us.

"Wanda Woman," he smiled, referring to the DC comic book superhero.

"She is that," I agreed.

Tom Williams, my boss, showed up with Richard DeVries, the Taper's literary manager. Richard had also been the producer of my *Sonora*

Town play. During our final rehearsal, he asked me to make some last-minute changes to the play's script. I didn't like the changes and decided not to make them. I thought his suggestions would only hurt the play. Richard disagreed with me, and ordered me to make the changes anyway. During the opening night performance he noticed I hadn't followed through with his orders. He didn't say anything to me, but I could tell he was pissed. I had no regrets though because I was the one who'd discovered Carlos Cruz's novel, pitched the original idea, and wrote the adaptation. In the theater, a playwright always has the last word. Anyway, that's the way it was supposed to be.

"So, where's this new player?" Tom asked, with Richard standing nearby.

"She'll be here," I said.

"She?" asked Tom and Richard at the exact same moment.

"Don't worry," said Hank, who'd also been listening. "She'd kick both of your asses without even breaking a sweat."

Just then, Wanda Jefferson made her entrance into the gym. She wore her old WPBL warm-up outfit, with the team name, the Dallas Diamonds, embossed across the front. She held her gym bag in one hand and dribbled a basketball in the other. She strutted in like the pro that she was, cocky and self-assured. A few players on the opposite team noticed her and pointed. I waved to Wanda and she came right over, a big smile on her face.

"Niko," she shouted, tossing me the basketball.

"Wanda, you're here," I said, catching the ball with both hands.

Hank came over to greet her. "What's up, Wanda?" he asked.

"Pilsner," she shouted, giving him a high five. "Every time I say your name, I want a cold one."

"Afterwards, I'm buying," he offered.

"Deal," she replied, sliding her gym bag under our team's bench.

I introduced Wanda to Tom and Richard, and they spoke briefly. Tom handed her a black *Zoot Suit* jersey, which she slipped on over her t-shirt.

While we tossed the ball around to loosen up, Daryl, a stage carpenter, and Martin, a scenic artist also showed up and joined in. While everyone was warming up, Richard pulled me aside to talk.

"Your *Sonora Town* play did pretty well," he admitted. "How would you like to write another play for the Literary Cabaret, maybe based on Cruz's other novel, *Edendale*?

"That would be great," I said.

"If you can get your adaptation done, we can cast it, and then go into rehearsals right after the Olympics. We could even make it the first show for next season."

"I'll get right on it."

"You'll have to talk to Carlos' widow," he said. "We'll need her permission again."

"I can do that," I said, knowing that would mean a trip up to Pasadena.

After the warm-ups, Tom gathered us at one end of the gym. The opposing team looked to be a group of young Latino players. A few of them made positive comments about our *Zoot Suit* jerseys. For some reason, I thought I'd seen these guys before.

As usual, Hank was playing center, so he made his way to mid-court for the tipoff. Wanda would play guard along with Tom. The rest of us took our customary positions. It was only when we picked our man to guard on defense that I realized who these guys were on the other team. These were the same guys I'd seen earlier that day on the street corner in the Pico Union neighborhood. In fact, the guy guarding me was the same one who'd asked me for the time.

"Hey, man," he said, looking at me curiously. "Don't I know you?"

"Uh, I don't think so," I lied.

When the referee threw the ball up to start the game, Hank tipped it to Wanda. She took the ball and immediately drove the lane for a slam dunk. For a moment, everyone just stood there in disbelief, then cheers filled the gym. Tom gave me a thumbs up, and Richard pumped his fist. We all fell back into our defense.

"Wanda Woman!" barked Hank.

The other team had some good players, but they didn't have a Wanda Jefferson. Not only was she the best player on the court, she was probably better than the rest of our team combined. We all watched Wanda put on a show. It was like Meadowlark Lemon and the Harlem Globetrotters playing the Washington Generals. Hank scored his share of points, while I played defense and rebounded. We ended up winning the game fairly easily. The only real problem occurred after the game was over. The other team told us that they really liked our *Zoot Suit* jerseys and wanted to buy them. They even raised their offer when we said no. We could see they weren't willing to take no for an answer.

Our team huddled together to talk over the situation. Tom decided that instead of selling these guys our jerseys, we should just give it to them as a public relations gesture. Tom promised us we'd have new jerseys before our next game. We peeled off our old jerseys and handed them over to the players on the other team. They looked at their sweaty *Zoot Suit* jerseys adoringly, like they'd been handed the winning ticket for the California Lottery.

∞ ∞ ∞

From Echo Park, Wanda, Hank, and I headed over to Barragan's Mexican Restaurant on Sunset Boulevard. Barragan's was a large neighborhood place with good food, a full bar, and cold Mexican beer. They seated us at a booth by the window, then took our order. We munched on tortilla chips and drank beer while we waited for our grub. I looked over to Hank, who was munching on a tortilla chip.

"How was the Chili Cookoff?" I asked, knowing he'd just returned from Catalina Island.

"It was crazy," Hank said. "Jared scored ten free cases of tequila. When I wasn't drinking, I was helping him bartend."

Hank had grown up on the island and still had many friends there. Jared was the proprietor of the Thirsty Marlin, one of the island's many watering holes.

"Tequila can be the foundation for any good party," said Wanda, sipping on her Corona.

"You should come over next time, Wanda," Hank said, dipping a chip into salsa. "You can't imagine how much fun you'll have."

"I don't know, Pilsner," she smiled." I got myself a pretty good imagination."

I told them both about my burglary, and Randy, whom they both knew, was now a Los Angeles cop.

"No way," Hank barked. "How did he get past the background check?"

"I have no idea," I replied, "but he did."

"Randy's one crazy white boy," Wanda said.

"He's exactly the type that the LAPD wants to hire."

"What do you mean?" I asked.

"My brother, Bobby, and I went to the IHOP in Pedro for a late-night snack. Randy was already there with some friends. His group finished eating before we did, and on their way out, Randy stopped at our table to talk to Bobby. Randy was acting all nice and everything."

"Randy likes Bobby," Hank said. "They played ball together."

"And Bobby was okay with Randy," she said, "until that night."

"So, what happened?" asked Hank.

"They're talking to us, all friendly like, and then Randy leaves. When we go to pay our bill, we found out Randy had switched checks on us. He'd taken our small bill and paid it, leaving us their big bill."

"That's Randy," I sighed, shaking my head.

"He thought he was playing a joke," Hank said.

"Yeah, some joke," she said. "We didn't have the money, and they wanted to call the police on us. Finally, we were able to prove it wasn't our bill."

"That's not cool," I said, "not cool at all."

"Did you ever talk to Randy about it?" Hank asked.

"Oh yeah. We found him that night, and he claimed he was sorry, that it was just a little joke." Wanda looked directly at both of us. "Let me tell you, when you're black, having the police called on you is no joke."

We both apologized for the actions of our stupid friend, as if we'd somehow been responsible just by mere association.

"Now, Randy is the police," she said. "Ain't that a bitch?"

Just then, the waitress delivered our food. Everything looked good and smelled even better. Hank ordered us another round of beers.

"Wanda," Hank said. "I don't understand. Why aren't you on this year's Olympic team?

"I turned pro after 1980," she explained. "I can't play in the Olympics anymore because I played professionally."

Professionalism had always been a dirty word with the International Olympic Committee. Even the great Jim Thorpe, maybe the greatest Olympian of all time, lost the medals he'd won after it was revealed that he'd played professional ball. Today, some U.S. Olympians find sponsors, while others find jobs that are unrelated to sports. But some, like Wanda, just had to make a living using their athletic abilities.

"In 1976," Hank said, "the Soviet women's basketball team won the gold. Then again in 1980, when your USA team boycotted."

"We would have beaten them in 1980," Wanda said. "We had the best team, and I was pretty good back then."

"Pretty good?" I corrected her. "Wanda, you were best player in the world."

"I know," she said, nodding. "I just wanted to hear somebody else say it."

Wanda went on to tell us how disappointed she'd been about the 1980 Moscow Games boycott. How she'd been at her peak as a player, and her team would have been favored to win a gold medal. Wanda was grateful to be playing professional basketball again, even though it was in Europe. She was also genuinely excited for this year's women's Olympic basketball team, and for her brother, Bobby, whose sprinters would be competing for gold medals. We finished off our food and downed the last of our beers. Hank even picked up the check.

Since I was only a few blocks away from Angelino Heights, I decided to visit my artist friend Danny Sanchez. I knew he liked to work late into the evening and didn't mind an occasional interruption. Three years ago, he'd bought an old Victorian home on Carrol Avenue, turning the separate garage into his art studio. The neighborhood had a collection of beautifully restored Victorian homes. During Christmas time, the area resembled a painting by Currier and Ives, minus the snow of course.

The other day, while stuck in traffic on the Hollywood Freeway, I found myself stopped beside the mural Danny had painted on the freeway's retaining wall. The mural was titled, *"Mi Casa, Su Casa,"* and it included images of palm trees surrounding MacArthur Park's Lake, a star-filled night sky, and the city's skyline silhouetted in the distance. I was overwhelmed by the beauty and sheer joy the mural exuded. Danny had been one of several artists who'd been commissioned to create these Olympic themed murals.

When I pulled my Firebird into Danny's driveway, I could see the lights were on in his garage and the doors were wide open. As I got out of the car, I saw Danny with brush in hand standing near a large canvas suspended against one wall. The Spanish language song, "Sabor a Mi," by Los Lobos played over a large boom box. Danny waved to me, then went over and turned down the music. He picked up an old coffee can and started using the contents to clean his paint brush. His purple 1964 Chevrolet Impala lowrider sat off to one side of the driveway.

When I first met Danny, he had just returned from serving in Viet Nam. He'd been a lowrider in high school, and when he got out of the army he learned how to do custom car painting and designs. At that time, we both owned 1954 Chevrolet Bel Aires and shared an appreciation for classic cars. For a while, Danny made a living doing the most outrageously beautiful custom paint jobs. His designs were vibrant, intricate, and reflected the Chicano culture he'd grown up in.

Then, out of the blue, Danny stopped working on cars altogether. He applied for and then received a full scholarship to attend the Otis Art Institute. He wanted to expand his artistic horizons and go in a completely different direction. At Otis, he met a group of like-minded Chicano artists who were also talented and determined. They created a movement that added richness and culture to L.A.'s art scene.

For the Olympic Art's Festival, Danny was asked to join another team of artists to create murals that would celebrate the city and the upcoming Olympic Games. Long gray freeway retaining walls were transformed into enormous murals, painted to share the artist's vision of Los Angeles as an Olympic city.

"I saw your mural," I said, "while I was stopped on the Hollywood Freeway."

"What did you think?" he asked.

"It's amazing," I replied, "it's so L.A."

"Thanks, man," he said, putting down the coffee can. "Murals are a grind."

"I believe it," I said. "I can't even imagine all the work that's involved."

"Yeah, and while you're working, you get to breathe in all that good freeway air," he smiled.

I'd already managed to see about half of the Olympic themed murals. On the Harbor Freeway, I saw Judy Baca's *Hitting the Wall* and James Wyatt's *James and the Spectators,* and over on the Hollywood Freeway, there were Glenna Avila's *LA Freeway Kids,* and Frank Romero's *Going to the Olympics.* Every mural was wonderful, and together they were a loving gift to the people of Los Angeles and these Olympic Games.

Danny attended the opening night of my play *Sonora Town,* but hadn't stuck around for the party. He never actually told me what he thought of it.

"I'm going to write another play," I told him, "using more of Carlos Cruz's writing."

Danny turned and glared at me; his brow furrowed.

"Maybe you should let a Mexican write this one," he declared.

"What?" I asked, not sure I'd heard him correctly.

"The story is about a Mexican kid," he answered. "Written by a Mexican kid, Carlos Cruz. You're just a Croatian kid from San Pedro."

"Are you serious?" I asked.

"Dead serious," he answered, applying paint to a pallet which he held in his other hand. "Maybe you should let Chicanos tell their own stories."

I was surprised by Danny's reaction. Carlos Cruz had died, and since had almost been forgotten. My play helped to spark a renewed interest in his work.

"I love Carlos Cruz's writing," I said, defensively, "and I wrote my play to honor him."

"Well, now you've honored him," he said, adding more paint to his pallet.

I didn't really know what else to say, so I just stood there watching Danny add paint to the canvas. I finally remembered something that I'd once read.

"Back in the 1940s, L.A. author, John Fante, who wrote *Ask the Dust,* was going to write a novel about the Filipinos, whom he'd work with at a Terminal Island fish cannery. They fascinated him, and he felt their plight. He hoped to write a great novel, comparing what he aspired to write to John Steinbeck's *The Grapes of Wrath.*

"Yeah, so?" Danny asked.

"The Filipino community protested his involvement because Fante was an outsider. He tried to explain that the story would be a sympathetic portrayal of their people and culture, but they wouldn't accept him because he wasn't Filipino. Fante dropped the project, and never wrote that great novel he felt he had inside of him."

"Oh, well," he said, dabbing paint onto the canvas.

"He never got over it, and it tormented him. Years later, he wrote the short story *Helen Thy Beauty is to Me,* about a Filipino cannery worker who falls in love with a dime a dance girl."

"I've read it," he admitted. *"It's maravilloso."*

"I agree, and it was only a taste of what his novel could have been."

Danny didn't say anything. He just continued dabbing paint onto his canvas. Another song by Los Lobos began playing over the boom box. He finally looked over toward me.

"You have the right to exploit our culture," he said, "but that doesn't make it right."

I understood what Danny was saying, but was it really that simple?

"Niko, I liked your play. It was good because Carlos Cruz's novel was good."

"It's still Cruz's work. I'm just adapting it for him. If he was here, he could do it himself and probably better than me."

"Yeah. For many reasons."

Maybe Danny was right, maybe I was just another white guy trying to play Charlie Chan.

ↂ ↂ ↂ

Heading home from Angeleno Heights, I noticed a large billboard that towered over the intersection of Sunset and Alvarado. The billboard advertised the upcoming Olympic Games, and reminded me of what I'd seen earlier that day at USC. Sometimes when I'm on campus now, I try to imagine what it would be like to be back in college. Although, when I was there as a student, I couldn't wait to graduate. Now I look back on those years with nostalgia. What was John Fante's quote? "Nostalgia is the whore to memory."

Just before my senior year, I was informed I needed to select a class in either political science or sociology to fulfill a graduation requirement. My roommate's girlfriend, Emily, recommended professor Michael Lafayette's class, *California in Politics and Culture.* Lafayette had a reputation for being a brilliant and demanding professor. Emily always took the most challenging courses and still maintained a 4.0 GPA. She was even in the school's marching band, which required an inordinate amount of her time. Still, she excelled, got good grades, and was a serious student. I, on the other hand, did just enough to get by, trying not to take any class that would screw up my GPA.

In order to continue receiving my financial aid, I was required to maintain a 3.2 GPA. If I lost my funding, I would be shown the proverbial door. I was happy at USC, but I never felt completely comfortable there. In every class, there were always students with famous surnames, civic leaders, Hollywood, or big business types. These students were the scions of the well-to-do. I, on the other hand, was a tuna fisherman's son from San Pedro, a first-generation immigrant, who spoke Croatian before he spoke English. I knew I was boxing well above my weight class and sure that my professors were also aware of this. "Why is this hapless welterweight competing with all of these prized heavyweights?" They undoubtedly asked themselves over cocktails at Julie's.

"Professor Layfette's class will be one of the most challenging courses you'll ever take," Emily told me. "He'll really make you think."

Having to think deep thoughts concerned me on many levels. First, it all sounded like way too much work. Next, I wondered if I could compete with students who'd attended prep schools and had private tutors. And finally, what if I just wasn't up to it? That would be the end of my USC education, and I'd be banished to where a miserable wretch like myself probably belonged in the first place, cast out among the common folk. Had I any sense, I would have run for the hills, or at least back to the registrar's office to sign up for an easy class to pad my borderline GPA.

"I've heard he's a good professor," I told Emily, "but I also heard he assigns a lot of work, and he expects you to know what you're talking about."

"Yes. But isn't that what college is for?" she asked. "Don't you want to stretch yourself?"

Even when I played sports, I usually did just enough stretching to get by. Anyway, I finally took Emily's advice and signed up for professor Lafayette's class, *California in Politics and Cul-*

ture. I was right, the class proved to be challenging. But Emily was also right, it turned out to be the best class I ever took.

63

Wednesday
July 18

●◆ Jeanne Cruz was still having breakfast when I phoned her. She was excited about an Olympic Arts Festival dance event she'd attended just the night before.

"They were from West Germany," she said. "And they performed right here in little old Pasadena."

I didn't know much about dance, but I liked dancers. They were usually attractive, athletic, and they often had the most incredible legs. Yes, I'm that shallow, I'll admit it.

"Was it a good performance?" I asked Jeanne.

"It was wonderful," she replied, "so original."

As a young woman, Jeanne had studied dance and considered herself an authority on the subject. She was also a supporter of the arts, and a founding member of the Los Angeles Music Center's Blue Ribbon 400, Dorothy Chandler's influential cabal of female fundraisers. Jess Unruh, the longtime California politician, once defined money as "the mother's milk of politics." This group of ladies provided the Music Center with its "mother's milk."

"I met a German dancer the other night." I told Jeanne. "She might have been with that dance company you saw last night."

"Where was this?" she asked, curiously.

"At the Variety Arts Club," I replied. "It's the Olympic Art's Festival's official gathering place. Everyone goes there after their shows."

"How exciting," she said. "All those different cultures getting a chance to mingle."

Even though Jeanne and I had only met at the first performance of *Sonora Town*, we'd somehow developed a friendship. Before that first show, I was so nervous knowing she would be in the audience. More than anyone else, I wanted her to like the play. Carlos died only a year earlier, and she was still in mourning. Fortunately, she loved the play and was pleased with how faithful I'd been to her late husband's novel. Her kind comments gave me validation and hope. Maybe all of those rejection letters I received were wrong.

After that opening night, Jeanne asked me to call her the next day, and we ended up talking for hours. She had once studied ballet with dreams of becoming a ballerina. This reminded me of my studying theater. Jeanne later invited me to have lunch at her home. It was great to see the place she'd shared with Carlos. The books I saw in his personal library gave me insights into his thinking, and she even allowed me to sit at Carlos' writing desk in front of his Underwood typewriter.

After that visit, I invited Jeanne to lunch at the Hollywood Brown Derby, the sister to the original restaurant that had been demolished on Wilshire. Having lunch at the Brown Derby was special for me and something I'd always wanted to do. We had drinks and both ordered their famous Cobb salad.

After Jeanne finished telling me all about last night's dance performance, I finally got to the point of my phone call.

"The Taper is interested in doing another play based on Carlos' work."

"Which book?" she asked.

"The producer thinks that *Edendale* might be a good choice."

"That would be wonderful," she replied, sounding genuinely excited.

"Could we get together sometime? There are contracts you'll need to sign."

"How about tonight? I could make us some dinner, nothing fancy. I might even ask my granddaughter, Isabella, to join us."

I'd met her granddaughter, Isabella, when she attended our play, and she wasn't what I expected. For a girl who'd grown up in Pasadena, I imagined a buttoned-up, preppy type. Instead, Isabella Cruz was a punk rocker, and in an all-female punk band called the Cherri Tarts. A concert flyer I'd seen stapled to a Hollywood telephone pole referred to them as: "Nasty bitches with nasty attitudes." Her band had recently opened for the Circle Jerks at the Starwood in West Hollywood.

"Tonight would be good," I replied. "If we could do it early; I have a performance tonight."

"Be here at five," she said, "and we'll dine by six."

"Great. Is there anything I can bring?"

"Bring a bottle of red wine."

"Perfect," I smiled. "I'll make sure the bottle has a cork instead of a screw top, only the very best."

"You are a class act," she chuckled.

This would all work out, since I already had plans to be up in Pasadena anyway. Richard DeVries had recently hired a new assistant, Cynthia Aldrich, to help him wade through his ever-growing stack of play submissions. Cynthia was lovely, with big brown eyes and long mahogany brown hair. She had the most wonderful, breathy speaking voice, that reminded me of a young Jackie Kennedy. Cynthia had grown up in South Hampton, New York, attended exclusive private schools, and graduated from an Ivy League university. She had recently returned from Oxford, England, where she had been a Rhodes Scholar. I should have been intimidated as hell, but Cynthia was so soft-spoken and sweet she instantly put me at ease. Since she was new in town, I offered to show her around Pasadena and provide her with a picnic lunch.

She was staying with her uncle's family. He was a scientist at the Jet Propulsion Lab. "Damn," I thought to myself. "He was a rocket scientist, and she was a Rhodes Scholar." I couldn't have been more out of my league. Why Cynthia was interested in spending even a day with me, I'll never know. But I wasn't going to squander the opportunity.

When I called Richard to tell him I would be meeting with Jeanne, he suggested he could send Cynthia's uncle a fax with the papers Jeanne needed to sign. I told him that was a good idea.

The Arroyo Seco Parkway, from Los Angeles to Pasadena, was Southern California's very first freeway. It acquired its name from the mostly dry riverbed that channeled rainwater from the San Gabriel Mountains to downtown Los Angeles. The parkway was a little eccentric because it was a first draft of what freeways would eventually become. I enjoyed the parkway's sharp curves, its narrow tunnels, and its odd landscaping. I even liked its white-knuckle, "merge or die," on-ramps and off-ramps. I found it all quaint, like a vintage knick-knack you might find at the Assistance League Thrift Store. None of the newer freeways had the same charm; they were all ordinary and boring. The Arroyo Seco Parkway was one of a kind.

Besides the city's museums, I often visited Pasadena to explore its fine California Craftsman style architecture. I was hoping to share some of that architecture today with Cynthia.

Her uncle's family lived in the Old Town area of Pasadena. I met everyone, and we talked briefly. They all seemed friendly and treated me well. Before we left, Cynthia handed me the contracts Richard faxed over for Jeanne.

For some reason, Cynthia looked especially radiant today. Her brown eyes were bright, and her complexion was fresh-scrubbed and glowing. Her flowing brown hair rested gently on her shoulders. Having just arrived from England, Cynthia hadn't had the time to acquire a Southern California wardrobe. Instead, she was dressed more for the climate of Oxford, England. Her proper blouse and conservative skirt made her seem like a character in a J.D. Salinger short story.

To get food for our picnic, we headed over to the Trader Joe's Market there in Pasadena. There were now about a dozen of these markets scattered around the Southland, but this store was the original. For our lunch, we stocked up on a variety of fruits, cheeses, dried meats, and bread. Cynthia also helped me pick out two good bottles of wine; one for our picnic and another for my dinner with Jeanne.

From Trader Joe's, I steered the Firebird onto the Foothill Freeway headed east.

"Why are we getting on the freeway?" Cynthia asked. "I thought you were showing me Pasadena?"

"The person's house I wanted to show you is in nearby Monrovia. He did live in Pasadena first, but that house is now buried somewhere under this freeway."

"Okay," she smiled, slipping on a pair of retro sunglasses. "I'm just along for the ride."

"I like the sunglasses," I said. "They make you look mysterious."

"Thanks. I just bought them."

We rolled down our windows to allow in some fresh air. The breeze tossed her hair and caused her skirt to billow up. I got a glimpse of her legs. She had great legs; they could have been dancer's legs. I tried not to stare.

We immediately exited the freeway near the Santa Anita Racetrack. After just a few minutes, we stopped in front of a small two-story Spanish Colonial Revival home. Two round-arched windows flanked the ornate entrance, and a pair of Eugenia trees grew beside those two windows. We stood on the sidewalk and looked earnestly at the home.

"Cute house," she said. "What year was it built?

"Sometime in the early 1920s," I said. "The resident bought it in 1941, and lived here until 1968 when he died."

"Okay," she smiled. "I think I know whose home this was."

"Are you serious?" I asked, surprised that she would know this.

"I'm a Rhode Scholar, remember."

"Yeah. I guess you are."

"He wrote *The Jungle,* didn't he?" She asked.

"He did," I said, smiling. "He also wrote a novel called **Oil,** about Southern California during the oil boom. He wrote about a hundred books in all."

"Upton Sinclair," she answered. "We studied him at Oxford. He was friends with H. G. Wells and George Bernard Shaw."

"I believe he was," I said.

"I think he was a socialist, right?"

"Yes. He was introduced to socialism by his best friend, a man named Gaylord Wilshire."

"Wilshire? Of Wilshire Boulevard?"

"The very same. Wilshire was a wealthy land developer, who usually plowed his profits back into socialist causes."

She wanted to go inside, but I had to tell her it was a private residence and the owner didn't allow tours.

"Didn't Sinclair run for governor of California?" she asked.

"He did, in 1934, as a Democrat, under the slogan 'End Poverty in California,' or EPIC- he lost."

"Interesting," she said.

"During the 1923 IWW labor strike at the L.A. Harbor, he was thrown in jail when he tried to read from the U. S. Constitution. That incident led to the creation of the Southern California Chapter of the ACLU, something that Sinclair was very proud of."

Cynthia studied me through her dark glasses, then she looked back at the house. I mostly just looked at her, admiringly. She was so beautiful and so damn smart.

By reversing our path to Monrovia, Cynthia and I returned to Pasadena, exiting the freeway near the Rose Bowl. The day was clear, and the San Gabriel Mountains rose up crisply in the distance. From Orange Grove Boulevard, I turned the Firebird onto a small side street named Westmoreland Place. Cynthia was looking elsewhere when she suddenly turned and noticed the large house on its grassy knoll. I heard her gasp, as if completely taken by surprise. Her eyes grew large as she stared.

"My god," she blurted. "That house, what is it?"

"That's the Gamble House," I answered. "That's what I wanted to show you."

I parked our car on the street, and we made our way up the red brick driveway. There was a peaceful quiet, and the scent of roses sailed through the air. The home's faded green shingles gave it a soft patina and made the old building look very appealing. The low-pitched roof and its overhangs echoed the angle of the nearby mountains. The natural materials used in its construction made it appear the house had not been built by men, but rather had sprouted up from the soil, like a tree.

From beneath her dark glasses, I watched a tear roll down Cynthia's cheek. She found a tissue in her pocket, then raised her sunglasses to dab at her eyes. She seemed embarrassed by her show of emotions.

"That's okay," I offered. "I also got emotional my first time here."

"It's just so beautiful," she stammered. "I don't usually get like this."

"I understand, believe me."

"Everything works so well together," she said, drying her eyes, "the home, the landscaping, the setting."

"And it's a sunny, clear day. It's all a little over-whelming."

"What year was it built?"

"1908, by the brothers Charles and Henry Greene of Pasadena. They were craftsmen before they were architects. The home reflects their attention to detail. You've probably noticed the Japanese influence.

We climbed the dozen or so steps to the spacious brick porch that wrapped itself around the home. Cynthia gasped again when she noticed the two stained-glass panels, that flanked the stained-glass front door, creating one large panoramic image.

"How lovely," she sighed. "Isn't that a tree?"

"It's a depiction of a California live oak, the kind you might find down near the arroyo. You should see the door from inside with the sunlight illuminating the stained glass."

"I'd like to," she said, enthusiastically.

"Good, you will. There's a tour starting soon."

I led Cynthia around to the rear of the home. From the wide brick porch, she surveyed the expansive lawn that rolled over the backyard. She stood over the lily pad filled pond and reached her hand out to touch one of the floating lily pads, dampening her fingers. A yellow-flowered lotus floated out of her reach. For a moment, she scanned the area, turning in a complete circle, trying to take everything in.

When it was time, a small crowd gathered in front of the home for the first tour of the day. A young female docent would be our tour guide. I'd been on this tour so many times I thought I could have led it myself, but I remained silent and allowed the docent to do her job. First, she shared some of the history of the architects, Greene and Greene, describing how they began in Pasadena and some of their earlier commissions. Then she told of David B. and Mary Gamble of the Procter and Gamble company who commissioned the building of the home. Finally, we made our way into the main entry hall. Just as I'd told Cynthia earlier, the morning sunlight illuminated the stained-glass door producing a truly magical effect.

"You were right," Cynthia whispered. "It's stunning."

I wanted to lean over and tell her "You're not so bad yourself," but of course I didn't. Cynthia relished the tour like a child opening presents on Christmas morning. She loved the amazing hardwoods of the walls and stairs, rubbed as smooth as satin. She loved the carefully articulated details of even the smallest items. She loved the original furnishings that still remained in place after all these years. Cynthia seemed to revel in everything she saw.

After the tour, we made our way back to the Firebird, and drove the short distance to Brookside Park, which overlooked the arroyo. Cynthia hardly spoke, as if she was still processing what she'd seen. We found a perfect spot on the grass under a large shade tree. I laid out an old blanket and helped Cynthia carry the food and wine. I opened the bottle and poured some wine into two clear plastic cups. After I handed her a cup, I proposed a toast.

"To the Gamble House," I proclaimed, cup raised. "May it never change."

We clinked plastic cups and sipped our wine. Then we proceeded to unwrap the food. I'd brought a small cutting board and knife so we could slice the meats and cheeses. I tore off a small piece of bread from the baguette and stole a bite. Cynthia looked as if she was still thinking about the tour.

"I couldn't believe someone actually wanted to paint all that amazing woodwork white," she complained, referring to when the Gamble family almost sold the home to a wealthy buyer.

"I know," I agreed. "It would have been like whitewashing the Sistine Chapel."

"Just because people have money doesn't mean they have good taste."

At that moment, I thought it couldn't get much better than this — a lovely setting, a beautiful woman, tasty snacks, and good wine. It was obvious Cynthia enjoyed seeing the Gamble

House, and it pleased me I was able to share it with her.

"Do you miss England?" I asked.

"A bit," she admitted. "But I really miss my friends there the most."

"Hopefully you'll make new friends here."

"Well, it seems that I've already made one," she said, giving me a shy smile.

We sat there on the blanket, eating, drinking, and talking. Cynthia had a wide range of interests. Her focus at Oxford had been English Literature, so she could discuss books with anyone.

"I know you were a theater major," she said. "But what was your main interest?"

"I did more directing than anything, and I also took a bunch of film courses."

"I'm interested in film too," she said, smiling, "even more so than theater."

She didn't seem to mind when I leaned over and gently kissed her. Her lips tasted sweet, like the strawberries she'd been eating. I thought she was an awfully good kisser. Maybe she studied that at Oxford too, on the side anyway.

"That was nice," she said. Then she leaned over and kissed me back. We finally came up for air, looking into each other's eyes.

"I'm having fun," she said, brushing the hair away from her face.

"Me too," I admitted.

Cynthia was wonderful, and I didn't want to

mess things up on our first date. I figured that I should take it slow. She was someone who I really wanted to get to know. The last thing I wanted to do was rush things.

"How would you like to come to the show I'm doing with the Drama Geeks?" I asked. "If you come to the last performance, you can even go with me to the closing night party."

She thought about it for just a moment.

"I'd like that," she answered. "I've heard they're a funny group."

"They're also a little crazy, but that's what makes them so much fun."

After our picnic, I returned Cynthia to her uncle's place. At the curb, she gave me a tasty kiss and thanked me again for showing her a good time. I told her I'd had fun as well, and I looked forward to next time. She smiled that great smile, turned, then walked toward the front door. She had a stride like a model, long and elegant. I watched her until she went inside. Cynthia had class, brains, and looks. She was in the major leagues, while I was maybe on a triple-A roster. But I wasn't going to tell anyone I didn't belong in the big leagues. This was my opportunity, and I was going to give it my best shot.

Since it was much too early to head over to Jeanne's I knew I had some time to kill. I turned onto Lake Avenue and took it until it ended at the foothills of Altadena. I parked my Firebird near the wrought iron gates which led to Rubio Canyon. I had some old running shoes in my trunk, so I put them on and started walking. The trail was dry and dusty. I noticed the wild poppies and the scattered chaparral and heard a hawk cry out in the distance.

On this very spot, back in 1893, a man named Thaddeus Lowe opened the Mount Lowe Railway, which he called "The Railway to the Clouds." It operated in the San Gabriel Mountains high above Pasadena. The railway ran its last trip in 1937, and by 1940, everything had been completely abandoned.

When I first joined the Los Angeles Conservancy, I attended a film screening where they showed old movies of the Mount Lowe Railway during its heyday. The old black and white images were other-worldly and a bit surreal. Now all that was left of "The Railroad to the Clouds," were the pictures, moving and otherwise. If it weren't for these preserved images, no one would believe such a place ever existed. They might assume that it was all just a folk tale, or just some myth.

☙ ☙ ☙

Jeanne Cruz's home on South El Molino Avenue had been in the family for generations. When her parents died, Jeanne, the only child, inherited their substantial estate. Jeanne was surprised by the inheritance because she'd long been estranged from her parents over her marriage to Carlos. Even after Carlos and Jeanne had blessed them with three grandchildren, Jeanne's parents still maintained their disapproval. Jeanne could only imagine at the end, her parents simply preferred she inherit their wealth rather than to have it passed on to total strangers.

Carlos and Jeanne's unexpected windfall turned out to be both beneficial and harmful. It gave the young family financial security, but it also made Carlos complacent. The early novels he had written during times of hardship now seemed pointless and unnecessary. Though his books had always received favorable reviews, none of them had sold particularly well or provided much of an income.

Now with the family's sudden wealth, there were no more financial struggles. But instead of the inheritance providing support for Carlos to continue his writing, he decided to give up writing altogether. Instead, he took up a life of leisure: playing golf at the Brookside Golf Club, enjoying a liquid lunch with friends at the Huntington Hotel, or wagering on the ponies over at the Santa Anita Racetrack. Jeanne longed for the days when her talented husband had no other choice but to write. The wonderful novels he'd once written now faded away into obscurity. Jeanne shared this story with me during our lunches together. She even shared with me how the two had originally met.

Back in the mid 1930s, after she'd just graduated from Stanford, Jeanne and a female friend were attending a play at the Pasadena Playhouse while Carlos and a male friend were there as well. In a moment of pure serendipity, Jeanne and Carlos found themselves seated right next to each other in the audience. There was an instant chemistry and a strong attraction. Carlos introduced himself, and they struck up a conversation.

As the curtain rose, Jeanne's thoughts were not on the play but rather the handsome Latino man with whom she shared an armrest. She noticed the pleasant smell of his aftershave. She noticed his joyous laugh. She noticed his raven black hair, which she hoped to run her fingers through.

Carlos was also smitten with this affable young woman. He loved her perfectly coiffured blonde hair. He loved her piecing blue eyes. He loved her subtle perfume, which reminded him of the well-heeled women he'd bumped into at the Bullock's department store.

The rubbing of their elbows, and the bumping of their knees, only made them long for more substantial contact. The drama on the stage was nothing compared to the drama they felt in their hearts. During the play's intermission, they exchanged phone numbers and planned to meet.

Finally, the two met at the Rialto Theatre in South Pasadena for a movie. But instead of watching the film, they began to kiss during the opening credits. After a few minutes, they fled the theater to his Plymouth and drove up the hill to a nearby lover's lane. There, in the back seat of that car, with a panoramic view of the valley below, Jeanne lost her virginity. Carlos then made love to her once again, just to make sure. She was pleased he was so thorough.

After that evening, they were hardly ever apart. Once, they even managed to sit through an entire movie at the Rialto without escaping to his Plymouth. Without telling their families, they were married by a county judge in his chambers.

Prior to meeting Carlos, Jeanne had accepted a spot in the *corps de ballet* for a San Francisco ballet company. Her family, although not exactly encouraging, had always accepted her choices for a career. Now, married to Carlos, she informed the ballet company she wasn't coming.

Jeanne's family were descendants of one of the founding Anglo families of Pasadena. Their ancestors had bought much of the original Spanish rancho, which Pasadena had been a part of. Over the years, her family had sold off large portions of the land, making enormous profits each time.

Carlos, ironically, had been one of the descendants of the last Mexican owners of that very same

Spanish rancho. Whereas the Anglos had seen their stock advance and their relatives flourish, the Mexican descendants saw their lives diminish in ways they could have never imagined. As the previous owners of the rancho, they were a kind of royalty themselves. But after waves of newer white settlers arrived, those Mexican families were now looked down on. The newcomers only saw the color of their skin, and they didn't care that they had once owned all the land that their eyes could see. The Mexican families were now little more than peasants on the very land that they had once been kings and queens. Carlos, from that original rancho owning family, lived better than most but not nearly as well as his white counterparts.

Early on, Carlos demonstrated a talent for writing. He attended Pasadena Junior College at first, then transferred to the University of California at Los Angeles, where he eventually graduated. He was determined to write stories about his Mexican American culture and the Southern California he loved so much.

After giving up her dream of a life in the ballet, Jeanne plowed her energies into her husband and her family. She eventually became a patron of the arts, supporting dance and music whenever she could.

C⊛ C⊛ C⊛

It was about 5:00 pm when I steered my Firebird up the driveway of Jeanne's impressive home. I parked beside a 1961 turquoise and white Nash Metropolitan convertible. I figured this car belonged to her granddaughter, Isabella, the punk rocker. I grabbed Jeanne's papers and the bottle of red wine I'd purchased earlier.

After I rang the doorbell, it was Isabella who opened the large door. She had the same contemptuous look on her face I remembered from our first meeting. Isabella couldn't have been more than 20 years old, yet she was a veteran of the L.A. punk scene. Her makeup was crude, and her badly cut hair was piled to one side, concealing one of her hoop earrings. She wore a black tank top with a vintage, country-western shirt over it. Her short skirt revealed tattered fishnet stocking.

"I like your car," I said, pointing to the Metropolitan.

"It gets me around," she scowled. "Come on in."

The entryway's pastel green walls were capped by the ornate crown molding, which encircled the high ceiling. Thick oriental rugs led us into the foyer where a smiling Jeanne was waiting. She wore a flowery summer dress, and her blonde hair was perfectly coiffed.

"Niko, it's so good to see you," she said, giving me a warm hug.

"It's good to see you too, Jeanne," I said, handing her the bottle of wine.

"Thank you," she said, taking the bottle. "Let's get comfortable, shall we."

"Sounds good," I replied.

Jeanne led us into the walnut paneled study, which was filled from wall to wall with books. Jeanne stepped over to the wet bar.

"What will you have?" she asked.

"Jack Daniels on the rocks, if you have it."

"I sure do," Jeanne said, reaching for the bottle. "And you, Isabella? You're almost twenty-one, I'm sure you indulge."

Isabella glanced over toward me. "I'll have what he's having, if that's okay?"

"It is," Jeanne replied, pouring our drinks, and pouring herself a Scotch.

She handed us our glasses, and then we sat down on the soft leather chairs.

"You brought the papers," Jeanne said, indicating the forms in my hand.

"Yes, these are for *Edendale*, I said, handing her the two documents.

"She looked them over quickly. "It's just like what we agreed to with *Sonora Town*.

"Yes, exactly."

"You know," she admitted. "I don't make much money on these. But if it helps to get Carlos' books in bookstores again, then I'm all for it."

"I don't make much on it myself," I replied. "But that's okay."

"The big money is when the books are sold

to the movies," she said. "Not that I need the money."

We sat sipping our drinks and talking.

"I liked your play," Isabella said, quietly. "I don't usually go to the theater."

"Thanks," I said. "Hopefully, now you'll go more often."

Isabella nodded and even smiled. This smile softened her harsh appearance and actually made her look quite attractive.

Jeanne finished examining the documents, then picked up a nearby pen and signed both papers. She then handed them to me.

"That should do it," she declared. "But now the real work begins for you."

"Yes. Pretty soon I'll actually have some time to write."

"You should go out to Malibu to get away," Jeanne stated. "We have a trailer there; you're welcome to use it."

"A trailer," I smiled. "That sounds more like Bakersfield than Malibu."

"I assure you," she said. "It's quite nice. It's at Paradise Cove."

"It is nice," added Isabella. "And there's even a nude beach close by."

"Well, that seals it," I said, smiling. "When can I move in?"

Instead of dining in the formal dining room, we had a simple dinner at the kitchen table. The pasta was good, and my wine went well with everything. Isabella was a part of the conversation, and I was able to see a completely different side of her. Besides her music, I also learned that she was an artist. Her sketch pad drawings, which she shared, were surprisingly good. Physically, Isabella resembled the Latin side of her family. She had beautiful dark features and glowing brown skin. I definitely saw some of her grandfather, Carlos, in her.

"Niko, I don't even know," Jeanne asked. "Do you have a girlfriend?"

"Grandma," Isabella blurted. "That's rude."

"Why is that rude?" Jeanne asked. "Niko and I have shared many things about ourselves."

"That's okay," I said. "No, I don't have a girlfriend exactly, but I have started seeing a young woman from the Taper."

"You mean, Cynthia?" Jeanne asked.

"Yeah," I answered, surprised. "How do you know Cynthia?"

"She introduced herself at the play, and we spoke once on the phone. She seems very bright and ambitious."

"Yes, she's very smart," I admitted. "And to be honest, I kind of like her."

"That's wonderful, a budding romance," Jeanne said.

After we finished our deserts, I thanked Jeanne for the meal and apologized for having to leave so soon. She handed me a key and the address to her trailer at Paradise Cove, suggesting again I should take advantage of her offer. She told me I wouldn't regret it. I said my good-byes and left for the play.

In 1928, the two-story Spanish style building on the corner of 10th Street and Fairfax Avenue was a grocery store called the Monterey Market. It was an old-fashion Southern California market with a storefront that opened up, and a produce section that extended out right onto the sidewalk. A canvas awning shaded the fresh fruit and vegetables from the sun. Inside, the meat cutter would wrap your T-bone steaks in pink butcher paper, and the baker's oven would send the smell of freshly baked bread drifting through the morning air. Anyway, that's the way it was back in 1928.

Then in 1932, the city changed the name of 10th Street to Olympic Boulevard in honor of the 10th Olympiad, which Los Angeles was then hosting. I'm not sure when the building stopped being a market, but in 1978, it was leased by The Drama Geeks, and suddenly, this old grocery store became a theater. It seemed appropriate that the group's show for the Olympic Arts Festival was a play set during those 1932 Olympics, when 10th Street first became Olympic Boulevard.

After driving all the way from Pasadena, I managed to get to the theater with time to spare. As a stage manager, I needed to prepare everything for the evening's performance. At the Taper, I usually had an assistant or two. That wasn't the case here, but the demands weren't as great, and everyone was always willing to pitch in.

Our play, since it was partly improvised, required nightly audience suggestions to fill in key details of the story. For this reason, no two performances were ever exactly the same. Doing improvisation in front of a live audience was like constructing a bridge while you were trying to cross over it. This group of performers made improvisation look incredibly easy.

What most people think of as improvisational theater started with a woman named Viola Spolin, who developed and began teaching certain acting exercises or "theater games" in Chicago back in the mid-1950s. One of her pupils was her son, Paul Sills, who then founded the improv group, The Second City. Their acting exercises or "games" were used to free the performer's creativity and unlock their self-expression. In 1963, Spolin published her book *Improvisation for the Theater,* which became the "bible" of improvisation. In 1976, she opened a school in Hollywood where the founding members of the Drama Geeks all took classes.

As I finished my preparation for that night's show, I used a checklist to mark off everything I'd completed. Finally, I put up that evening's sign-in sheet so the performers could sign in as they arrived.

Peggy Terry was the first of the cast members to sign in. Peggy had blue eyes and wore her blonde hair in a medium bob. She also handled business matters for the theater. Peggy was a nice Jewish girl from New York with a wonderful sardonic sense of humor.

Walt Wagner strolled in next. I quickly noticed that Walt had gotten his dark hair cut and his mustache trimmed. Walt was my buddy; I enjoyed his dry sense of humor and his caustic wit. Because of his rich baritone, he often worked as a radio announcer. He also played the guitar and loved to sing.

Janie Leslie walked in behind Walt. Janie could seem unassuming and a little shy. But in spite of her gentle demeanor, on stage she performed with reckless abandon. The contradiction between what you were expecting and what you got was part of her appeal.

Kevin McGeorge signed in next. Kevin was our corpulent cast member. He was much loved and always the first to poke fun of his own weight. He seemed to wear his girth as a badge of honor. Kevin also did some comedy writing on the side.

Tim Spillman, as he'd done many times, stumbled into the theater pretending to trip over the door's threshold. He landed on his stomach, then smiled. Tim was an expert at physical comedy, and he was always willing to take a pratfall. He felt no sight gag was too cheap, as long as it got a laugh.

Kelly Kirkland entered next. Kelly was my favorite performer. Not only was she our best female comedian, but she was one of the nicest people I knew. Kelly wore her hair short, like a blonde Audrey Hepburn. I imagined one day she would have her own situation comedy on TV.

Frank Kaiser was the last one to arrive. Frank was our star, and amazingly gifted. Walt referred to Frank as "the foundation," as if every show had to be built on his shoulders. Frank was the focal point and the cornerstone of everything the group did. In short, Frank was "the foundation." Everyone believed he was going to be a big star.

Our show, *Sam Sphincter Private Eye Proctologist,* was first developed from a skit Frank had improvised during one of the group's weekly shows. Before every Drama Geeks' show, the performers always take suggestions from the audience. That particular night, Frank asked the audience for his character's occupation. Someone shouted out "proctologist." Frank said: "Great, lucky me." Then he requested another occupation, which the character might do as a second job. Someone shouted, "private detective," and that's how *Sam Sphincter Private Eye Proctologist* was born.

Thinking the character had potential, Frank decided to develop some scripted skits. So, he and Kevin got together and started to write down ideas. Finally, Ted Folger, a founding member of the Drama Geeks, was brought in to direct the show. They took all of the "film-noir" detective clichés and turned them on their ear. They shamelessly borrowed characters from Hammett, Chandler, and other detective movies. The rest of the Drama Geeks transformed themselves into the supporting cast of eccentric characters.

"Half hour!" I announced, letting everyone know it was thirty minutes before curtain.

"Thank you!" I heard several voices shout.

Actor's Equity had struck a deal with The Olympic Arts Festival, placing all of the performers and stage managers under Equity contracts. This meant we would all get paid well and have health benefits. I was the first Equity stage manager the Drama Geeks had ever hired. I would stay with them forever if I could, but when this show is over, that's it for me.

Ted Folger, the director, entered the backstage area followed by what looked like a small

TV news crew: a camera man, a sound man, and the reporter. Ted led them over to me.

"Niko," Ted said. "These men are from German television, and they're going to tape a few minutes of the show. Then after the play, they'd like to interview Frank."

As the Actor's Equity Representative, it was my job to make sure that any after-hours interviews were allowed under our union contract.

"You're giving them permission to tape part of the show," I replied. "But I'll need to make sure the interview is okay."

The German cameraman suddenly erupted with anger.

"Come on!" he shouted. "What's wrong with you people? This is for television!"

The sound man tried to calm his friend down, but for some reason, the cameraman remained angry.

"Let us do our damn job!" he yelled. "We're doing you all a favor!"

I had no idea why this guy was so upset, but I certainly didn't like him telling us what to do.

"You aren't doing us any favors," I snapped back. "Maybe this attitude of yours works back in your country but not here."

Several of the cast members came out of their dressing rooms to see what all of the shouting was about.

"We're going to put you on television!" the

camera man shouted. "You should be grateful."

"Normally, we'd thank you," I replied. "But you can't just come in here and tell us what to do."

The reporter came over to me to apologize, while the sound man tried to restrain his angry friend.

"I'm sorry," the reporter said. "It's no excuse, but we've had a difficult day. We're going to set up to tape the show. Please let us know if we can do our interview afterwards. If not, that's okay too."

"We'll see what we can do," I said.

The German TV crew began to set up their equipment so they could record the show. I looked at my watch and saw it was almost showtime.

"Five minutes!" I announced, making sure that everyone heard me.

There was a copy of our Equity contract pinned to the bulletin board near the sign-in sheet. I pulled it down and thumbed through it, quickly finding the language that told me the interview would be okay. I found Ted backstage and let him know what I'd learned. He thanked me and said he would tell the German crew. The house manager reported to me the audience was now seated, and it was time to start the show.

"Places!" I shouted, making sure everyone backstage heard me.

Janie peaked out of her tiny dressing room and gave me a shy smile.

"Thanks for sticking up for us," she smiled.

"You're welcome," I replied.

When I entered the control booth, the lighting and sound operators were both already there. I put on my headphones and spoke into my microphone.

"Okay, everybody, here we go," I announced. "House lights to half."

The audience lights dimmed, letting the audience know the show was about to begin.

∽ ∽ ∽

That night was one of our better shows. The audience participation was good, and the performers were all in rare form. I could tell the audience went home happy. Backstage, Walt told me the actors were headed to the Variety Arts Club for a little libation.

"After your run-in with the German, you might need a drink," Walt smiled.

"Probably two," I answered.

After the TV interview with Frank, I locked up the theater and took Olympic Boulevard all the way to downtown. The Tom Petty song "The Waiting" played over my car's speakers.

The Variety Arts Club was the brainchild of Milt Larson, who also started the famous Magic Castle in Hollywood. Milt bought this building in 1977 from the Friday Morning Club, a progressive women's club that flourished from the

1880s through the 1940s. Milt's goal was to do for Vaudeville what he had done for magic. Built in 1923, this six-story Italian Renaissance Revival style building contained a 1,100-seat theater, a 250-seat theater, a basement comedy lounge, and a large restaurant on the fourth floor. The building's décor always reminded me of Rick's Café from the film *Casablanca*.

After I parked, I took the elevator up to the fourth floor. The doors opened to the crowded bar area. It was a lively party. There were so many people talking, laughing, and drinking. I heard a good amount of English, but I also heard French, German, Italian, and even some Chinese. Every group seemed to be a mix of cultures. There were individuals in each group that translated for the other members. I imagined United Nations gatherings were something like this, but I couldn't imagine them being as much fun. The world, I thought, had come to Los Angeles.

While I was at the bar getting my drink, Walt Wagner shouted my name and waved me over. When I got there, he was in a conversation with two attractive French women, whom he introduced as Celine and Adele. Celine knew some English, so she translated for her friend.

"This is Niko," Walt said to them with a wicked grin. "He's a famous American porn star."

Celine's eyes grew large, and she scanned me from head to toe. She then translated for her friend Adele, who also gave me the once over. I wanted to correct what Walt said but instead just went along with the improvisation. While the four of us were doing our best to carry on a conversation, I felt a tap on my shoulder. It was Kelly Kirkland. She took me by the arm and led me away from Walt and the two French women.

"Excuse me," I said to the others, then followed Kelly over to Janie Leslie, who was engaged in a conversation with two Italian men. Janie introduced them as Giovanni and Rossano. Neither of them spoke English, but they both seemed friendly enough.

"This is Niko," said Kelly. "He's our stage manager."

"*Ah, Buono,*" Giovanni said, "*direttore di scena.*"

"*Si,*" I said, hoping he was correct with his translation.

"I really liked how you dealt with that German," said Janie.

"Yeah," said Kelly. "He had some nerve."

"I still don't know what made him so angry," I said.

Just then, I felt a hand on my shoulder and turned to find that it was that German cameraman himself. But this time, he had a smile on his face instead of a scowl.

"I wanted to tell you I'm sorry," he said, "for being an... How do you say it in English?"

"An asshole," Janie offered. "Sorry, I don't know the German word for it."

"Okay," he smiled. "I deserve that." He offered to buy me a drink to make amends.

"Sure, Jack Daniels on the rocks," I said, "but it's not necessary."

"No, I insist," he said, making his way over to the bar. Kelly, Janie, and their two Italian friends made their way over to the two arched windows that opened up to a view of the city.

I noticed the German soundman and the reporter were also there. They were in a conversation with two German-speaking females. Eventually, the cameraman returned with our two drinks. He handed me mine, then raised his glass for a toast.

"Prost," he declared, then took a large sip.

"Cheers," I replied, doing the same.

He then stuck his right hand out, offering me a handshake.

"Wilfred," he announced, introducing himself.

"Niko," I replied, shaking his hand. "So, what part of West Germany are you from?"

"Munich," he answered. "Do you know Germany?"

"No," I replied. But then I remembered Munich hosted the 1972 Summer Olympics. "Were you there in Munich during the Olympic Games?"

"Yes," he answered, hesitantly. "I was seventeen and still in school."

"I was in school at that time myself," I added. "Did you get to attend any of the Olympic events?"

"We had tickets," he answered. "But we were never able to use them."

"Why not?" I asked, wondering why they'd buy tickets and then not go.

"My father was a police officer at the time, and he was killed while trying to save the Israeli athletes from the terrorists." He looked down at his drink, swirling the ice cubes around in his glass.

I suddenly realized who Wilfred was. During the 1972 Olympic Games in Munich, the Palestinian terrorist group Black September killed eleven Israeli athletes and coaches. One West German police officer was also killed. That police officer must have been Wilfred's father.

"My God, Wilfred. I'm so sorry."

"It was such a horrible thing for everyone, not just our family." He paused. "After the terrorists were captured, they postponed the Olympics for thirty-four hours before finally continuing them."

I remembered the U.S. team sent the swimmer, Mark Spitz, home because he was Jewish, and they worried about his safety.

"When I was sent here to cover your Olympic Games," Wilfred said, "I was asked if I would be okay with it, emotionally. I couldn't imagine I'd have any problems since it was so long ago. But after seeing all of the Olympic banners and decorations, it brought me right back to those awful days."

Wilfred paused for a moment before continuing.

"In Munich, we were like you people from Los Angeles, proud of our city, and looking forward to hosting the world. But instead of recognition for all of our efforts, and the joyous celebration we had planned, we had terrorist killings instead," he paused. "Now, no one wants to remember Munich in 1972 because it was a permanent stain on the Olympic Games."

I bought us another round of drinks, and Wilfred and I talked until most everyone else had gone. He told me his television crew was planning to cover the opening ceremony and then some of the athletic events. There were a few West German athletes he was hoping would do well in the competition. I told Wilfred I would be rooting for them as well.

∞ ∞ ∞

From the Variety Arts Club, I headed straight home. When I went to bed, I experienced another earthquake dream, but this one was completely different from the ones before.

This time, I'm up in Beverly Hills, on Coldwater Canyon. It's a bright, sunny day and I'm driving a white Jeep Wrangler convertible with the top down, and the Eurythmics song "Sweet Dreams Are Made of This" is playing over the car's stereo. I turned onto a long driveway, and then parked the Jeep in front of a sprawling hilltop home. The place was one of those great mid-century modern mansions built by fashionable Hollywood types back in the late 1950s. I recognized the place because I'd actually been there once before.

Months earlier, Richard DeVries asked me to drop off a playscript for the Music Center's other tenant, the Ahmanson Theatre. Charlton Heston needed a script for *Detective Story* because he was going to do that show. Mr. Heston was no stranger to the Ahmanson, having starred in five previous plays there over the last several years. That day though, I never did get to meet the famous actor because I had to hand the script to a woman who'd answered the door.

But in my dream, with script in hand, I rang Charlton Heston's doorbell, and Heston himself answered it. He stood there, all 6 feet 3 inches of him, wearing a white tennis outfit ala Jimmy Connors. But for some reason, Mr. Heston was made up to look like the Mexican drug enforcement officer, Ramon Miguel Vargas, whom he played in the movie, Touch of Evil. His hair and mustache had been dyed jet black, and his dark facial make-up was supposed to make him look like a Mexican. I was half expecting Orson Welles to make an appearance as the disheveled police captain.

Heston had me follow him, then led me to a separate building just past the tennis pavilion.

"You must really like tennis," I said.

"Si, mucho," he answered in a Spanish accent."

Inside the building, there was a large photography studio, and past that, we entered a home movie theater. I thought to myself, "Wow! How Hollywood can you get?" The theater had three rows of comfortable seats and a large movie screen. Just then, the movie projector started up and the lights dimmed. Mr. Heston's 1974 movie, Earthquake, began to play on the screen. We quickly grabbed seats, and Heston found two boxes of candy, offering me one.

"Raisinettes?" he asked.

"Sure," I said, taking the box. I wondered how he knew that Raisinettes were my favorite movie candy?

We sat and watched the movie for some time. Heston's acting was okay, but the storyline was hokey and predictable, and frankly, could have used some humor. Finally, the movie got to its climactic earthquake scene. During this scene, the shaking grew stronger and louder. The shaking in the film seemed to transfer to the walls of Heston's home theater, which were now shaking violently. The room actually began to break apart, like a scene from the movie. Heston and I were frantically trying to dodge falling debris. I thought that we were both going to die right there and then. I even imagined the headlines in tomorrow's Daily Variety; "Charlton Heston Killed in Earthquake, While Watching His Movie, Earthquake."

I finally woke up, perplexed that my earthquake dream had somehow morphed into a bad Charlton Heston movie.

Thursday
July 19

●❖ Obviously, I still had earthquakes on my mind. I remembered back to my class with Professor Lafayette. Our textbook had been Carey McWilliam's *Southern California, an Island on the Land*. Lafayette had actually known McWilliams and considered his book the definitive history of the region.

During our first lecture, Lafayette asked for a show of hands to see how many students had heard of the writer Louis Adamic, a good friend and colleague of McWilliams. I noticed my hand was the only one up.

"Mr. Petrovich," Lafayette said, referring to his seating chart to find my name. "You've heard of Louis Adamic?"

"Yes," I admitted. "I wrote a paper on him back in high school."

The other students glared at me as if I'd just said Farah Fawcett was having my love child. Professor Lafayette smiled broadly, surprised by my answer.

"How did that come about, exactly?" he asked.

"I guess because Adamic was from San Pedro, like me."

Lafayette gave me a long stare, trying to size me up.

"Someday you'll have to tell us more about it," he said.

"I'd be glad to."

As he continued on with his lecture, my classmates eyed me with suspicion. Who was this guy from San Pedro? They figured the only good thing to come out of San Pedro was tuna.

After his lecture, Lafayette assigned us to read Carey McWilliams 1933 article, "The Folklore of Earthquakes." That was so long ago I couldn't remember exactly what it said. Fortunately, I thought I might still have the article. I looked through my file cabinet, and to my amazement, there it was. I pulled out the article and began to read:

"On the basis of their reaction to the word 'earthquake,' Californians can be divided into three classes: first, the innocent late arrivals who have never felt an earthquake, but who go around avowing to all and sundry that 'it must be fun'; next, those who have experienced a slight quake and should know better, but who nonetheless persist in propagating the fable the San Francisco quake of 1906 was the only major upheaval the state has ever suffered; and last, the victims of a real earthquake--for example, the residents of San Francisco, Santa Barbara, or more recently, Long Beach (The Sylmar quake was still many years away). To these last, the world is full of terror. They are supersensitive to the slightest rattles and jars and move uneasily whenever a heavy truck passes on the highway."

Maybe that's all there was to my earthquake fears. Since I've experienced a real earthquake, I'm now supersensitive. I put the article back into its file folder.

On the front page of the morning *Los Angeles Times*, there were several photos of athletes arriving at Los Angeles International Airport for the Games, their nation's flags held proudly. While I had my coffee, I opened up the sports page and read a long article about the various U.S. Olympians that were competing for medals. Carl Lewis and Edwin Moses were the two favorites in track and field, and the U.S. men's and women's gymnastics teams were expected to do well, Mary Lou Retton was one of the names mentioned. The U.S. men's basketball team was also a favorite. They had an excellent group of young college all-stars, including a player from North Carolina named Michael Jordan.

After I finished the sports page, I wanted to get right to work on my adaptation of Carlos Cruz's novel *Edendale*. But there was only one problem, I didn't have the book. And since the novel was long out of print, getting a new one was going to be impossible. I'd checked it out before at the library, but now I needed a copy I could markup. I could never deface a library book. To me, that was sacrilegious. Luckily, there were over a dozen great used bookstores right up on Hollywood Boulevard. I was sure I could find the book there.

I didn't always love books. In first and second grade, I would rather be outside playing than reading. But at the beginning of third grader, I somehow discovered comic books. "Bang!" "Pow!" "Boom!" "Zap!" My timing couldn't have been better because I'd started buying comic books right at the inception of Marvel Comics. At my neighborhood drug store, I bought all the premiere issues that were just being introduced. *The Amazing Spider Man*, *The Fantastic Four*, *The X-Men*, *Captain America*, *Iron Man*, *The Incredible Hulk*, *Thor*, and *The Avengers*. Then I continued to amass a collection. I took meticulous care of each magazine as if it was the *Guttenberg Bible*. Every book was carefully stacked in numerical order and placed on the top shelf of my closet.

After several years, I eventually stopped buying comic books. My passion had waned. But I kept my collection intact because I'd heard collectors were now placing a value on collections like mine. But one day, my father cornered me in my bedroom.

"You need to get rid of all those comic books," he said, pointing to my closet shelf.

"Why?"

"They're just taking up room, and you don't even read them anymore."

"I'm keeping them as an investment."

"They're comic books," he chuckled. "You paid twelve cents for them. How much do you think you're going to make?"

"Dad, people collect them," I tried to argue. "Do you know how much an original *Superman* goes for?"

"Why, do you have one of those?"

"No. Action Comics # 1 came out in 1938. You were around then, not me. I have *Amazing Fantasy # 15*, the debut of *Spider Man*. That was 1962, and I have every issue after that."

"They're all just taking up space."

"It's my closet," I argued. "And they're not in anybody's way."

"Get rid of them," he demanded, then walked out of my room.

This was so unlike my dad. He'd always been easy going, and pretty much let me do my own thing. But for some reason, he'd drawn a line in the sand, and there was no changing his mind. There were a couple of collectors in town who cherry picked the best of my collection, and then a local comic book store bought the rest dirt cheap. I felt like I'd hardly gotten anything for my prized possessions. My dad, on the other hand, was so happy I actually made any money at all off of what he perceived as junk.

"Look at that nice empty space," he said, proudly pointing at my now empty shelf.

"Yeah," I agreed, "It's definitely empty."

It took a while before I put anything else on that shelf. It had been reserved for my comic book collection, a place of great honor. It had been filled with super heroes and magical worlds.

Eventually, I filled that shelf with stuff, ordinary stuff. But there was an emptiness in me that took years to fill. I was always a picky reader, and if a book didn't hook me right away, then I just couldn't finish it. Finding a good book, was like finding a copy of *Amazing Fantasy # 15*.

Earlier this year, when I was assigned to adapt *Sonora Town,* I had written two drafts before I finally got it right. I'd never collaborated with anyone before, so I took copious notes from the creative team, thinking that's what I needed to do. They gave me plenty of ideas of what they thought should be in the play. Everyone had suggestions, so I took all of their ideas and incorporated them into my first draft, trying hard to please everyone else. But when I handed them that first draft, which fulfilled every one of their requests, they hated it, absolutely hated it. I sat there listening to them tell me how awful it was, how uninspired it was. Where did I get all of those stupid ideas?

The truth was they were stupid ideas because they were their stupid ideas, and I had foolishly listened to them. I'd tried to give them exactly what I thought they wanted, instead of what I knew the story needed. I sat there taking in all their criticism, realizing the mistake that I'd made. Instead of responding to their criticisms, I simply asked for a chance to write a second draft. Since I'd barely used half of my allotted time, I thought it was a fair request. They reluctantly agreed to give me one more chance. As I was leaving Richard's office, I threw all of their notes into the trash.

When I gave them the new second draft, which was based on what I thought the story needed, they all loved it, and said that it was exactly what they'd always wanted. "Why didn't you just give us this the first time?" they asked. Again, I didn't reply, I just smiled. The one lesson I learned from that experience was: trust your own judgment above all others.

∞ ∞ ∞

Vidor, my neighbor, was just coming up the stairs carrying a basket of clean laundry, while I was going down the stairs carrying my 12-speed. Vidor wore a baby blue baseball cap with the letter "N" in white.

"Hi, Vidor," I joked. "Are you using up all the hot water again?"

"Niko," he laughed. "You know me, I'm always in hot water."

"I didn't know you were a baseball fan." I said, referring to the ball cap he was wearing.

"I'm not," he frowned. "My aunt sent this hat. It's my father's team, Nicaragua. They're playing in the Olympics; he's their coach."

"Your father?" I asked. "Wow, that's great."

"Back in Panama, he was once a famous baseball player. He was handsome, strong, and he probably fucked every woman in the stands."

"He was a ballplayer, that's really cool."

"He was the best pitcher on a championship team that once beat Cuba, Puerto Rico, and the Dominican Republic all in the same year. He also played in the Negro Leagues here in this country. Had he been white, who knows, he might have played in the Major Leagues."

Vidor said all this in a matter-of-fact way, with little enthusiasm for his father.

"I'm attending some Olympic baseball games," I said. "I'll look for your dad."

"You can't miss him," Vidor said. "He'll be the one trying to get all the girls' phone numbers."

From Koreatown, I rode west on Fourth Street, and right into the Windsor Square/Hancock Park neighborhoods. I loved the area's elegant homes, its wide streets, and its mile high palm trees. Sidney Mordechai had once pointed out the red brick Tudor mansion on the corner of Fourth and Muirfield. The house had once been the home of the famous black entertainer, Nat "King" Cole. In 1948, Mr. Cole and his young bride, Maria, bought the home as a place to settle down and raise a family. Unfortunately, after some of the neighbors learned of his new purchase, they weren't pleased. They didn't like having a black family in their neighborhood, and an all-white homeowner's association was formed with the goal to remove the Cole family.

In the 1920s, when the neighborhood had first been established, a 50-year restrictive covenant was instituted to prevent any non-white family from living there. Just before the Coles had bought their home, the Supreme Court of the

United States ruled such covenants were uncon-stitutional, striking down the validity of these long-standing practices.

But this court ruling didn't stop these white home owners. They tried various tactics to "solve their problem." First, they offered to buy the home from the Coles, offering them a slight profit, but the Coles declined. Then, someone placed a sign on their front yard with an ugly racial slur. When the sign didn't intimidate them, a gunshot was fired into their window. Finally, a cross was burned on their front lawn. But none of those threats caused the Coles to want to leave.

Through all of the turmoil, Mr. Cole and his wife remained surprisingly calm. When Nat spoke to reporters, he simply let everyone know he and his bride were good citizens, they loved their new home, and they planned to stay, as any other American citizen would. He made it clear to everyone his family was not going anywhere.

Over time, the Hancock Park neighbors began to slowly warm to the Cole family. They started to realize the Coles were actually good people. The other homeowners even began to take pride in the fact a celebrity of Cole's stature lived in their neighborhood. This acceptance didn't happen overnight, it took a long time, but it did happen. Everyone finally acknowledged the Cole family was a valued part of the community. Nat "King" Cole was living in this home in 1965 when he developed cancer and eventually died at the age of forty-five. The very neighbors who once protested his family's arrival, were now saddened by his untimely death.

From Hancock Park, I rode into Larchmont Village, passing the Le Petite Mustache, Jules and Betty's French restaurant. At Melrose, I switched over to El Centro and followed that street up to Hollywood Boulevard. I began my search at Gilbert's Book Shop, the street's oldest bookstore. Mr. Gilbert, the owner, was married to the daughter of author Edgar Rice Burroughs. So, there were probably a few Tarzan books on his shelves, but sadly, no copies of Cruz's novel *Edendale*. I also had no luck at several other nearby bookstores.

Whenever I could afford a new book, I usually headed right over to the Pickwick Bookshop. Opened in 1938 by Louis Epstein, it was considered the "anchor tenant" for Hollywood Boulevard's many book shops.

There are at least two different versions of how Mr. Epstein, earned the capital to purchase the bookshop's building. In one version of the story, Paramount Pictures is making the movie *No Man of Her Own,* with Clark Gable and Carole Lombard. In the film, Lombard is supposed to be a librarian, so the prop department needed books to stock her library. Epstein ended up loaning Paramount over 20,000 books for the duration of their filming. Under the arrangement, he had not only negotiated excellent financial terms, but the right to sell any individual book he had loaned out to the studio. This included Epstein's customers being allowed to travel to the Paramount sound stage and pick books right off the shelf. Epstein even sold books to extras who were working on the picture. That's one version of the story.

In another version of the story, a movie studio (not sure which one) rented 5,000 books at five cents a day per book for thirty days. After the thirty days, Epstein called the studio and asks for the return of his 5,000 books, but his requests are ignored. Finally, the books were returned an entire year later. Now, the studio only wanted to honor the original thirty-day contract, but Epstein expected payment for the entire year. Finally, his lawyers convinced the studio to pay the full amount. With that money, Louis Epstein bought the building on Hollywood Boulevard and opened his Pickwick Book Shop. I can't really vouch for either story, but they both sounded pretty good.

Only a block away from Louis Epstein's Pickwick Book Shop, Jerry Weinstein and his brother-in-law, Alan Siegel owned Hollywood Book City, the street's preeminent used book store. With a quarter million books, the number of titles seemed endless. The Weinstein family had a long history as knowledgeable bibliophiles. If they didn't have a particular book you needed, they could help you find it. Their place was well stocked and spacious. Having started with a single storefront, they'd already expanded to three full storefronts with the possibility of adding more in the future. At the front counter, I saw Jerry and asked him if he had a copy of *Edendale* by Carlos Cruz.

"I think so," he said. "Follow me."

He led me through the catacombs of book shelves, down one isle, then up another. He finally stopped in the fiction section for authors whose last names started with "C." Among the authors, I noticed: James M. Cain, Erskine Caldwell, and Albert Camus. Finally, on a shelf just above my head, there was a single copy of *Edendale*.

"Here you go," Jerry said, pulling down the old hard-cover book and handing it to me.

Even though it was missing its dust jacket, it still looked damn good.

"Great," I said, opening the book and looking through it.

I noticed it had a publication date of 1938, and Jerry's price had been written on the front inside cover in pencil, "$4.99." Inside the back cover, I saw a small sticker which read: "The Stanley Rose Book Shop, Hollywood," with an image of a centaur firing a bow and arrow.

"We still find those sometimes," Jerry said. "But not as many as we used to."

"Wasn't that bookstore nearby?" I asked.

"Yeah, right across the street, next to Musso & Frank."

The Stanley Rose Bookshop was a legendary 1930s hangout for many of the famous writers of the day. They often gathered in the backroom after hours to drink and bullshit.

I paid Jerry for the book, then decided to make one more stop. Larry Edmond's Bookshop was the first book store anywhere to specialize in all things cinema. Whether you needed a movie poster, movie script, publicity photos, or even books on various filmmakers, you could find them all here. While I was scanning the shelves, I notice the female owner, Git Luboviski, speaking to an older gentleman who was standing at the counter. The man had bushy eyebrows and a full head of silver hair. He appeared to be jotting something down on the title page of a book. This made me think the man was an author signing one of his own books. I tried to get closer, so I could get a better look. The man finished by signing his name, then shut the book to reveal the dust jacket's cover. It read: *What Makes Sammy Run*, a novel, by Budd Schulberg.

Here I was, within a few feet of the great Budd Schulberg. His *What Makes Sammy Run* was one of my very favorite Hollywood novels. Schulberg also wrote the screenplay for the Oscar winning film *On the Waterfront,* among other things. After the Watts Riots in 1965, he surprised everyone when he put his writing on hold and helped to create the Watts Writers' Workshop in South Central L.A.

I wanted to introduce myself to this great man, but I thought better of it because I didn't want to seem too pushy. I didn't want him to see me as a version of his character, Sammy Glick from *What Makes Sammy Run.* Sammy was the prototype of the ruthless, self-serving, Hollywood jerk, willing to do just about anything to get ahead. I didn't want Budd Schulberg to think I was anything like Sammy Glick.

I watched from a distance while he spoke to Git, the bookstore's owner, and then handed her the book he'd just signed. Without saying a word, I retreated from the bookstore. Once outside, I began to feel I'd blown a golden opportunity, and I then became frustrated with my own inaction. My friend, Randy, used to say: "No guts, no glory." I suddenly felt like a lousy failure, defeated by my own self-doubt. It was too early to have a drink, but there was still one place I could drown my sorrows.

C. C. Brown's Ice Cream Parlor had been on Hollywood Boulevard since 1929. It was a classic, old-fashioned, ice cream parlor, which claimed to be where the first hot fudge sundae was served. I locked up my bike, grabbed the book off my rack, and walked through door. I considered grabbing a stool at the counter but decided on a booth instead. I ordered their famous hot fudge sundae, then cracked open *Edendale* and began to read.

Just then, Budd Schulberg walked right into C. C. Brown's. Schulberg seemed completely at ease here, like it was a place he knew well. He headed straight for the counter and grabbed a stool. When his waitress arrived, I heard him order a Buster Brown, which I believe was a banana split. I heard Schulberg mention to the waitress he'd been coming here ever since it opened in 1929. I'd blown my first opportunity to meet him, but now I had a second chance. Before my ice cream arrived, I grabbed my book and slid onto a stool beside him.

"Mr. Schulberg," I said, nervously. "My name is Niko Petrovich." I extended my right hand. "I'm a writer, and I just had to say I admire your work."

"Call me Budd," he said, graciously shaking my hand. "It's always good to meet a fellow writer."

"Earlier, when I saw you at Larry Edmond's, I wanted to introduce myself, but I didn't want you to think I was pushy like Sammy Glick."

He laughed, which put me at ease. The waitress brought out my vanilla ice cream with its small pitcher of hot fudge.

"You know," he said. "When I wrote that book in 1941, Sammy was the villain of the story, he was a cautionary tale."

"Yes. He was the model of who not to be like."

"That's right, because he was ruthless, cut-throat, and wouldn't stop at anything to get ahead. You simply introducing yourself to me wouldn't have qualified as being pushy."

As I poured the hot fudge over my ice cream, the waitress brought Schulberg his Buster Brown. We both sat enjoying our desserts.

"About ten years ago," he said, "the perception about Sammy started to change."

"How so?" I asked.

"I was speaking to a college class about the book, and afterwards, a young student approached me. He told me how much he admired Sammy's rise to power, and how it was an example of how he should lead his life in order to succeed. Then others started telling me the same thing. I was horrified."

"My God," I said. "They entirely missed the point."

"Yes, completely. But back then, at least they had some awareness to the irony of being so despicable, they were at least aware that what they were doing was morally wrong, even if they were going to do it anyway. But now, there's not even any consideration of such matters; morals and decency are considered old-fashioned.

Sammy has become their role model; someone they should aspire to be like." He paused for a moment. "What the hell have I done?"

We discussed the unintended consequences of creating such a character, and how they can develop a life of their own. I then set my copy of *Edendale* on the counter beside Schulberg. He took the book, tilting it to read the title and author's name from the book's spine. A look of recognition appeared on his face. He then opened the book to the inside back cover and noticed the sticker for the Stanley Rose Bookshop.

"I know this book," he said, smiling, "and its author, and this bookstore."

"All three, really?"

"Carlos was never a regular at the Stanley Rose Bookshop like some of us, but he was around when he'd published a new book. That's when I first met him. I thought he was a very good writer and unique because of his Mexican-American heritage. But then later he just seemed to vanish, no books, no stories, nothing."

"The Mark Taper Forum produced my adaptation of his book *Sonora Town* at their Literary Cabaret."

He congratulated me on getting my play produced, and we talked a bit about the process. I then asked him what he was currently working on.

"I'm supposed to be covering the Olympic boxing," he said. "But I'm still waiting to hear."

I knew Schulberg had covered boxing for Sports Illustrated and other publications. He also wrote the fine boxing novel *The Harder They Fall,* which had been turned into a movie with Humphrey Bogart.

"How do you think the U.S. boxers will do?" I asked, remembering the great boxing team from the 1976 Montreal Olympics.

"With the Soviets and the Cubans boycotting, we should do well. Look for Evander Holyfield and Pernell Whitaker, they're as good as it gets."

"I will," I nodded. "Anyone else?"

"One of our best boxers didn't even qualify for the team, a kid named Mike Tyson, tough as nails, but unfortunately he lost his qualifying bouts."

We talked boxing for a while, and then I asked him about his involvement with the Watts Writer's Workshop. He smiled from ear to ear and his eyes lit up.

"It was the best thing I ever did," he said. "When I went down to Watts, buildings were still smoldering, there would be a block that had burned down, but one building had somehow survived. I put up flyers, 'Writer's Workshop, every Wednesday at 3 pm,' but for weeks nobody came. Then one person showed up, then another, and another. I wasn't there to lecture anyone; I wanted a dialogue. John Steinbeck had been on the NEA council, and he made sure we received a grant. That grant allowed us to get a building. Some of the members of the workshop were homeless. So, they slept at the Douglas Center where we held our meetings. We eventually had two dozen writers and poets. We were doing so well, then an FBI informant torched our building. I still can't comprehend why someone would do such a thing."

Schulberg said after that, he moved back east, where he focused his energies in founding the Frederick Douglas Creative Arts Center in Harlem.

"What so many people don't understand about Watts," he said, "is how depressed the economics of the community are. Unemployment is thirty-five to forty percent for adults and seventy percent for young men. The crime and drug use are symptoms of a society that has allowed poverty to destroy a community. There is so much untapped potential there. We can't go on ignoring the problems and just assume they'll just go away. The question isn't if we'll have another uprising like Watts, but when."

As we were finishing the last of our ice cream, I asked if he would sign my copy of *Edendale*. He protested at first, saying it wasn't his novel to sign, but finally agreed when I told him he could sign it on the back page near the Stanley Rose Bookshop sticker.

"For the old gang in the backroom," I said.

Schulberg took the pen and wrote:

"To Niko,

You're no Sammy Glick, but that's a good thing.

With best wishes,

Budd Schulberg"

꩜ ꩜ ꩜

From C. C. Brown's, I made it to Cedars-Sinai in under a half hour. Last time I saw Beryl, we tried to think of a way to save her photo collection, but we didn't come up with anything. It was once again time for us to put our heads together and try to come up with a solution.

Beryl looked a little better than the last time I saw her. She had a little more color in her face and also seemed more alert. For a while, we brainstormed ideas, trying to come up with something that might work. When Beryl got tired, we'd take a break for a while. Fortunately, her photographs were safely locked up in her vault and secure for now. After she rested a bit, Beryl told me of another problem she had. Well, actually two other problems.

"Niko," she said. "I need you to do me a big favor."

"What kind of favor?" I asked.

"My sister was supposed to grab my two cats, but she couldn't find them. She left them food and water, but by now they'll be hungry and thirsty and need more."

I came here to help Beryl save her photo collection; I wasn't here to offer pet care for her two cats.

"I wish I could help you, Beryl, but I'm pretty busy, and to be honest, I'm just not an animal person."

"There's plenty of food in the cupboard, just put some out every day with a little water."

"Beryl, I've never even had a pet, unless you count the goldfish we had to flush down the toilet."

But Beryl wouldn't take no for an answer, and she went on and on about her two cats. She was getting so upset I was worried she'd have another stroke, so I reluctantly gave in.

"Okay," I said. "I'll do it. Just tell me what I need to do."

"Wonderful," she smiled. "I knew I could count on a fellow Trojan."

"Yeah, yeah," I said. "I've already agreed to help. You don't need to butter me up."

Beryl went into detail about how to care for her two cats, Maggie and Dottie. The two, she told me, were named for Margaret Bourke-White and Dorothea Lange, two famous female photographers whom Beryl had actually known. My instructions included how to clean the cat box. "Oh, goody," I said. "I can't wait." She also told me where I'd find her hidden house key. Beryl then looked at me wistfully.

"When I got those two, they were just kittens. Now, I don't know if I'll ever see them again."

"You'll see them again, Beryl, I promise." I wasn't so sure I could actually keep that promise.

It didn't take me long to ride to Beryl's house from Cedars. The hidden house key was right where she said it would be. When I unlocked the door, I had to crawl under the boards that had been nailed across its opening. Inside, it was warm and musty. One of Beryl's cats, Maggie, the Calico, came out from under a table. She rubbed against my leg and meowed. Then Dottie, the tabby, also made an appearance. As I walked to the kitchen, they both followed me. The food was right where Beryl said it would be, so I put out a healthy amount, along with two good size bowls of water. They ate and drank ravenously. While they were eating, I went to the back porch and changed their litter box, a truly shitty task.

While I was washing my hands in the kitchen, I heard someone call out "Hello" at the front door, and I hurried to the entryway to find Nina Levenson standing there on the porch peering in through the nailed-up boards.

"Hi, Nina," I said.

"Niko, what are you doing here?"

"Beryl asked me to take care of her two cats."

"Oh," she said, crawling under the boards to get inside. "I'm here to do some inventory for the estate sale. I've also acquired the listing to put the house up for sale, so I also need to determine a good asking price."

"When are you planning to list the house?" I asked.

"Right after the estate sale. The place is a tear down, so we really don't need to spruce it up any."

"A tear down?" I asked, shocked they would be tearing down such a wonderful old house. "Isn't there a chance it can be saved?" I asked.

"Not really," she answered. "Someone will want to build either apartments or condos."

I knew Nina was right because Mr. Lee, my landlord, even offered to buy Jules and Betty's house just so he could knock it down and put up a new apartment building.

"How about Beryl's photo collection?" I asked. "I know she wants to keep it intact."

"Well, that's very nice," Nina said. "But her family expects me to make them as much money as possible."

Nina let me know she had her own key to the house, so she would lock up when she'd finished her inventory. She was also hoping to find the combination to the vault where Beryl kept her photographs. I returned Beryl's key to its hiding place and got back on my bike.

∞ ∞ ∞

As I approached my block, I noticed my friend Jules out walking his two dogs, Mimi and Rodolfo. Jules' head was down, and his expression looked pained. I could tell something was wrong.

"Hi, Jules," I said, pulling up to the nearby curb. "Everything okay?"

Jules shook his head no, while choking back emotions. His two dogs sniffed around the grass for a place to do their business.

"What's wrong?" I asked. "Maybe I can help."

"I fired Betty's friend, Matteo," he answered.

Matteo was a young actor who Jules hired to work as a waiter at his restaurant.

"What happened?"

"Betty said she was headed to the gym, and she asked if I wanted to join her. I told her I couldn't because I was expecting an important phone call. But right after she left, I got that call and finished my business. So, I grabbed my bag and headed to the gym. But when I got there, there was no Betty, and nobody had even seen her."

Mimi found a spot on the lawn and squatted to pee.

"So, where was she?" I asked.

"I was getting suspicious about the two of

them, so I drove to the address I had for Matteo, and Betty's car was parked right out front. I wanted to get out of my car and knock on his door, but I didn't."

I watched him wipe tears from his eyes with his sleeve. After he'd regained his composure, he finally spoke.

"So, I came home and waited for her. When she got here, I asked how the gym was. She smiled and said she had a great workout."

I cringed.

"I told her where I'd found her car when she was supposed to be at the gym. She tried to deny anything happened, and actually got angry at me for following her. I immediately got on the phone and fired Matteo. She started calling me every name in the book. I told her if she ever saw Matteo again, I'd be filing divorce papers."

"I don't know if I could be so forgiving," I admitted.

"I know," he said. "But I need to give her one more chance. Could you come by the restaurant tonight? I could use a friend."

"Sure," I told him. "But I can't stay long. I have a show tonight."

Rodolfo finally found a good spot on the grass and took a healthy dump. I couldn't help thinking the dog's steaming pile perfectly represented how Jules was feeling at that very moment.

ↄ ↄ ↄ

Once home, I took a quick shower. I was meeting my ex-girlfriend, Carol, for lunch, and I wanted to look my best. Carol was getting married in a couple of days, and I knew that this might be our very last time together. Her fiancé, Douglas, didn't like me much. After I threw on a shirt and a pair of jeans, I walked over to the Four Coins Sidewalk Café on Wilshire. Since Carol was so busy with the renovation at the Wiltern, we'd decided to have lunch right across the street in the McKinley Building.

When Carol's architecture firm first began their restoration of the Wiltern, they had no idea what bad shape the theater was in. Besides missing it's seats and many Art Deco fixtures, several of the murals had water damage, and much of the theater's plasterwork was crumbling. A portion of theater's ornate ceiling had even collapsed. Carol assured me that the theater would once again look like it did when it opened back in 1931.

The Four Coins Sidewalk Café was located right across Wilshire in the central courtyard of the old McKinley Building. The McKinley, built in 1927, was an elegant two-story Spanish Revival structure with a row of cute shops on the street, and a large Spanish courtyard in the center. A three-story Spanish tower stood majestically over everything.

Carol was standing by the courtyard's large outdoor fountain when I arrived. Her blue eyes sparkled, and her blonde hair bounced as she walked toward me. We hugged and kissed each other on the cheek.

"You look happy," I said, smiling. "Things must be going well."

"I have a lot to be happy about," she beamed.

Carol practically glowed, and I knew why. Career wise, she loved her job and was doing exactly the kind of work she'd always wanted to do. Her architectural firm specialized in historic preservation, and they had a flood of projects lined up after the Wiltern. And this weekend, she was marrying a man she loved and who loved her right back.

A waitress seated us at a small table near the fountain and then brought us our water and two menus.

"I don't know if Douglas deserves you," I frowned.

"Maybe I don't deserve him. Did you ever think of that?"

I suddenly felt very sad. Douglas was going to be her husband and not me. I felt like something inside me was slowly dying. She began to tell me about where they were going on their honeymoon and the new home they planned to build. I tried to smile, and even told her how great it all sounded. Carol was the one woman I could honestly say I loved, and here she was marrying someone else.

"Are you seeing anyone?" she asked.

The question perked me back up and took me out of my funk.

"As a matter of fact, I am." I smiled. "Her name's Cynthia, and I really like her.

"That's great. What's she like?"

I began to describe Cynthia in detail. I also told her about the day Cynthia and I spent together in Pasadena.

"Is she good in bed?" Carol asked, with a grin.

I was a little taken aback by her question. I certainly would never have asked her the same thing about Douglas, although maybe she wanted me to so she could brag about how great the guy was in the sack.

"We haven't gotten to that yet," I sighed. "But I'm hopeful."

"Is she ambitious?" Carol asked. "Is she someone who is going to put her career above all else?"

This was a strange question, and one I never really considered. Carol had a career when I first met her, so I just assumed most women wanted the same thing.

"I don't know," I said. "She's well educated, so I assume she'll want to do something with her education. Why do you ask?"

"I just don't want to see you get hurt," she frowned. "You're pretty sensitive."

Where was this coming from? I thought. Carol was moving on with her life. Why was she so worried about mine?

"I don't understand your concern," I said.

"You're ambitious, Niko, but not overly so. You need to find a woman who cares about you and not just herself."

"Are you saying that I'm not tough enough, or what?" I asked.

"No, not at all. The answer is complicated."

"Why don't you try to explain then?"

Carol thought for a moment, not wanting to say the wrong thing.

"When you, Niko, come to a closed door, if it's locked, you figure the room just wasn't meant to be, and you go try another door. Some people don't simply give up on that first room. Even if they have to break down the door. They aren't concerned with how their actions affect others or even if someone gets hurt along the way."

"Are you saying nice guys finish last?"

"No. I'm just hoping you'll find a woman who's not just in it for herself."

After the waitress took our order, we changed the subject and talked about mutual friends. Carol also told me more about the work she was doing across the street, which all sounded so fascinating. I then shared with her my plans to adapt *Edendale,* and this pleased her. She'd seen *Sonora Town* and liked it.

When the lunch was over, I walked her to the crosswalk on the corner. While the light was red, we turned and hugged. It was a long embrace, as if neither of us really wanted to let go. But we finally did when the light turned green.

"Good luck, Niko," she said.

"You too, Carol, with everything."

She started across the street, and I watched her walk. When she reached the theater, she showed the security guard her pass, then disappeared into the Wiltern.

Back in the apartment, I cracked open my copy of *Edendale* and tried to read. But instead, I kept thinking about Carol. After a while, I finally returned to reading Carlos Cruz's novel. As I read, I underlined passages and scribbled notes in the book's margins.

From downstairs, I began to hear Vidor playing his piano. It was one of Chopin's Nocturnes. I slid open my balcony door and allowed the music to come in. I spent the afternoon listening to Vidor's piano while reading *Edendale*. I finally had to stop when it was time to head over to Jules' restaurant.

It was early so I managed to find a parking spot right out front. Just as I was parking, the restaurant's door swung open, and Matteo, their former waiter, stepped out onto the sidewalk. He carried a letter sized envelope, which I watched him open. He pulled out what looked like a check and examined it. It was easy to see why this young actor appealed to Betty. He was handsome, with wavy brown hair, chiseled features, and an olive complexion. Matteo finally slid the check back into its envelope, got into his red, BMW 1600, and drove off. Only then did I get our of my car and go into the restaurant.

Jules and Betty's place was a casual bistro with exposed brick walls and a high wooden beamed ceiling. The hanging plants and ivy-covered rear wall added to its rustic charm. As I entered, Betty was seating a group over at the other end of the room. She noticed me and made her way over.

"Hi, Niko," she said, smiling. "It's so good to see you."

She seemed friendly. But I didn't know if that was genuine, or she was just being a good actress.

"Good to see you too," I said, trying to be equally pleasant.

Betty seemed unfazed by Matteo's departure. Maybe this whole thing with him was really over, just a quick fling, and now she and Jules could begin to mend their lives together.

"Just you tonight?" she asked.

"Yeah, just me."

Betty grabbed a menu and led me over to a small table.

"Tonight's special is the *bouillabaisse*," she said. "Although, I know you usually order the *Soupe à l'oignon*."

"Tonight, I might try something different."

"We're short a waiter," she frowned, "so I'll be your waitress."

I assumed the waiter she was referring to was Matteo.

"Would you like something to drink?" she asked.

"Just water for now. Oh, and by the way, I have my Drama Geeks show tonight, so I can't stay long."

"I understand. I'll be back with your water."

When Betty returned, I ordered the *bouillabaisse* and a glass of white wine. Betty must have told Jules I was here because he came out to see me.

"Hi, Niko," he said, pulling out a chair and joining me.

"How's everything going?" I asked. "I just saw Matteo leaving."

"Yeah," he said. "He came in for his final paycheck."

"Good. Then he'll have no reason to return."

Jules told me he and Betty were really trying their best to make things work. He admitted getting past the whole Matteo thing wasn't going to be easy. Finally, Betty returned with my dinner. When Jules stood up to leave, she surprised him with a kiss on the lips. Their eyes met, and they shared a loving smile. For me, this sign of affection was encouraging. Jules returned to the kitchen as I dug into my *bouillabaisse*.

℘ ℘ ℘

Just as I was finishing my backstage tasks, the house manager found me and told me the audience was seated and I could start the show. He also handed me a folded-up sheet of paper. As I unfolded it, I saw it was a concert flyer for Al's Bar in downtown. I noticed Isabella Cruz's band, the Cherri Tarts, were one of the bands playing there tonight.

"Some punk rocker chick just gave this to me," he said, with a smile.

"Thanks."

"Nothing personal," he said, "but she doesn't seem like your type."

"I didn't know I had a type," I smirked.

"She also wrote something on the back."

I turned the flyer over and read Isabella's message:

"Hey Niko, I'm here to see your show. I've been drinking, so I hope I don't act too crazy. This isn't exactly my scene. At midnight, our band is playing at Al's Bar, downtown. I'd love for you to come hear us play. We're a riot, sometimes literally! I promise, I'll make it worth your while. Teasingly Yours, Isabella Cruz."

Isabella Cruz was the last person I expected to see tonight. But her note did pique my interest. I loudly called out "Places," letting everyone know our show was about to begin. I took my seat in the control room, and then looked down through the control room window and found Isabella there in the audience. She was seated next to another young woman with a similarly wild hairdo. I watched as her friend handed her a pint-sized bottle of liquor, which she proceeded to drink from.

From my yellow notepad, I tore off a sheet of paper and wrote out a message, telling Isabella I would love to see her band perform tonight and we should meet out in front after the play. I gave the note to the house manager, and asked him to please give it to her during intermission.

The house manager was correct about one thing, Isabella wasn't exactly my type, and we were also at opposite ends of our twenties. But what the hell, for an evening, it might be fun to take a walk on the wild side.

After the play, I found Isabella and her friend out front among the crowd. The two both sported ripped fish-net stockings and short skirts. Isabella had what looked like a skate key dangling down from one of her earrings, while her friend simply used safety pins through her earlobes and what looked like a dog collar around her neck. Both of them also appeared to be a bit drunk.

"Niko, this is Brenda," Isabella said, introducing me to her friend. "She plays lead guitar for our band."

Brenda gave me an indifferent hello as she adjusted the array of bracelets that adorned both arms.

"I like your bracelets," I said.

"Thanks," said Brenda, with a snarl. "They're cock rings, do you want one?"

"Uh, no thanks," I replied, patting my front pocket. "I always carry my own."

She laughed at my reply.

"This guy's alright," Brenda said. "He's quick."

"It's all the improv," I said. "It's probably rubbed off on me."

Brenda took out a pack of Marlboro cigarettes, placing one between her teeth, then lighting it with a Zippo lighter.

"We really liked the show," said Isabella, taking out a stick of Juicy Fruit gum and putting it in her mouth.

"Yeah," said Brenda. "It's some funny shit."

"Where did you park?" I asked. "I'll get my car and follow you downtown."

"No way," said Isabella, taking me by the arm. "You're riding with us."

"You're our guest tonight," said Brenda, taking my other arm. "We want you along for the ride."

"But what about my car?" I asked.

"You can get it later," smiled Brenda. "Or not at all."

"Neither of us are twenty-one yet," said Isabella. "So, we need you to buy us some booze."

"Oh, sure," I said, remembering back before I was of legal drinking age. "I guess I can do that."

"Great," said Brenda. "Because nobody rides for free."

They escorted me over to Isabella's Metropolitan, which was parked nearby.

"If you weren't buying us booze," said Isabella. "Then you'd have to pay for the ride with sexual favors."

I wondered if this is what Ronald Reagan meant when he said "There's no such thing as a free lunch."

I climbed in the back seat while the ladies put down the convertible top. Isabella then slammed a punk rock mix tape into the car's cassette player. The first song was loud, fast, and violent. The harsh music and angry words almost radiated from the vehicle. Isabella pulled the Metropolitan onto Olympic Boulevard and headed east. It was a warm night, and the wind felt good blowing against my face.

"This is real head banger stuff," I shouted, referring to the music. "Is this what your band sounds like?"

"No," said Brenda, turning down the volume. "This is hardcore punk; it attracts the 'Clockwork'

Orange County rowdies and the valley 'Surf Nazis.' It's all about testosterone. Unfortunately, hardcore is what most people now consider punk rock. We have a very different sound."

"Punk isn't a musical style," said Isabella. "It's a state of mind. When punk started, the scene was much more diverse and inclusive."

"Yeah," agreed Brenda. "It was okay to be a female band, and it was okay to be a gay band. Now, with the hardcore scene dominating, women don't feel comfortable with the physical violence, and if you're openly gay, you're going to get your ass kicked. The crowd has changed for the worse."

"I've listened to some punk," I admitted. "But I just don't understand it."

"That's because you're old," said Brenda, "You're not supposed to get it. You're supposed to be listening to the fucking Eagles."

That comment hurt. I was twenty-nine; I hadn't realized I was already over the hill.

"Hey, ease up on Niko," said Isabella. "He still needs to buy us some booze."

"Oh yeah," said Brenda. "I forgot."

As we rolled down Olympic Boulevard, I thought back to when I first began listening to rock and roll.

"The first record album I bought was Jimi Hendrix," I admitted. "And the second was The Doors. So, yeah, I guess I am old."

"The Doors," smiled Brenda. "We love the Doors."

"Yeah," said Isabella. "And Hendrix was amazing."

Isabella and Brenda started to explain how punk rock was a reaction to the way rock and roll had become so corporate and so removed from their fans. Punk rock was a DIY alternative and a back to basics.

"Rock music is supposed to be simple," said Brenda. "It's not supposed to have violins and a fucking orchestra."

"Go back to its roots," said Isabella. "Carl Perkins, Chuck Berry, Wanda Jackson, Eddie Cochran, and of course Elvis, before he got so damn fat."

We were almost to Koreatown before we finally found a liquor store that was open. Isabella and Brenda didn't have any preference so I just bought us a pint of Jim Beam and a six pack of Eastside Beer. They approved of my choices, and we each cracked open an Eastside for the drive. We passed the Jim Beam bottle around as we made our way toward downtown.

Al's Bar was located on the ground floor of the old American Hotel in the warehouse district of Los Angeles. It was easy to find the place because some clever artist had attached a brightly painted Cessna airplane to the side of the building. He called his masterpiece "Pinned Butterfly." I would have called it "Airplane Hanging from Building," but what do I know about art?

I'd been to Al's Bar once before to play a game of pool. But not being a punk rocker or an artist, I felt a little out of my element. The place had become a home for L. A.'s burgeoning punk rock scene. Bands like The Blasters, X, The Gun Club, The Plugz, Fear, and San Pedro's own, Minutemen played there nightly.

A group of punk rockers had gathered on the sidewalk out in front of Al's Bar. At the door, a guy with a mohawk was taking their entry fees. After circling the block, Isabella managed to snag a parking spot on Hewitt. While walking over to Al's, I noticed a blue Econoline van parked on the curb in front of the bar. As we approached, the van's rear doors flung open, and two female punk rockers jumped out. Both were Hispanic looking, and their hair and clothing seemed to mirror Brenda and Isabella's. One of the girls noticed our group.

"Brendita and Bella," the girl shouted. "Glad you sluts could finally make it."

The other girl noticed me.

"Who's this guy?" she asked, eying me with suspicion.

"I'm with the band," I answered, with a smirk.

"Okay, roadie," she said. "Grab some equipment and bring it in."

"I can do that," I replied, grabbing a guitar amp and carrying it to the door of the bar. The mohawk guy waved me right in. As I stepped through the door, the pungent aroma of stale beer, cigarettes, and puke hit me like a comedic pie in the face.

"Oh, man," I gasped. "That smell." I'd somehow forgotten the room's pungent odor.

"Welcome to Al's Bar," said Isabella, carrying in a guitar case right behind me. "Wait till the crowd gets all sweaty from pogoing."

"I can't wait," I replied, setting the guitar amp down on the small stage.

The room's dominant feature was its long and crowded bar. Behind that bar, stood two female bartenders, both were blonde and surly. Above the doorway to the restrooms was a neon sign that glowed: "Tip or Die." I figured this was only hyperbole, but considering the intimidating appearance of the two female bartenders, I wasn't going to take any chances.

The walls in the bar were covered in a collage of crap. There were so many layers of graffiti you couldn't really decipher any of the words. Scattered on top of the graffiti was an assortment of concert flyers, artwork, and inexplicable artifacts. The large steel support beams were an earthquake retrofit, installed after the Sylmar

Quake had done some damage. Against the rear walls, were a number of booths with green vinyl benches. Near those booths, was a pool table, and near the pool table was a jukebox. The song "Los Angeles," by the band X played over that jukebox. The crowd mingled with their drinks in hand.

I helped the band bring in their drum cases, more guitars, and more amps. While schlepping, I got to meet the other two band members. Everyone called the drummer, Renee Rojas, Nae Nae. Nae Nae wasn't very talkative, or maybe she just didn't think I was worth talking to. I finally met Valentina Martinez, who sang the lead vocals and also played rhythm guitar. Unlike Renee, Valentina couldn't stop talking, although what came out just seemed like a rant. She instructed me to call her Val and threatened to hurt me if I ever called her Tina. I gladly swore I wouldn't.

After we finished setting up, the band checked their instruments, did some tuning, and then took their places on the stage. Val grabbed the microphone and let out a loud belch, gaining the crowd's immediate attention.

"Ah, now I feel much better," Val sneered. "We're the Cherri Tarts, and we're here to rip you a new one."

A smattering of hoots, hollers, and even some applause came from the crowd, then Val continued.

"This song is from our album, *The Rich Taste Like Chicken,* and it's called 'Castration Club.'

And if any of you guys act like dicks," she threatened, using her index and middle finger to represent scissors, "snip, snip."

With that, Renee, the drummer hit the rim of her snare drum four times, and then the band jumped right into their song. They played loud and fast, and I was amazed at how good they sounded. The crowd began to pogo furiously. While Renee kept the aggressive beat on her drums, Isabella's bass complemented that beat with a pulsing rhythm. Brenda was on lead guitar, laying out a melody and riffing some solos. The song's lyrics, what I could understand of them, were angry and mean. But the music had a rockabilly twang to it, giving it a classic rock sound. Besides her lead vocals, Val also contributed some with her rhythm guitar.

The song's beat was much faster than I was used to, but I liked the music, and it was obvious they were good musicians. For some stupid reason, I hadn't imagined females could really rock and roll. The fact that the Go-Go's had started out as an L. A. punk band should have already convinced me. The Cherri Tarts now left no doubt in my mind.

I found I couldn't take my eyes off of Isabella; I was mesmerized. She was focused on her bass playing and her backup vocals, and she had a great stage presence. When she caught me staring at her, she smiled and winked. I thought she looked so damn hot. Amazingly, for the first time in my life, I felt like a fucking groupie.

The band played a few of their own original songs: "Real Hell," "Losing Control," and "Ripe Papaya," which I found out had nothing to do with the fruit. All of the songs were fast, loud, and nasty. The audience stayed right with them, and they all shared a violent and kinetic energy.

It was interesting to watch the crowd move. As long as their movements were vertical, everything was okay, but when they started to move laterally, that's when the pushing and shoving occurred. A few fist fights broke out, but they were quickly extinguished. Just before things went completely south, the band finished playing their final song of the evening.

Before packing up their equipment, The Cherri Tarts decided to take a much needed break. Since they were the last band scheduled, the bar's audience began to slowly file out the door. I offered to buy the band a round of drinks, which they gladly accepted. They shouted me their drink orders, as they grabbed the large semi-circular booth in the corner. A bartender eventually brought over our drinks. Miraculously, no IDs were ever checked.

"Your band is really good," I said, sipping from my Jack Daniels.

"Thanks," said Isabella, grabbing her beverage. "We work hard."

"You can be our roadie anytime," said Val, sipping from her Margarita.

Everyone sat enjoying their cocktails and catching their breath.

"Niko is a writer," Isabella told them. "He adapted my grandfather's novel into a stage play."

"No shit?" said Renee, enjoying her Jose Cuervo and lime. "Are you famous or something?"

"No. I make a living as a stage manager," I admitted, "But I work hard at it, just like you ladies."

"All of us have daytime jobs," Brenda said. "Nae Nae and I clean houses, and Val is a waitress."

"I work at Aron's Records on Melrose," Isabella added. "It has its perks."

I knew the Cherri Tarts had one record album out, and they played shows all over town. So, I was a little surprised everyone still needed day jobs.

"How long have you all been playing together?" I asked.

Isabella set her glass down before answering my question.

"Before we joined this group, Brenda and I played in a band called The Lips. We played all of the Hollywood clubs: The Starwood, Club 88, The Whiskey."

"We played our last gig with Black Flag and DOA," Brenda added.

I was amused by the band names, and thought I'd be a comedian.

"Are those the names of bands or two different insecticides?" I asked, grinning.

Nobody laughed at my so-called joke, so I returned to my drink.

"Val and I played together in an East L.A. band called Las Chicas," Renee said.

"We played all over the east side," Val added. "Back then, there were really two completely separate punk rock worlds in L. A.; Hollywood, with the places that Isabella mentioned, and then there was East Los, with The Vex and all of the backyard parties. If you were a Chicano band, you never left the east side, and if you were a white band, you stayed in Hollywood."

"We had a lot of good East Los bands," said Renee, "The Brat, The Stains, Los Illegals, The Plugz. Every band had something good to offer."

As Renee was sipping her tequila, I noticed the date "February 3, 1959" tattooed on her forearm. She was too young for it to be her birth date.

"Your tattoo," I said. "That must be an important date."

Everyone in the band glared at me as if I'd said something really stupid.

"Niko," Val asked. "Haven't you ever heard the term, 'The day the music died?'

I quickly thought back to the song "American Pie," by Don McClean, which came out back when I was in high school.

"You mean Buddy Holly's death?" I asked.

"Well, yeah, that was obviously tragic as well," said Val.

They waited a moment for me to figure it out, but then Renee finally spoke.

"Richard Steven Valenzuela," Renee said.

"Who?" I asked, realizing that was probably another stupid question.

"Richie Valens," Val answered. "One of our own."

Of course, I thought. There were three musicians on that flight: Richie Valens, Buddy Holly, and The Big Bopper. Along with their pilot, they all died on February 3, 1959 when their plane crashed into an Iowa corn field.

"Richie was a seventeen-year-old Mexican kid from Pacoima," Renee said. "He already had a number one record and several other hits. There's no telling what else he could have done with his life."

The band members shared a moment of silence, as if to contemplate what could have been.

"He inspired all of the Chicano bands that followed after him," said Val. "Because until you see someone who looks like you being successful, you can't imagine what's possible for you."

I thought for a moment before I finally spoke. I didn't want to make another stupid comment.

"Maybe the music didn't die that day," I said, "because so many musicians were inspired by him."

They all looked at each other with amazement.

"Wow," Val said. "Maybe this guy isn't as dumb as he looks."

"Thank you," I said, accepting whatever compliment I could get.

We were putting the last of the band's equipment into the van just as Al's Bar was switching off its lights. I said my goodbyes to Val and Renee and told them I'd enjoyed hearing them play. Just as they were climbing into the van, Brenda stopped them and asked for a ride home. I immediately wondered why she wasn't going back with Isabella and me. I thought maybe Isabella had something in mind for just the two of us. I started to imagine the possibilities. Now that I was a punk rock groupie, there's no telling what was possible. Brenda and I exchanged goodbyes and then she moved over toward Isabella.

"Come here, girl," Brenda shouted, with her arms extended.

"Yeah, Brendita," Isabella replied, moving toward her.

To my surprise, the two embraced and began to kiss. They weren't just smacking lips; they were feverishly sharing spit. If I didn't know bet-ter, I'd of thought Brenda was trying to swab Isa-bella's tonsils with her tongue. When they finally separated, Brenda got in the van with the others while I just stood there like a deer caught in the headlights. Finally, Isabella grabbed her guitar case and started down Hewitt Street motioning for me to follow.

"I didn't realize you and Brenda were a cou-ple," I said.

"We're not," she laughed. "We're free to see anyone we want to see."

"Oh," I replied, somewhat confused. "But you're both gay, right?"

"Not exactly," she declared. "We're more what you might call gender fluid."

"Gender fluid?"

"Yeah. Brenda's more into girls than I am," she clarified. "I usually like guys more, especially when I'm sober. But sometimes when I'm drunk, I prefer women."

This was something new for me, alcohol as a determinant of sexual identity. I wondered if Freud had factored that in to his theory of penis envy.

"What condition are you in right now," I asked, "drunk or sober?"

"Neither," she said, "I just have a good buzz on."

She placed her guitar case into the trunk of the Metropolitan, and then I helped her put the car's top down.

"Thanks for giving me a ride back to my car," I said.

"I'll get you back to your car," she smiled, "but not just yet."

Okay, I figured. Maybe I should just enjoy the ride.

Isabella drove us into the old part of downtown, passing once glamorous movie palaces and shuttered department stores. In the city's old financial district, we passed wonderfully ornate office buildings that were now completely empty, their corporate sponsors having fled to newer and shinier buildings further west.

On Figueroa, Isabella turned and headed toward the Bonaventure Hotel. Compared to the city's older structures, the Bonaventure's 1970s modernism stood out like a magical island. The hotel was visually striking and looked new. With its tall cluster of cylindrical glass towers, and its exterior elevator pods, the hotel stood apart from its more conservative surroundings.

Isabella pulled her Metropolitan into the hotel's valet parking area. She said something to the parking attendant, who simply handed her a ticket. We stepped past the self-opening doors and right into the hotel's soaring atrium.

"Where are we going?" I asked, wondering what she had planned.

"You'll see," she smiled, leading me onto one of the escalators.

The escalator took us up to the hotel's outdoor plaza. I'd been here many times for their afternoon jazz concerts. But I'd never seen it in the evening, or should I say, early morning. Unlike those well attended events, Isabella and I were the only ones here. It was dark and a bit eerie. The tall buildings loomed over us making it feel like we were standing on the floor of a canyon.

At the end of the long courtyard was an elevated swimming pool area. Isabella led me over to the locked gate, which led to the pool deck.

"It looks like you need a key," I said.

"No," she answered. "We do this all the time."

Isabella reached into her small purse and pulled out a thin hair comb. She slid the comb between the lock and the door jam, easily retracting the latch bolt. With that, she pulled the gate open. We entered and then climbed the stairs up to the pool deck. The pool lights were on giving the water a magical blue glow.

To our right, the Union Bank Building loomed large. To our left, was the Los Angeles Central Library and its marvelous pyramid top. Directly in front of us were the ARCO Plaza's twin office towers, fifty-two stories of polished granite and glass. Unfortunately, I was well aware of the architectural masterpiece these towers had replaced.

"Your grandfather wrote eloquently about the building that once stood right there," I said, pointing straight ahead. "It was his favorite building in all of Los Angeles."

"Really?" she asked. "What was the building?"

"It was called the Richfield Building," I said. "It was built in 1929 to be the world headquarters of the Richfield Oil Company. It stood there until 1969, when it was finally demolished."

"That's forty-years," she said, gazing over to the new building's smooth granite and glass. "What did it look like?"

"It was like nothing anyone had ever seen before," I said. "Back then they called the style 'Jazz Moderne,' later it would be called 'Art Deco.' The building was twelve stories high, which was the height limit back then, and it was covered in black terra-cotta tiles embossed with gold leaf. It was topped by a huge tower with the name 'Richfield' spelled out vertically in giant neon letters. The building was gaudy, elaborate, and extremely beautiful."

"And my grandfather wrote about it?"

"He did. He compared it to a female of the 'Jazz Age,' a flapper, Louise Brooks or Clara Bow, all dressed up in her finery, headed out for a wild night on the town."

Isabella looked at me for a long moment, then proceeded to remove her clothes.

"Let's go for a swim," she said, kicking off her shoes.

"Uh, I don't have a swimsuit," I tried to argue.

"That's okay, neither do I."

She had her fishnet stockings off before I even finished unbuttoning my shirt. As she removed each item of clothing, she'd toss them aside arbitrarily, leaving everything strewn in disorder. I was down to my boxer shorts when she removed the last of her garments. She had a great body, lean and firm. Her dark Latin skin was a glorious brown. Isabella seemed as comfortable naked as she was clothed.

"Come on," she announced, diving head first into the water.

What am I doing? I thought to myself. She said she likes guys more than women, but how much more? Isabella poked her head out of the water and looked right at me.

"Well," she asked. "Are you coming in?"

"Yeah," I replied, reluctantly pulling down my shorts and setting them on a chair. Isabella chuckled for some reason. This embarrassed me so I dove into the water to reclaim my modesty. When I broke the surface of the water, Isabella was there to greet me, her big brown eyes giving me a tender gaze.

"Hi," she said, smiling.

"Hi," I replied, gazing back at her.

She placed both hands on my shoulders as I wrapped my hands around her waist. She leaned forward and kissed me. It was a nice long kiss. She certainly knew how to kiss a man, I thought.

That was a good sign.

"This is my first time here with a guy," she smiled.

"Really? How do you like it so far?"

She thought for a moment. "It's different." She chuckled, then kissed me again.

After the kiss, Isabella placed both hands on my head and dunked me. She laughed, then took off swimming toward the shallow end of the pool. Isabella was feisty and playful, which I liked. But for some unknown reason, I started thinking about Cynthia Aldrich. This was crazy. I'm here in a pool, naked, with Isabella, and I'm thinking about Cynthia. I swam after Isabella and finally caught her at the shallow end of the pool. There were steps there and a handrail that led out onto the deck.

"This is a good spot," she said. "I've had a lot of fun in this part of the pool."

I could only imagine what fun she'd had here, especially since I knew I was the first male she'd brought.

"Did you bring a condom?" she asked.

"No. I didn't," I grimaced, thinking maybe I'd messed up. "When I left home, I didn't know I'd need it."

"That's okay," she smiled. "I always carry a supply."

Isabella climbed up out of the pool, went over to her scattered clothes, and found her purse among the mess. She pulled a single packaged condom from it, then dropped the purse back on the ground. She walked to the steps and then climbed down into the pool. She handed me the condom.

"I assume you know how to use one of these?" she grinned.

"I think I can figure it out," I smiled, peeling open the wrapper.

The sex was wet, wild, and wonderful. I'd never had so much fun in a pool. This certainly beats swimming laps, and forget about water polo, this was a hell of a lot better.

Afterwards, we laid there on the steps spent, exhausted, and trying to catch our breath.

"You were amazing," I said, touching her cheek.

"Yeah," she said. "That was fun."

She was right, it was fun. What's that old saying? 'That was the most fun you can have with your clothes on.' Well, this was the most fun you can have with your clothes off.

We suddenly heard some noise coming from the other end of the pool deck and realized we were no longer alone.

"Alright," shouted a male voice from the darkness. "What do you two think you're doing?"

Two uniformed security guards appeared, flashlights out. The taller one was doing all the talking while the other one looked around and found us two towels.

"We got a call from one of the hotel's guests," the tall one said, "asking if the two skinny dippers were part of the hotel's free entertainment."

"We were just taking a little swim," I tried to explain. Thankfully, I'd already thrown away my used condom.

"Well, we can see that," he replied. "Right now, you both need to get your clothes on."

"Sure," I answered, climbing out of the pool and taking both towels from the guard. I wrapped myself in one and held the other for Isabella to climb up into. She took the towel and wrapped herself in it.

"Are you two guests of the hotel?" the guard asked, giving us a stern glare.

"No," I admitted, "we're not." I managed to slide my boxers on over my damp body.

"We're here from Canada," Isabella announced. "We're Olympic Swimmers here for The Games."

I looked at her and then decided to go along with the ruse.

"Yeah," I said. "Up north we always swim in the buff just before a big competition. It's an old Canadian custom."

"You Americans are such great swimmers," Isabella said. "We're just hoping to compete."

I held Isabella's towel for her so that she could get dressed behind it.

"Well," he said. "Maybe you should get back to your Olympic Village. Which one are you staying at, USC or UCLA?"

I answered "USC," while Isabella simultaneously answered, "UCLA."

They both looked at us with some confusion.

"I'm staying at UCLA," said Isabella. "While he's staying at USC."

"Yeah," I stated. "They try to keep us apart because of our chronic bad behavior. We're always getting each other into trouble."

"Yes," Isabella said, "We're like oil and water. You should never put us together."

Once we were dressed, the two guards escorted us back down to the atrium level and watched as we exited the hotel. After they'd gone back in, we started laughing.

We finally stopped laughing while we were traveling west on Wilshire. Even though Isabella and I were not the perfect couple, I actually liked her a lot. She was outrageous and fun, maybe too much fun. She was right at that nexus of fun and trouble, which I unfortunately liked. In the heat of the moment, I'd forgotten all about Brenda, and I'd put Cynthia completely out of my mind. But now, I was back to thinking about those things. Evidently, they really hadn't gone away, they'd just been pushed into the background. Because we were getting close to my apartment, I suggested that Isabella could just drop me off there.

"Are you sure?" she asked. "I don't mind taking you back to your car."

"No, that's okay. I can get my car tomorrow."

She turned on Serrano and then pulled up near my apartment building. When she parked, she looked over at me.

"Would you like me to come up?" she smiled. "I think I might have another condom in my purse."

Well, I guess this is where the rubber meets the road, so to speak. Do I invite Isabella upstairs? Or, do we just call it a night? I'll probably regret it as soon as she leaves, but I really needed time to sort through my thoughts. I liked Isabella, but I still didn't know whether I was comfortable with her sexuality, not that she was doing anything wrong. I just needed to figure out where she fit into my life.

"I'm pretty tired," I told her. "I think we should both just get some sleep,"

"That's fine," she smiled. "I could use the sleep myself." She thought for a moment. "Did you really like our band tonight?"

"I really did," I said. "You girls rock."

Isabella reached over and pulled out a boxed cassette tape from her glove compartment. The box read: *"The Rich Taste Like Chicken,"* by The Cherri Tarts. It also had a crude drawing of a businessman hanging from a spit over an open fire.

"Here," she said, handing me the tape. "You've already heard most of the songs."

"Thanks," I said, accepting the tape.

"Tomorrow I'm working at Aron's Records. You should come by."

"I just might," I smiled.

I gave Isabella a long kiss, all the while wondering if she would rather be kissing Brenda instead of me. "Damn, I'm so messed up," I thought. Here is this great young woman, sexy, creative, and completely uninhibited, and all I can think about is she might be wanting to kiss some other woman.

Friday
July 20

•❖ The next morning, I grabbed my copy of *Edendale* and a pencil. But as I read, I kept flashing back to Isabella in the pool: clothes off, wet, and wild. Even though there were no strings attached, and no commitments, I still wished I'd been able to share with her my conflicted feelings because she was so honest with me. Hopefully, I'd have time today to get over to Aron's Records.

Since I'd left my Firebird overnight at the Drama Geek's Theatre, I grabbed my bike and headed over to Beryl's place to feed her two cats.

I didn't want the ASPCA making me their poster child for animal neglect. When I got there, I found the house in a flurry of activity. Cars were parked everywhere, and people were entering and exiting. I'd forgotten that Nina had scheduled her estate sale for this day and time. I watched as dark room equipment, cameras, and lighting equipment were all being carried out the door.

Inside, a crowd of shoppers were perusing merchandise that had been set out on tables. When Nina saw me, she hurried over.

"Niko, I need your help," she pleaded. "The combination I have doesn't work, and I can't get to Beryl's photos. I need to get into her vault."

"I don't have the combination," I tried to explain. "All I have is her house key."

"What am I supposed to tell these collectors?" she asked, angrily. "Some of them are from out of town."

I tried to sound sympathetic, even though I was actually happy as hell.

"That's awful," I said, trying to sound sincere. "Have you tried her sister?"

"That's where I got this combination," Nina barked. "And that old fool won't even talk to me."

It didn't surprise me that Beryl was putting up a fight. This photo collection was her life's work.

"Maybe she doesn't want her photographs scattered everywhere," I said. "Maybe she wants them to remain in one place, as a collection."

"Well, that's her problem," Nina answered. "I'm just trying to make us all some money."

Nina kept pestering me until I finally agreed to help her.

"Okay," I said. "After I feed her cats, I'll go over to Cedars and talk to her."

"I wish you would, Niko," she pleaded. "Without her photos, my estate sale will be a complete flop."

In the kitchen, I put out more cat food and water, but I didn't see the cats anywhere. When I went to the back porch to clean out their litter box, I found them huddled together behind a chair. I approached them slowly, then stroked their fur. After a while, they finally started to purr.

∽ ∽ ∽

When I entered Beryl's room at Cedars, I noticed there were two new flower arrangements on her side table and several new get-well cards pinned to her wall. Beryl had a Cheshire Cat grin on her face.

"Nina's not happy with you," I said, sitting down at her bedside.

"Frankly my dear, I don't give a damn."

"Well, you might give a damn if Nina charges you for a locksmith and then sells your photos anyway."

"I think I've finally come up with a plan that might work," she said, smiling. "But I'm going to need your help."

"That's why I'm here, Beryl," I said. "What's your plan."

Beryl told me her plan, and I thought it all sounded pretty good. But we still needed someone in the right position to help us. I thought of the perfect person to put our plan in motion. After we finished discussing all the details, two young nurses brought in Beryl's lunch. As she ate, I got up to read some of the new get-well cards on her wall.

"How are Maggie and Dottie doing?" Beryl asked, while picking at her food.

"They're fine," I said, "but they didn't like having all those people around."

"I'm sure they didn't," she agreed. "I miss the little runts."

On one of Beryl's cards, someone had thanked her for the pictures she'd sold them of the old Richfield Building downtown.

"I was just telling Carlos Cruz's granddaughter about the Richfield Building," I said. "Losing it was such a shame."

"I took my first pictures of it in 1929 on the day it opened, and I was also there in 1969 when it was demolished." She paused. "The company they hired to tear it down balked when they first saw the building. It was amazing because these were tough, unsympathetic men, who did this work for a living." She thought for a moment before she continued. "When they arrived, they toured the old building, admiring its garish charm and elaborate detail. They were completely taken by its beauty. They couldn't comprehend why anyone would want to destroy something so lovely. They told their bosses there had to be some mistake because this was one of the most beautiful buildings they'd ever seen. When they were then told there was no mistake, they simply refused to follow orders, and told them they didn't want their blood money." Beryl paused, looking right me. "Can you imagine that?"

"Good for them."

"Of course, they were finally forced to do their job. You could tell how pained these men were, and how bad they felt about what they had to do. It was such a damn shame."

I noticed the stack of newspapers by Beryl's bed. On the very top of that pile was a special Olympic Games Section.

"It looks like you've been reading up on the upcoming Olympics?" I asked.

"Yes. I plan to watch as much of it as I can." Beryl glanced out the window facing the Hollywood Hills. "Back in 1932, I was there with my camera for the opening ceremonies. It's not every day the world pays you a visit," she paused. "It was an amazing sight: the sold-out crowd in the

Coliseum, all the athletes; the parade of nations, and our own USA team wearing navy blue, red, and white," she paused. "It made me proud to be an American. It made me proud to be a citizen of the world."

∞ ∞ ∞

From Cedars, I rode southeast on San Vincente to get my car. I liked Beryl's plan to save her photo collection, and I thought it might just work. But I also knew we needed to move quickly since Nina wasn't going to wait around forever. Beryl needed me to make an important phone call to someone I hadn't spoken to in years. Without this person's help, everything might not come together in time.

When I turned onto Fairfax, I was happy to find my Firebird right where I'd left it. But as I got closer to the car, I saw the driver's side rear window had been bashed in, and shards of broken glass were spread over the asphalt.

"Crap!" I shouted, dropping my kickstand. When I opened the door, I could see the glove box was open, and its contents were strewn out on the floor. The ashtray, which I'd kept filled with coins, now sat empty on the passenger seat. Finally, I noticed the gaping hole in my dashboard where my car stereo used to be. Just like when my apartment was burglarized, I now felt angry and helpless at the same time. I knew my auto insurance only covered liability, so I would have to pay for these repairs out of my own pocket.

Fortunately, under the hood, everything looked okay, and the contents of the trunk looked untouched as well. I pulled my bike rack out and mounted it on the rear of the Firebird. After I'd secured my bike to the rack, I climbed in the car and turned the key, just hoping it would start. To my relief, the car started right up.

Needing immediate help with my Firebird, I headed over to see my friend Jake Polanski at Tinsel Town Picture Vehicles. Jake's storage yard was in a multi-level parking structure in West Hollywood. The entire structure was packed with a large variety of different vehicles. A stunning yellow Lamborghini Countach was parked directly in front of Jake's office. I could see Jake inside talking to someone on the phone.

Jake was of medium height, with dark features and boyish good looks. Back in high school, Jake got into fist fights almost daily. He had a serious chip on his shoulder, and he didn't take crap from anybody. Once, I watched him fight three guys at one time. Hank and I were there to jump in if he needed us, but he took care of business all by himself. After he finished his phone call, he came out to greet me.

"Remember," he said. "When you're ready to sell your Firebird, I want to buy it."

Jake had been bugging me forever to sell him my car.

"Maybe someday, Jake," I said. "But not today. I came here because I need your help."

Jake stepped over to the other side of the Firebird and noticed the broken window.

"What happened to your window?"

"I left it at the theater overnight, and this is how I found it today."

Jake examined the opening where my window had once been.

"I think I can help you replace it," he said.

"How?"

"We just got our 1967 Camaro back from Universal Studios. During one of their stunts, they accidentally totaled it. The insurance already paid us off, so we're just waiting for the car to be hauled to the wrecking yard."

Jake and I both knew the 1967 Camaro and the 1967 Firebird shared many of the same parts. In fact, most of them were built on the very same assembly line in Van Nuys. Except for just a few differences, the two vehicles were practically the same car.

"What are we waiting for?" I said "Let's do it."

Jake grabbed some tools and led me out to the street where the 1967 Camaro was parked. He was right, the rest of the car was a wreck, but fortunately, it still had that one rear window we needed. Jake and I removed the rear window assembly, and then we did the same with the Firebird's. Finally, we installed the Camaro's window into my Firebird. All that took less than an hour.

"Thanks, Jake," I said. "I owe you one."

"Just give me a good price when you're finally ready to sell it. Okay?"

"I promise."

After Jake put his tools away, he found me admiring the yellow Lamborghini. It looked so sleek and sexy. Jake pulled a latch, causing the passenger side door to scissor up into the air. I'd never seen a door open like that, and I was impressed. I peeked inside, and the interior looked like a race car, no frills, just functional and clean, with deep bucket seats and simple analogue gauges. The gear shift revealed a 5-speed synchromesh transmission.

"It's got twelve cylinders and six carburetors," Jake said, nodding his approval."

"The Italians are really good at three things," I replied. "Mobsters, pasta, and cars."

"There are no wiseguys around, and I can't offer you any spaghetti," he said. "But how about a spin in one of their cars?"

"Let's go."

Jake got into driver's seat and I got in right beside him. When he turned the key, the car roared like an angry lion. Jake moved the car out onto the street, locked up the building, and then hung up a sign which read: "Back in one hour."

❧ ❧ ❧

Jake was behind the wheel of the Lamborghini, and I was seated next to him. We were on Sunset Boulevard turning left onto Laurel Canyon, and the road ahead looked wide open. We got the green light at Hollywood Boulevard, so Jake dropped the Lamborghini into third gear, and I hung on for dear life. Jake pushed down hard on the accelerator, and the car shot forward like a rocket. The force pushed me back into my seat and the houses along the road became a blur of earth tones. Finally, a car turned onto the road ahead of us, forcing Jake to slow down to a somewhat normal speed.

That's when I was finally able to tell Jake about my burglary and seeing Randy Ferlinghetti as an LAPD officer.

"I can't believe Randy's a cop," Jake said, shaking his head. "I guess they'll take anybody."

"It sounds like he's finally cleaned up his act."

I then told Jake about my wonderful evening with Isabella and about her complicated sexuality, which still bothered me. He liked the idea of us doing it in the pool, but he didn't understand the problem I had with Isabella's bisexuality.

"Niko, that's not a problem," Jake said. "That's a golden opportunity."

"What kind of opportunity are you talking about?"

Jake's eyebrows arched and his eyes grew big.

"A threesome," he said, "a *ménage a trois.*"

"You're kidding, right?"

"No. It's always been one of my fantasies. One fortunate guy and two very lucky ladies."

"Jake, just because Isabella is attracted to men and women, doesn't mean she wants them all thrown together in one bed."

Jake was having difficulty explaining to me why I should find his idea appealing.

"Think of it like a dessert," he said. "I know you like dessert, right?"

"Of course. But what does that have to do with anything?"

"Well, some women like ice cream, and some like pie, and some women like their ice cream on top of their pie."

I didn't know what the hell he was talking about. Who said anything about dessert? "That's called a pie ala mode," I said.

"Exactly," Jake replied. "And some of these women go for that stuff in a big way."

I couldn't figure out if Jake was getting his sex tips from "Playboy After Dark" or the House of Pies.

"That's not the case here," I said. "Isabella sent Brenda home so the two of us could be alone."

"Maybe you're right," Jake said. "But just think of the possibilities."

I wasn't remotely interested in Jake's possibilities. If I had a group of women in bed with me, I'd feel like the only guy at a Tupperware party. With my luck, I'd just be the odd man out.

Up at Mulholland Drive, Jake turned the Lamborghini around and headed back toward Hollywood. He offered me a chance to drive, but I passed.

co co co

After my unhelpful and rather confusing conversation with Jake, I decided to head over to Melrose Avenue to visit Isabella. Melrose, between La Brea and Fairfax, had become the main shopping street for the city's punk and new wave crowd. There were vintage clothing stores, cafés, and quirky shops. There were also record stores, like Rene's All Ears, Vinyl Fetish, and Aron's Records, where Isabella Cruz was working.

For places to eat, I liked The Burger that Ate L.A.: a burger joint shaped like a giant cheeseburger. This was Melrose's version of the now demolished Brown Derby.

For a touch of the surreal, there was always the street's decades old retirement home. Here, polyester clan seniors lounged on their patio and watched a parade of grungy punk rockers go by. I considered these seniors the luckiest old folks in the city. Even though I was only twenty-nine, I thought, "Man, this is where I want to retire."

After dropping some coins into the parking meter, I made my way into Aron's Records. The place wasn't very busy, and I found Isabella stocking the bargain bin. She said we had some time to talk.

"Have you listened to the cassette I gave you?" she asked, dropping records into the 99-cent bin.

"No, not yet." I told her about how both my home and car stereos had been stolen, and now I had nothing to play music on.

"That's awful," she frowned. "I couldn't live without my music."

She showed me some of the album art on display and started telling me about the various punk bands. She made each album sound like it was the greatest record ever.

That's when I remembered why I was there.

"Isabella, I need to tell you something," I said, pausing. "Because I really like you."

"Before you say anything," she said, stopping me. "I need to tell you something first."

I'll bet this is where she tells me she regrets cheating on Brenda with me, and how she really prefers women. After all, I was the first guy that she'd brought to that pool.

"This morning, I got back together with my boy-friend," she said. "We broke up several weeks ago."

"Are you talking about a guy?"

"Yeah, of course. And we're kind of serious, so I don't think I'll be able to see you anymore."

"But last night, you and Brenda?"

"Brenda and I are very casual, she has other girlfriends, and then I met you. Last night was great."

Well, I definitely didn't see this coming.

"He and I have a lot in common," she said, "and he doesn't have any hang-ups about my sexuality. He loves me for who I am." She paused for a long moment. "Now, what were you going to tell me?"

"It's not that important anymore," I smiled. "What's your boyfriend's name?"

She looked at me kind of funny, like I just said something really dumb. I seem to get that look quite a bit.

"You know him," she smiled. "In fact, I met him at your *Sonora Town* play. I was seated right next to him, and we just clicked somehow, even though he's much older than me."

"At my play?"

"Yeah. Then he invited me to his art exhibit in Little Tokyo. Afterwards, we went out for sushi and then hooked up. He's an amazing artist, and he likes my stuff too. He thinks I could be an artist if I wanted to be."

"Who are we talking about here?" I asked.

"Danny Sanchez," she replied. "He told me you two were old friends."

After I got over my initial surprise, this actually made sense to me. She and Danny were both artists, and they were also both Latin.

"Danny is a great guy," I said. "But he's been through an awful lot."

"I know, Viet Nam," she answered. "Sometimes he still has nightmares."

I suddenly remembered last night's little adventure in the pool. "You're not going to tell him about us, are you?"

"I already did," she smiled. "He's cool with it since he and I weren't together at the time. Believe me, he's had his flings too. Besides, he likes you, and was just glad it wasn't some loser."

"Okay," I sighed. "I hope you two are together for a long time."

Isabella laughed. "We'll be lucky if we can stay together for a month. But I have no regrets about last night, because for a pretty straight dude, you were fun."

"So were you, Isabella," I smiled. "A little too much fun."

We said our goodbyes, then Isabella went back to work.

∽ ∽ ∽

On my drive home, I looked up and saw the Griffith Park Observatory high up on its hilltop. Weeks ago, I decided to ride my bike up to the observatory just to take in the view. After climbing the hill's long and serpentine road, I finally made it to the very top, where I admired the great view of the city below.

Just below the observatory, on that very same hill, was a unique home that stood behind a large ivy-covered wall. The house looked more like a Mayan fortress than a single-family home. It was the Ennis-Brown House, and it was one of several Southern California homes built in the 1920s by the famed architect, Frank Lloyd Wright.

During my time at USC, our class, California in Politics and Culture, was invited to have our Christmas Party at this unique home. Professor Lafayette knew the owner, Mr. August C. Brown, who had suggested to Lafayette his students might learn something about residential architecture by visiting his amazing dwelling. That was a huge understatement.

As a child, I'd been raised a Catholic, but Catholicism never stuck, there was never much religion in my life. It wasn't until I saw the Ennis-Brown House that I had, what some might call, a "religious experience." I would have sung out with the Hallelujah Chorus, from Handel's *Messiah,* but I didn't want my classmates knowing what a complete dork I was.

Mr. Brown, I would learn, had collaborated with Harry Bridges in 1934 to form the ILWU longshoreman's union. The ILWU played a vital role in shaping the L. A. Harbor where I'd grown up, as well as every other west coast port. Brown was the eighth owner of this Frank Lloyd Wright home, and he cherished being its guardian and caretaker.

To prepare us for our visit to the Ennis-Brown house, Professor Lafayette spent an entire class session teaching us about Frank Lloyd Wright's Los Angeles architecture. Lafayette began by discussing Wright's first home in the area, which he designed for Aline Barnsdall, called the Hollyhock House. This home was Wright's link between his prairie style, and this new Southern California style he was developing.

Wright chose the pre-Columbian designs from Mexico as the foundation for his new architecture. By incorporating Aztec and Mayan influences, he hoped to create a completely new and indigenous style.

For his constructional material, Wright used what he called: textile-block construction. These were 16 inch by 16 inch molded concrete blocks, made on site. These blocks were then fastened to a lattice of steel rods.

Wright built the first of these homes for Alice Millard in Pasadena, which he called "La Miniatura." Wright adored it. "I would rather have built this small house than St. Peter's in Rome," he wrote.

The next home that Wright built was the Storer House in Hollywood for Dr. John Storer. Unfortunately, after Dr. Storer died, the home never received the care it required and now was in a state of disrepair. Fortunately, the home was recently purchased by Hollywood Movie producer, Joel Silver, who was planning a massive restoration.

The third home Wright built, was the Ennis-Brown house, which I'd visited with my class. It was the largest and most imposing of Wright's L. A. homes. As I approached it, I couldn't believe it was just a single-family home, because it looked more like a temple. It was dramatic, and there was a sense of mystery about it. Mr. Brown told us it had recently been used as a location for the 1982 film, *Blade Runner,* to depict a dwelling in the dystopian Los Angeles of far off 2019.

Inside the house, art glass windows dominated the rooms, bringing light and warmth into an otherwise cold interior. Most of the students thought that the views of the city were breath-taking, but not all of them loved the house itself. Some said it reminded them of a mausoleum or a crypt. But I found the place magical. In fact, no other building had ever made such a powerful impact on me. It was my first visit to a Frank Lloyd Wright home, and like they say, you never forget your first.

Finally, in 1924, Wright designed and built the Freeman House in the Hollywood Hills for Samuel and Harriet Freeman. The couple had fallen in love with Wright's architecture while staying overnight at Aline Barnsdall's Hollyhock house, that first home that Wright had built in Southern California. The Freeman House was considered the most modest of his textile-block homes, and the last one he ever built.

∞ ∞ ∞

When I got home, I knew I had to hurry to make it to tonight's Drama Geek's performance. But I noticed a new message on my answering machine so I quickly played it:

"Hello, Niko. This is Marvin Grossman, and I need your help. And yes, there's money involved. But I'm a cheap bastard, so it won't be much. I know your show at the Drama Geek's is closing tomorrow night, and I'm hoping you can help me out the next day. I'm casting a television commercial, and I need a stage manager to help with the auditions. It'll be like old times. In other words, you'll be doing all of the work, and I'll be taking all the credit. But, if you're here by noon, I'll even take you out to lunch. Call me."

It was good to hear Marvin's voice because I'd always enjoyed working with him. Before he was a casting director, Marvin had been a successful TV actor with a hit series under his belt. When that show was cancelled, he started directing stage plays with the goal of becoming a television director. That didn't exactly work out for him, but while he was trying to become a director, he got to know all the actors in town, and he excelled at casting the right actor for the right role. Other directors quickly noticed his casting skills and started asking him to help cast their shows as well. Marvin finally opened his own casting agency. He was always busy, and sometimes had more work than he could handle. Since I didn't have anything going on that day, I decided to help him out and make a few bucks in the process. I called Marvin back but his receptionist told me he was busy, so I gave her my name, and told her to tell Marvin I would be there for his auditions, and that I expected lunch beforehand. She promised to give him my message.

That night, at the theater, I made a list of everything to be accomplished after tomorrow night's final performance. For most shows, that list would be long and detailed. But because the Drama Geeks were an ongoing improv group, my list would be amazingly short. Our second to last performance was a little lackluster because everyone was focused on tomorrow night's last show. Tomorrow, everyone had friends or family attending, and then there was the closing night party. Also, closing nights usually meant unemployment, so everyone was already starting to look for new work. Me, I was waiting to hear if Len Sebastian's play was going to be re-staged. That show would keep me employed for twelve weeks, a lifetime in theater terms.

With everything planned out for tomorrow, I went home to get a good night's sleep. But when I sat down in front of the TV, I noticed in the TV Guide that the 1937 film *The Prisoner of Zenda,* was coming on in a few minutes. *Zenda* was a wonderful old adventure film, and a classic swashbuckler. The film starred Ronald Colman, the greatest voice in motion pictures. Coleman could read the telephone book, and his velvet voice would make even that sound like poetry.

The Prisoner of Zenda also starred Douglas Fairbanks Jr., a young David Niven, and the beautiful Madeleine Carrol. The film was set in a picturesque European kingdom. The whole thing was like a fairy tale: with a wayward king, an evil stepbrother, and a beautiful princess.

Like any good swashbuckler, the film culminated with a dramatic sword fight between the hero and the villain, in this case, Ronald Coleman and Douglas Fairbanks Jr. This particular sword fight was special for me because I knew the man who staged it. His name was Ralph Faulkner, and he was one of Hollywood's master swordsmen.

Faulkner arrived in Hollywood during the silent film era and worked as an actor and stuntman. While doing stunt work on one particular film, Ralph injured his knee and feared that he might never work again. For his rehabilitation, it was suggested that he try fencing exercises to strengthen the knee. Not only did the exercises help to heal Faulkner's knee, but he discovered that he a talent for fencing, and even began to win every fencing competition that he entered. Faulkner ultimately qualified for the 1932 Summer Olympics in Los Angeles.

Even before the Olympics, Faulkner staged sword fight scenes for the movies. His first major assignment though was the 1935 version of *The Three Musketeers*. Faulkner also helped to train Errol Flynn for the swashbuckler roles that made him famous.

I'd taken fencing back in college, because as an actor, I thought I needed the sword skills to perform in a Shakespearean or other play that required sword fighting. After I'd stopped acting, I continued with fencing because it was good exercise and I enjoyed the competition.

I considered staying up and watching *The Prisoner of Zenda*, but it was getting late, and I had a big day ahead of me tomorrow, so I just turned off the TV and went to bed.

That night, I once again experienced my Sylmar Earthquake dream. It had been several days, and I thought maybe I was finally done with it. Evidently, it wasn't done with me.

Saturday
July 21

●◆ When I went down to get the morning newspaper, I checked my mailbox for yesterday's mail.
Among the bills and the junk, was another postcard from my cousin, Vlatko. Vlatko owned the
most beautiful wooden hulled schooner, on which
he traveled the oceans of the world. I had an open
invitation to join him, but I never did. This new
postcard was from yet another South Pacific paradise. I added the postcard to the array of Vlatko's
postcards on my refrigerator. He always ended
each message with: "Wish you were here!"

Vlatko would be gone for months, sailing to any number of exotic locales. He would return to San Pedro just long enough to see family and to recruit a new all-female crew for his next journey. It was amazing, as he got older, the women somehow never aged. He always said he'd been inspired by his sailing friend, the actor, Errol Flynn, whom he claimed to know.

Vlatko was raised on the ocean, the way my father had been raised on the ocean, and the way their fathers had been. I looked at the postcards of all the beautiful places: French Polynesia, Bora Bora, Tahiti, and Aitutaki on the Cook Islands. There was even a photo of Upolu in Samoa, where author Robert Louis Stevenson lived out his final days.

On one of Vlatko's recent visits, he brought back an Aloha shirt from Hawaii. That's right, he visited Hawaii, and all I got was a shirt. But tonight, I could finally put that shirt to good use since our closing night party had a Polynesian theme. I did inform Cynthia of this fact, and she said she'd wear something suitable. I couldn't imagine her wearing a grass skirt, but I was sure she'd look good in whatever she wore.

It was through Vlatko that I first met Ralph Faulkner at his Falcon Fencing Studios. Evidently, Vlatko had done some extra work back in the 1950s, and he'd even been in some sword fight scenes. Faulkner was in his nineties now and required a cane whenever he assumed the *En-garde* position. His white hair, wrinkled face, and thick glasses gave away his age. But his posture was still straight and true, and his physical dexterity belied his years.

Besides *The Prisoner of Zenda,* my other favorite Faulkner movie sword fight was the comedic duel in *The Court Jester,* with Danny Kaye and Basil Rathbone. Faulkner called Rathbone the finest fencer in Hollywood and referred to him as "The Great Baz." Rathbone simply referred to Faulkner as "The Boss."

Before I headed to my fencing class, I stopped at Beryl's to feed her cats. Maggie and Dottie greeted me at the door. They both meowed and carried on as if they were glad to see me. Nina's estate sale had cleared the place out. There's something sad about an empty old house, especially when you remember the way it once looked.

The first time I walked into the Falcon Fencing Studio, I thought I'd accidentally stepped into a museum. In the lobby, there was a wall covered with the photographs of all the film stars Ralph Faulkner had trained. Near those photos, were display cases filled with the trophies and medals Faulkner had earned as a competitive fencer. There was a large photo of Faulkner with his

1932 USA Olympic Fencing team. He looked so dashing back then, as handsome as any of the movie stars on his wall.

In another part of the room, there were photographs of some of Faulkner's prize students. Several of which were females, and a few of them had even become Olympians. For me, there was something strangely seductive about an attractive woman holding a sword. I wondered what Freud would have said about that?

Through the practice studio windows, I noticed a fencing class going through their routines, but I didn't see Maestro Faulkner. Then, I heard his distinctive voice coming from inside his office. I poked my head in and saw him seated behind his desk and wearing his usual black fencing tunic. Across from him sat a woman, and they were engaged in a lively conversation. Faulkner stopped when he noticed me standing at his doorway.

"Yes, Niko," he asked. "How can I help you?"

"Sorry to bother you, Maestro. But I was wondering if we were still having class?"

The woman glanced over at me. She was in her fifties, blue-eyed, with medium-length, reddish-blonde hair. She wore a blue blazer, with the "Star-In-Motion" logo of the 1984 Olympics over her breast pocket. I immediately recognized her from her photographs in Faulkner's lobby. I'd also seen her picture in Heritage Hall at USC, where she'd once been a student athlete. Her name had been Janice York, but she changed it to Janice Romary when she got married. She was probably the finest fencers this country ever produced, male or female.

"We are having class," Faulkner answered. "But today you will be with one of my assistants. I'm visiting with a former student and old friend."

I looked over to Romary. "I'm sorry, but I recognized you from your photos."

This earned me a smile, and she stood to shake my hand. "Well," she chuckled. "I assume you're one of Master Faulkner's students."

"My name's Niko. I'm just a beginning fencer, maybe an intermediate by now."

"On his good days," Faulkner grimaced, waiting for me to leave the room. When I didn't leave, he finally offered me a seat.

"Thank you, Maestro," I said, grabbing the empty chair.

I knew Romary had stopped competing years ago, but her blazer logo made me think she was still somehow participating in these upcoming Olympics.

"It looks like you're still involved with The Games?" I asked.

"Yes. They asked me to be the commissioner of the fencing competition. My first Olympics as a fencer was 1948 and my last, 1968. I think this will finally be it for me."

I just sat there, listening to the two of them talk, the teacher and the student. They spoke about Romary's teenage years and all the training that led to her first Olympic Games. I felt a little bit like a fly on the wall.

"During your years of Olympic competition," I asked, "was there one special moment that stands out?"

Romary paused for a moment. "Yes," she answered. "It happened in Mexico City in 1968, at my last Olympics."

I remember watching those Mexico City Games on our first color TV. I also remember Tommie Smith and John Carlos raising their black-gloved fists in protest. 1968 as I remember, was a year filled with protests.

"Why the 1968 Olympics?" Faulkner asked. "Because it was your last as a competitor?"

"No, because that year, I was asked to carry the American flag during the opening ceremonies."

For every Olympics, one athlete is chosen to carry the American flag during the opening ceremonies. It's considered a huge honor.

"If I'm not mistaken, I believe you were the first woman ever chosen," said Faulkner.

"Yes," she said. "But it almost didn't happen."

"Why?" I asked.

"The USA Olympic Committee first asked Al Oerter, the four-time gold medal winner, to carry the flag. But Al said he couldn't do it and be ready for his first event. They weren't happy with him and told him he'd need to pick his own replacement. Without hesitation, Al Oerter said, 'That's easy, Janice Romary.'

"So, what was the problem?" asked Faulkner.

Romary looked at us for just a moment before answering.

"They didn't want a woman carrying the flag because it broke tradition."

Faulkner and I looked at each other in disbelief.

"That's some fine tradition they're upholding," frowned Faulkner.

"That's just stupid," I said. "And worst of all, it's not fair."

"Oerter was shocked and angry with their response," said Romary. "He told them how dumb he thought they were, but they refused to budge. So then, Oerter told a sports reporter friend about the committee's decision. When word got back to them a story was being written about that decision, the committee immediately changed their tune."

"Public humiliation can be a wonderful tool," Faulkner smiled.

I never made it to my fencing class that day because I just sat there listening to Faulkner and Romary share stories. I had to reschedule my class for later in the week, but that was okay because I learned a little piece of Olympic history. I also learned that Tommie Smith and John Carlos weren't the only athletes who protested during those 1968 Olympics. Al Oerter and Janice Romary had their own protest even earlier.

∞ ∞ ∞

That afternoon, I finally finished reading *Edendale*. I'd forgotten what a fine book it was. Back in his day, Cruz should have won some of the literary accolades that went to other less deserving writers. Maybe because he was a Mexican-American writer they didn't take him seriously. He just needed a little bit of luck, which he unfortunately never got. Now, I had to somehow condense Cruz's sprawling novel into a workable 90-minute play, but I'd done it before so I knew I could do it again.

Tonight's closing night party was being held at a once famous Hollywood restaurant. I'd heard so many great stories about the place, and I was looking forward to going there for the first time. I was also looking forward to having Cynthia there with me. In theater, it's a closing night custom to exchange small gifts or cards. I grabbed the cards I'd made out, threw on my Aloha shirt, and headed to the theater.

Over the stage door, someone had hung a banner which read: *"Aloha!"* which I assumed was the theme for the evening. I delivered my cards to the various dressing rooms before anyone else got there.

Peggy Terry was the first cast member to arrive. She wore a pink sun dress with grass skirted hula girls and bird of paradise flowers printed on it. Her blond hair hung down to a purple orchid, which she wore as a corsage. She gave me a hug and handed me a card from a bundle that she carried.

My friend, Walt Wagner arrived next. He wore a pale-green, Aloha shirt adorned with printed palm trees and coconuts. Walt carried in a ukulele, which he began to play. At first, he was just strumming a tune, but then he began to sing the old Hawaiian song: "My Little Grass Shack" Peggy knew the words and joined in.

Janie Leslie entered wearing a short, red sarong covered with white Hibiscus blossoms. She knew Walt's song and began to sing along as well.

Kevin McGeorge made his entrance wearing a straw beachcomber's hat and a pale-blue Aloha shirt adorned with a flock of parrots. Kevin also had his pet parrot, Rodney, perched on his shoulder. We'd all heard stories about Rodney but we'd never met him. Kevin adored the comedian, Rodney Dangerfield, and we'd heard he'd taught his parrot, Rodney, most of his jokes.

"I'm not saying you're ugly," Rodney squawked, "But I looked up ugly in the dictionary, and there was your picture."

"Sorry, folks," Kevin said. "There's nothing I can do, he's crazy about Dangerfield."

"I tell you," Rodney announced. "It's not easy being me."

Walt began to sing a solo of "I Wonder Where My Little Hula Girl Has Gone."

Tim Spillman, who was never one for understatement, arrived dressed as a giant pineapple, with pointy leaves as a hat. Somehow, a six-foot pineapple didn't seem out of place tonight. "I might be cold and prickly on the outside," Tim said, "but I'm warm and sweet on the inside."

Kelly Kirkland came in wearing a navy blue sarong. Images of yellow Hibiscus flowers covered the dress. Kelly began to sing along with Walt.

Frank Kaiser entered last. He wore a white skipper's cap and a red Aloha shirt covered with images of bananas. Frank carried in a live monkey in his open backpack. The monkey was dressed as a beachcomber. Everyone howled when they saw the monkey.

"For years," Frank joked, "I've been trying to get this monkey off my back."

Walt and the Kelly ended their song, and went over to meet Frank's monkey, whom he introduced as: "Thatcher." To keep Thatcher happy, Frank constantly fed him peanuts from his shirt pocket. Frank explained that his animal trainer neighbor allowed him to bring Thatcher here as his date.

"Would you believe it," Frank said. "He loves banana Daiquiris."

Even though everyone was ready for the party to begin, we still had one final performance of *Sam Sphincter Private Eye Proctologist* to get through. I could tell it wasn't going to be easy. I loudly announced "half hour," letting everyone know it was time to prepare for our final show. I asked Kevin and Frank what they'd planned to do with their pets during the play. Kevin said that he had a cage for Lucky, and Frank told me Thatcher's trainer would be here to babysit. I was relieved they'd actually made plans.

As the actors made their way to their dressing rooms, I headed for the theater's front lobby to see if Cynthia had arrived. I found her gazing up at the cast photos on the wall. She wore a white, flowered sun dress with a slight split at the bottom. A single white orchid was pinned over her ear. Her long brown hair covered her bare shoulders. To me, Cynthia looked like a tropical dessert.

"Hi," I said, indicating her white dress. "You look great."

"Thanks," she smiled. "I found it at a second-hand store." She spun around, giving me a 360-degree view. "I hope it's okay?"

"It's perfect," I smiled. "Everyone is into the Polynesian theme tonight."

"Good," she replied. "Then I won't stand out."

"No chance of that," I admitted. "Kevin brought

his parrot. Tim's dressed as a pineapple, and Frank brought in a live monkey. It's going to be one of those nights."

Cynthia laughed her charming laugh. It reminded me of a little girl who'd been caught being bad. I was certainly hoping I could encourage her to be bad with me. That would make for one fine evening. After I've had a couple of drinks, I'd allow her to have her way with me. Tonight, I was planning to be a slut, and I didn't care who knew it.

Just then, the house manager appeared holding a small xylophone. He played three notes as a signal, then announced to the audience the show was ready to begin. The crowd started moving toward their seats. I said goodbye to Cynthia, and told her that I would see her after the show. I made my way to the control booth, where I immediately announced "places" over my headset.

It turned out to be a good show, one of our best. The cast had fun, the crew had fun, and of course the audience had a great time. Everyone there could tell their friends they'd been a part of the Olympic Arts Festival, a historic event. When the last performance of *Sam Sphincter Private Eye Proctologist* was over, the audience gave the Drama Geeks one last standing ovation.

∞ ∞ ∞

He was born Ernest Raymond Beaumont Gantt in Limestone County, Texas. As a young man, it was said he traveled to Tahiti, New Guinea, Australia, and Jamaica. Sometimes the facts didn't always line up, so it was difficult to corroborate large portions of his life story. He was a "fabulist," an embellisher, a teller of tall tales. In my hometown, he would have simply been called a "bullshit artist." That doesn't mean we would have liked him any less, or been any less willing to fall for one of his schemes.

You see, the man had a vision, like Christopher Columbus in Spain, or Brigham Young in Utah, or Moses leading his people across the Red Sea. Well, maybe not exactly like those people, they were probably a tad more important than he was, but he had a vision none the less. His vision was to create a romantic place with the atmosphere of a South Pacific paradise, filled with tropical plants, Polynesian masks, and the delicious "rum rhapsodies," as he called his many tasty cocktails. He generously offered to share these libations with humanity. When I say share, I mean he would charge you a tidy sum, but it's only fair because even paradise costs money.

In 1933, just months after Prohibition was lifted, he opened his modern-day Mecca in Hollywood. He called his place Don the Beachcomber. It was the world's first Polynesian themed bar. It was ground zero, the Garden of Eden, and Los

Alamos, New Mexico all rolled into one. Every Tiki bar, or Polynesian restaurant you've ever heard of, seen, or experienced leads right back to this place. He even legally changed his name to Donn Beach, just to add a touch of authenticity to his new enterprise.

That same year, a gentleman named Victor Bergeron, who owned a restaurant in Oakland, California, called Hinky Dinks, visited Don the Beachcomber. It must have been a life altering experience because Bergeron went right home and changed the name of his restaurant to Trader Vic's, and adopted a menu suspiciously similar to Donn's. Trader Vic's was only the beginning of what would become a flood of imitators. What's the old saying? Imitation is the sincerest form of flattery? Well, Donn Beach was certainly flattered. But he was also pissed off as hell and went to great lengths to try and keep his drink recipes a secret. But all to no avail, because people knew a good thing when they tasted it.

Donn Beach eventually married an astute business woman who helped him turn this one Polynesian bar and restaurant into a successful chain. At one time, there were as many as sixteen from coast to coast. When the two finally divorced, she acquired all of his mainland businesses, and he left the continent for Hawaii, where he opened his new Don the Beachcomber on the beach at Waikiki.

I'd passed by the original Don the Beachcomber on North McCadden Place many times, and I knew of its history. I'd heard stories of Humphrey Bogart, Bing Crosby, and Clark Gable all patronizing the joint. Frank Sinatra always ordered their Navy Grog, and Marlene Dietrich enjoyed the Beachcomber's Gold. Most of the drinks were fruity, but they also packed a punch. There were so many incidents of customers getting pie-eyed that Donn had to impose a two-drink limit on some of his more potent concoctions. With at least eighty-four different cocktails to his name, Donn Beach was probably the most prolific mixologist of all time. Both he and Victor Bergeron claimed credit for the Mai Tai, but of course Beach's concoctions didn't stop there. His masterpiece was probably the Zombie, known for turning its drinker into one of the walking dead.

The Polynesian Tiki Bar craze Donn had started, eventually spread like wildfire. There were once Tiki bars all over the globe. But fifty years is a long time, and many of those fires have long since gone out. We'd heard rumors that this original Don the Beachcomber was in danger of closing. To me that was unimaginable since it was such a historic place, and the Tiki bar concept still had many fans. When the Drama Geeks heard rumors of its demise, they booked Don the Beachcomber for our closing night party, wanting to support the place any way they could.

When I saw Cynthia after the play, she was all smiles. She loved the show and was amazed by the level of improvisation. "They're all so funny," she beamed. "I've never laughed so hard in my life." I offered her a ride to the party, but she preferred to follow me there in her car. It was a relatively short trip, and it didn't take us long to get there. We parked in a nearby lot, and then walked over together. Other people from the show were arriving, and I had a chance to introduce them to Cynthia.

The inside of Don the Beachcomber looked exactly how I'd imagined it. Bamboo covered most of the ceiling and walls, with palm fronds hanging from the tree like pillars. The chairs and bar stools were all a rattan style. A long window opened to a tropical setting, lush with different exotic foliage. Netted glass float globes were hung randomly around the place. The sound of rain falling onto a tin roof blended with the gentle Hawaiian music. There was a scent of tropical flowers in the air, and a large portrait of Donn Beach was displayed prominently on one wall. Donn had a devilish smirk on his face and wore a safari shirt and a wide-brimmed beachcomber hat. A sign below the portrait read: "Don the Beachcomber — Host to diplomat, beachcomber, pirate, and prince."

The Filipino bartenders took our drink orders as fast as we could call them out. Peggy ordered a Tahitian Rum Punch. Walt, still carrying his ukulele, decided on a Q B Cooler, which he claimed was the original Mai Tai. Janie selected the Vicious Virgin. "Maybe I'll be recycled," she smiled, sweetly. Kevin asked for the Test Pilot with an extra a cup of Maraschino cherries for his parrot, Rodney. Tim ordered the Pi Yi, which was served in a hollowed-out pineapple. Needless to say, it was the first time I'd seen a pineapple drinking from a pineapple.

Kelly had some difficulty deciding which drink to order, but since she was a lapsed Catholic, she settled on the Missionary Downfall. She said: "It sounded rebellious." Frank ordered a Coconut Rum Swizzle, which was served in a hollowed-out coconut. He also ordered Thatcher that banana Daiquiri he'd promised him. The Daiquiri made Thatcher one happy monkey.

I asked Cynthia what drink sounded good to her. She looked at me and said: "A Shark's Tooth, because I want something with a little bite to it." She smiled wickedly and gave me a wink. Finally, I ordered the bar's most infamous cocktail, the Zombie. The Filipino bartender raised an eyebrow and reminded me I could only order two for the entire evening. I assured him two would be just fine. I then read aloud the quote on the drink menu for the Zombie: "Imitated, but never duplicated."

With drinks in hand, we took over the bar area, even spilling into the main dining room.

Some people stood while others sat on stools and chairs. As I scanned the room, I couldn't believe how great everyone looked. This scene could have been out of a 1940s Technicolor film. The gathering had a *Feliniesque* quality to it, like a Polynesian *La Dolce Vita*. Here we were, in the original Tiki bar, half a block up from Hollywood Boulevard, drinking with the ghosts of old Hollywood. Sure, the place was kitschy, a bit tacky, and well past its prime, but it was still great fun, and with a little imagination, you could imagine you were somewhere in the South Pacific, which I'm sure was Donn Beach's plan all along.

Large plates of Cantonese appetizers were brought out from the kitchen. There was fried shrimp, barbecued pork, egg rolls, and Hawaiian spareribs. Everyone took advantage of the finger food while they sipped their cocktails. Walt and Kelly joined Cynthia and me at a table.

"So, you work with Niko at the Taper?" Kelly asked Cynthia.

"I'm on staff, and Niko works on specific shows." Cynthia answered. "So, yes, we both work there."

"We've enjoyed having him in our group," Kelly admitted. "He fit right in."

"He doesn't know any Hawaiian songs," Walt said, strumming his ukulele. "But he's fine, otherwise."

"One of my many short comings," I added, taking a generous sip from my cocktail.

"Your group is incredible," Cynthia said. "That's the funniest play I've ever seen."

"Thanks," Kelly replied. "We've been working on this show for a while."

Cynthia began to describe why she liked the play so much. She explained everything in great detail, like a good review in the newspaper. Her explanation was analytical and thoughtful. I didn't know what Walt and Kelly thought, but I was really impressed.

Kevin and Rodney stopped at our table to say hello. We were their captive audience.

"My wife and I were happy for twenty years," Rodney squawked. "And then we met."

Walt gave Rodney a threatening glare. "It's a shame they don't have parrot on the menu."

Rodney let out a shriek. "I tell you," he cried. "I get no respect."

Kevin and Rodney moved on to the next table, looking for more appetizers and a new crowd. The four of us continued talking and sharing stories, all the while sipping our potent cocktails. Cynthia was a good listener as well as a good talker. She also revealed a sly sense of humor, which I found very appealing.

Frank eventually stopped at our table to introduce us to Thatcher, his monkey. Thatcher was still sipping from his banana Daquiri.

"Don't worry," Frank assured us. "Thatcher's Daquiri is a 'mocktail,' there's no alcohol involved."

"That's good," Walt replied. "Drunk humans are bad enough."

I'd never been very good at nursing a drink, and tonight I was no better. I finished my entire drink before anyone else was half way into theirs. That first Zombie was good, and I was now ready for round two. In the past, I would sometimes overdo it, and then I hate myself in the morning. It looked like tomorrow was going to be one of those mornings.

"Another Shark's Tooth?" I asked Cynthia, as I got up wobbly from my seat.

"No," she answered. "I'm fine."

I looked to the others, seeing if anyone else was ready for their second beverage, but they all shook their heads, no. "What were they waiting for," I thought? This is a party, a time to celebrate. Unfortunately, trying to walk to the bar turned out to be more difficult than I expected. The same bartender from earlier was there to greet me.

"Another Zombie," I said, with a big grin.

Nearby, I could hear Rodney performing his routine.

"I told my psychiatrist everyone hates me," Rodney screeched. "He said that was ridiculous because everyone hasn't met me yet."

After a moment, the bartender returned with my Zombie. It looked so damn good: tall, wet, and gorgeous. I thought it was the most beautiful drink I'd ever seen. I wanted to put a picture of it on a billboard, then hang it over Sunset Boulevard.

"Here you go," he said, handing me my drink. "Remember, that's your last one."

"Alright," I agreed, tasting the cocktail to make sure it was okay. I'll be honest, it was so much more than okay. The damn thing was perfect. I carried it back to our table with reverence, trying not to spill a single drop. I sat back down with the others.

"Cynthia wants to make movies," Kelly said. "Someday, we'll all be working for her."

Cynthia told me she was interested in films, so this was no surprise. She even claimed she knew several studio executives. We were in Hollywood after all, everyone wanted to make movies.

Walt stood up at the table with his ukulele. He then placed two fingers in his mouth and let out a loud whistle, getting the crowd's immediate attention. He asked everyone to grab one of the lyric sheets he'd passed out earlier, then he made his way to the small stage. Walt began singing "Hanalei Moon," a romantic Hawaiian tune. The song conjured up images of a sensuous Hawaiian evening. During the song, I caught myself staring at Cynthia. She looked so beautiful, the orchid in her hair, the white dress, those big brown eyes. The more I drank, the more attractive she became. By the time I'd finished my second Zombie, Cynthia was easily the most beautiful woman I'd ever seen.

Walt finished his song, took a bow, then came back and sat down with us. At that moment, I realized I felt no pain. The Zombie was working its magic. Kelly looked at me with some concern.

"Are you okay?" she asked.

"What?" I replied. "I'm fine."

"You don't look fine," Kelly said. "You look like a guy who's had too much to drink."

"No," I tried to reassure her. "I'm okay, really."

Glancing around the table, I noticed no one else had even finished their first cocktail. I couldn't figure out what was wrong with them. Kelly and Cynthia chatted while I spoke with Walt.

"Excuse me," Cynthia said, standing up. "Where would I find the restroom?"

Walt pointed to a hallway up near the front door. Since I needed to visit the little boy's room myself, I offered to escort Cynthia there. We carefully wove our way through the crowd. Cynthia entered her restroom as I entered mine.

While standing at the urinal, I had difficulty getting things to flow. I just couldn't open the spigot. So, I tried to imagine some of the famous Hollywood actors who might have peed at this very spot. Amazingly, this strategy worked, and the dam finally broke. I suddenly felt proud to be urinating where some of the greatest names in Hollywood had peed. This was better than standing in the footprints at Grauman's Chinese Theatre.

Even though I'd managed not to pee on myself, I still washed my hands afterwards, remembering the good hygiene I'd learned in kindergarten. I stepped out into the hallway and waited for Cynthia to come out. I hadn't kissed her since the other day in Pasadena and it had been far too long. Maybe it was the rum, but I suddenly felt emboldened. The moment Cynthia stepped out of the restroom, I met her with a big kiss. She seemed surprised at first but then responded in kind.

While we smooched, I felt her bare shoulders. They were smooth and wonderful. Then, out of nowhere, we heard someone clearing their throat. We stopped kissing and discovered Kevin standing there with his parrot, Rodney. Rodney was the first one to speak.

"I have good looking kids," he screeched. "Thank goodness my wife cheats on me."

"Niko," Kevin said. "Could you watch Rodney while I use the restroom?"

Before I could object, Kevin placed Rodney on my shoulder.

"Are you sure he's safe?" I asked, looking at Rodney warily.

"Don't worry," Kevin answered, hurrying into the restroom. "If anything happens, I'll pay for the stitches."

Before I could respond, Kevin disappeared into the restroom. Rodney gave me the stink eye.

"I told my wife that I was seeing a psychiatrist," Rodney squawked. "Then she told me that she was seeing a psychiatrist, two plumbers, and a bartender."

"Pretty bird," Cynthia said, admiring Rodney's fine plumage.

"When I was born, I was so ugly," Rodney declared, "the doctor slapped my mother."

"Oh, no," Cynthia replied. "You're beautiful."

Kevin finally came out and took back his loquacious parrot. Kevin thanked me, then they returned to the bar area, leaving Cynthia and me alone once again.

This was a good time to invite Cynthia back to my place. I wanted to get her between my sheets and give her a "Croatian sensation."

"I think I'd better get going," Cynthia said. "It's getting late."

"What? The party is just getting started." Even if she wasn't ready to go to my place, she couldn't leave this early. We had the whole evening ahead of us.

"I'm really sorry," she said," but Richard handed me a playscript this afternoon, and he expects me to have it read and evaluated by tomorrow morning." She gave me a quick kiss. "I really had a great time," she said, turning toward the front door. "Please say goodbye to Kelly and Walt for me."

"Let me at least walk you to your car," I offered.

"No, I'll be fine. You go and enjoy your friends."

Cynthia opened the door and walked out.

Well, that was disappointing, I thought. So much for a "Croatian sensation." This was more like a "Croatian deflation."

I went back into the bar and I found our show's house manager. I knew he was a health nut and never touched alcohol, so I asked him for one more favor. He was reluctant at first, but he finally agreed to order me that third Zombie. After he handed me my cocktail, I thanked him, then dove headfirst into it like a thirsty man finding an oasis in the middle of the desert.

I'd already passed out behind the wheel when my Firebird went through the intersection at Western and Santa Monica, so I had no idea whether the traffic light was green, yellow, or red. But when my car's rear fender clipped the light pole on the corner, the impact jolted me awake. I somehow managed to gain control of the car and keep it traveling within the white lines. I began to curse, first in Croatian, then in English, only stopping when I ran out of expletives. I knew I was less than a mile from home, and I figured if I could just keep my eyes open, I might be able to make it. I should have just pulled over but I didn't.

I was drunk, and my judgment was shit. When I finally reached the Villa Serrano, I slid my Firebird into its parking spot and got out to survey the damage. The rear fender was smashed in and paint was scraped down to the metal.

Climbing the stairs to my apartment was like conquering Mount Everest. But I somehow made it to the summit. After opening my door, I went right into the bathroom. In the mirror, I noticed I was still wearing my silly Aloha shirt — a dumbass stranger in paradise.

Maybe the Tiki gods were angry with me for desecrating their good name for the purpose of liquid libation. They had every reason to be pissed off at the whole foolish bunch of us, but I was the one they'd chosen for their human sacrifice.

I knelt down before the porcelain god and said my penance. I swore I would never do this again. Then, I suddenly began to puke. It was all pretty gross.

Sunday
July 22

●✦ "Oh, my head," I muttered, as I hid my eyes from the morning sun. My skull throbbed, and my stomach felt queasy. I notice I was still wearing my Aloha shirt, a sad reminder of last night's misadventures. I thought maybe I would just rest and recuperate today, but I then remembered I had agreed to help my friend, Marvin Grossman. I couldn't just call and cancel because he'd already scheduled everyone to be there.

When I saw my Firebird in the daylight, it looked as bad as I remembered. Before I could go help Marvin, I knew that I needed to feed Beryl's cats, so I went there first. Maggie and Dottie were glad to see me and happy to just get some food and water. I apologized to them for not spending more time, and promised I would try to do better in the future.

I arrived at Marvin's casting office just before noon. The receptionist was on the phone, and Marvin was in the lobby talking with two young actresses. I had a massive headache and my stomach was still sour. I don't think the aspirin I took helped with either issue.

Marvin Grossman was rail thin, with a moon shaped head, and a mop of brown hair. His round-rimmed eyeglasses gave him the appearance of a prep school nerd. As an actor, this look was his bread and butter. He'd probably played versions of the same character a hundred times. When the actresses left, Marvin came over to me.

"You look like crap," he said. "Don the Beachcomber, right?"

"Yeah. It was fun until it wasn't."

"Let's go eat. Maybe some food will help."

"Yeah, if I can hold it down."

I followed Marvin into the hallway, which led to the alley. Marvin drove us to Hamptons hamburger restaurant, which was located in a repurposed old house on Highland in Hollywood. The burgers there were insanely good and very different from most burger joints. Hamptons had a large variety of toppings and a huge selection of salads and side dishes. For some reason, the one item you couldn't order here, were French fries.

Marvin was a regular, and he'd already made us a reservation. The owner of Hamptons was a friend of the actor, Paul Newman, who supposedly invested in the restaurant. The two partners even wrote a movie together, which Newman then went on to direct. Sadly, the movie wasn't nearly as good as their hamburgers.

"I'm glad you were available," Marvin told me, as we sat down at a table. "We'll be seeing actresses all day."

"What kind of commercial is this?"

"It's for a new hamburger chain. In the commercial, a salesgirl is behind the counter and selling this guy a burger. We've already cast the guy, so today we'll be casting the girl."

Marvin ordered the Foggy Bottom Burger with peanut butter and sour plum jam. I considered the Frank's Fantasy with sour cream and caviar, but then settled on just a plain cheeseburger. My stomach wasn't in the adventurous mood.

Marvin said he heard my show with Sebastian could be coming to the Taper's main stage.

"It's not a done deal," I answered. "But they're close to making a decision."

"My New York friends tell me Sebastian is a real prick."

"Yeah, maybe," I said, "but it's a paycheck."

Marvin gave me a wry look.

"Niko, life's too short to work with jerks."

"Not everyone is as charming as you, Marvin," I smiled.

Marvin laughed, then began to tell me about the time he'd been cast in a Broadway show with a once famous TV comedian. The guy had been a huge star, but those days were long gone. The play was Marvin's first big break, and he was playing the comedian's nerdy son.

"During rehearsals, I had some really funny lines and got some big laughs."

"That probably made the old guy happy," I said.

"Just the opposite," Marvin frowned. "He had the director take all of my funny lines and give them to his character. So now, the lines don't make any sense and are no longer funny."

"Did you complain?"

"Of course. But the old guy was the star of the show, and I was a nobody."

We finished our lunch and then headed back to Marvin's office. By this time, the reception area was packed with young actresses. We parked the Jeep and entered through the backdoor.

The auditions were to be held in a tiny rehearsal room with two small windows and one door. Marvin and I set ourselves up at a table with notepads and sharpened pencils. There was also a tall stack of actor's resumes with photos. Marvin informed me I would be reading the role of the male customer. It would also be my job to escort each actress in for her audition.

Just as we were about to begin, a man I'd never seen before entered the room and sat down behind us near the wall.

"Niko," Marvin said. "This is John. He's going to be sitting in during the auditions."

I didn't know who John was, but I figured he might be the client or maybe just another casting person, although he didn't look the type. He looked more like a truck driver with the Teamsters.

I scanned the list of actresses' names, then suddenly stopped at the name Stephanie Davies. Stephanie was actually an old girlfriend of mine from high school. In fact, she was the one who talked me into being in my first play. I'd heard she was still acting.

When Marvin was ready, he had me bring in the first actress on our list. In the waiting room, I looked around for Stephanie but didn't see her. I wasn't sure I'd even recognize her after all these years.

This audition became something of an assembly line. It was one actress right after the other. Marvin would always have a question or two for each actress, and then they'd chat a bit. I would eventually read my part with them for their audition. After that, Marvin thanked them, and said he would let their agent know the results. I would then open the door for each one to exit. Sometimes Marvin would ask me what I thought of the actress, and other times, I would just offer my opinion unsolicited. Usually, Marvin and I were in sync. Truthfully, any one of these actresses could have done the role. This wasn't Shakespeare, it was just a burger commercial.

At various times during the auditions, John would ask Marvin to see the actress' resume. John would look it over, and then jot down some of their information. I finally became curious, and asked Marvin who this John guy was.

"He's just some guy," Marvin whispered. "He has an office down the street."

"Is he casting something?"

"The only thing he's casting are blow jobs," Marvin muttered.

"What?"

"He's looking to get laid," Marvin admitted. "He's a pretty shady character."

It took me a moment to fully comprehend what was going on. Here were all these young women coming in to audition for a TV commercial, and this guy is taking down their phone numbers. This whole thing was bad, and I felt dirty just being a part of it.

"Marvin," I said. "I don't like this one bit."

"Niko, I don't either, but John is a bad guy

with some equally bad friends. I was afraid to say no."

John did look pretty tough. If we were casting goons, he'd definitely get the role.

"Let's just get through this," Marvin pleaded. "We're almost finished."

"Fine," I said, in a way that let Marvin know that I wasn't fine with any of it.

Stephanie Davies was next on our list, so I went out to the waiting room and called out her name. Stephanie popped up from behind another actress. She hadn't changed one bit and looked just like I remembered her. She was still the same cute little blonde with the big smile.

"Hi Niko," she said, wistfully.

"Hi Stephanie," I muttered. "It's good to see you after all these years."

"You too."

Stephanie and I talked while I led her into the audition room. I then introduced her to Marvin. They spoke while he glanced down at her resume. Stephanie was relaxed and charming. She and I read the scene together, and I thought she did a great job; she was in the moment and natural. Marvin thanked her for coming in and told her he'd let her agent know. I opened the door for her.

"It was great seeing you," I said.

"You too, Niko," she said, smiling.

Stephanie walked out and I closed the door

behind her. I then looked over to Marvin for a long moment.

"What?" Marvin asked, sensing that I had something to say.

"I thought she was one of the best ones."

"She was. But there were also a few others."

"Yeah. It's just too bad you can only hire one," I smiled.

John stood up. "Can I see her resume?" he asked.

Marvin looked over to me.

"No," I replied. "You can't."

I took the resume from Marvin and returned it to our table, where I shoved it under a tall stack of other resumes.

John's angry stare practically burned a hole right through me. Then he looked over to Marvin. Marvin just shrugged his shoulders, as if to indicate it wasn't his call. John then moved right up to me, and without pause, punched me right in the eye. An array of stars floated past my face as I fell on my ass. I assumed he'd used a baseball bat, because that's how it felt. He then stood over me, just daring me to get up. But I couldn't, even if I'd wanted to. The little birdies were singing me a song. John finally returned to his chair, gathered up his papers and walked right out the door. Marvin then came over to me.

"Niko, I'm so sorry. That's what I was trying to avoid."

"Ow! My eye." I complained, trying to pull myself up off the floor.

Marvin helped me to my feet.

"You know," I said. "If I were bigger, stronger, and meaner, I could have kicked his ass."

"I'm sure you could have," he agreed. "I'll go get you some ice."

I sat down at the table, searching for Stephanie's resume from under the pile. Marvin returned with an ice pack. I put the ice on my eye, then handed him Stephanie's resume.

"You're going to give her the commercial," I said. "She's perfect for it."

Marvin looked like he was about to argue with me, but then just threw up his hands.

"Oh, what the hell," he said. "This is no time to start having scruples."

Hank Pilsner's bungalow court apartment was on Beachwood Drive near the Hollywood Memorial Park Cemetery. The neighborhood was more than a little seedy. At night, drug deals took place right out on his street, and male prostitutes hustled their wares over on nearby Santa Monica Boulevard. Hank just ignored the male hookers, but he sometimes took advantage of the drug deals. To him, it was like being a kid and having the Good Humor Man stop right on your block.

Last time I saw Hank, he'd asked me to come by to get my ticket for next week's Olympic baseball game. The USA team was playing Chinese Taipei at Dodger Stadium, and we would be sitting in our usual seats. Baseball was only a demonstration sport at these Olympics, but it would still be great if the USA team won.

Driving over to Hank's, I looked at my eye in the rearview mirror. The ice pack reduced the swelling, but the skin had already turned black and blue. When I got out of my Firebird, I waved to the friendly Iranian man who was always riding around the neighborhood on his bicycle. Hank called him "The Mayor," because he was usually patrolling the streets. Before the Shah of Iran was deposed in 1979, "The Mayor" had been a general in the Iranian army. Now his entire battlefield was reduced to this one block on Beachwood Drive. Also, when the Shah was deposed, Tehran, the capitol city, lost its claim to hosting the 1984 Summer Olympics, allowing Los Angeles to step in as the replacement. In other words, L. A. was extremely lucky to get these Olympic Games.

Hank's one-bedroom cottage was the first one off the sidewalk, and I could hear a Dodger game playing over his TV. I knocked on the door, and Hank shouted the door was unlocked. I walked in and found Hank reclining in his favorite chair. On his coffee table sat an opened beer and a framed photograph of the Casino Building on Catalina Island. Spread out on the photograph's glass, were several lines of cocaine. Hank immediately noticed my black eye.

"What happened to you?" he asked.

"Do you remember my ex-girlfriend, Stephanie?"

"Yeah. Why? Did she finally kick your sorry ass?"

I didn't answer him. Instead, I just walked over to his wall mirror and looked at my eye.

"Do you want a line of blow?" he asked, pointing to the cocaine. "It might take away some of the sting."

"I appreciate the offer," I answered, grabbing a seat, "but no thanks."

"Good," he smiled, "just more for me."

Hank picked up a short straw and leaned over the glass picture frame. He snorted a line of cocaine up each nostril. His eyes glazed over and he displayed a euphoric smile. He then leaned back and settled blissfully into his chair.

"So," he said, "are you going to tell me what happened?"

I told Hank the whole story about Marvin's audition with Stephanie, and how that John guy had punched me.

"Didn't Stephanie dump you back in high school?" he asked.

"Yeah, so?"

"So, you got your ass kicked over a girl who once dumped you?" he frowned. "And then you let some guy sucker punch you, instead of hitting him first? Hmm, not too smart."

Even though it was going to be painful, I needed to give "Father Hank" my full confession. It was like ripping off the Band-Aid and allowing the wound to heal.

"Before you see my car," I said. "I need to tell you the whole story."

"Oh, wonderful," he replied, "another shit-show."

I told Hank about Don the Beachcomber, and my car crash afterwards.

"You should have called a cab," Hank said. "Driving drunk is just plain stupid."

"You're right. What can I say?

Suddenly, from the street right out front, we heard the loud screeching of tires, car doors opening, and people shouting. We then heard what sounded like firecrackers going off.

"Fuck!" Hank yelled. "Those are gun shots!"

We waited to make sure the shooting had stopped, then we carefully opened the door and stepped outside. Sitting there, in the middle of the street was an LAPD patrol car, its lights flashing, with both front doors flung open. Two uniformed officers, still holding their weapons, were stand-ing over a black male who was lying face down on the pavement. There was a handgun lying on the ground nearby. A pool of blood began to form around the man. One officer kneeled down and checked for a pulse. Not finding one, both officers then holstered their weapons.

That's when I recognized the two cops. It was Randy Ferlinghetti, and his partner, Officer Watkins. I pointed Ferlinghetti out to Hank, who at first didn't recognize Randy because of his crew cut. As other patrol cars were pulling up, a small crowd of neighbors began to gather. Hank's neighbor, Gabe, who had been out walking his black Lab, joined us on the sidewalk. "The Mayor" was also there on his bicycle.

"What happened?" Gabe asked, holding tightly onto his dog's leash.

"It looks like a police shooting," Hank answered. "We know one of the cops."

"Wow," Gabe said. "No shit?"

"I saw the whole thing," The Mayor said. "That man was running away, when the police car pulled up. He then turned and started shooting at the officers. That's when they got out and shot him dead."

"You better go tell them what you saw," Gabe said. "They'll appreciate an eye witness."

The LAPD had a bad reputation when it came to officer involved shootings. It seemed like their motto was, "Shoot first, and ask questions later." This time, it appeared the shooting might have been justified. While the crime scene was being taped off, Randy and Officer Watkins were being questioned by some other officers. Watkins was still answering questions when Randy started walking back to his police car.

"Hey, Ferlinghetti," Hank shouted. "You got a minute?"

Randy looked over and saw Hank and me standing there on the sidewalk. A small smile formed on his face as he walked right over to us.

"What are you guys doing here?" Randy asked.

"I live here," Hank answered, pointing to his bungalow. "What happened?"

"We were the backup for a drug bust," Randy said. "We chased this guy across Santa Monica Boulevard to here, and he started shooting at us."

Over the last few years, there were many stories in the news about the LAPD shootings. Some of the shooting seemed more justified than others. Leading up to the Olympics, Los Angeles Police Chief Darryl Gates had been cracking down in the inner-city neighborhoods, and the complaints of police brutality were way up. The question most people were asking was whether this was a temporary policy, just until the Olympic Games were over, or was this the new normal? Knowing Chief Gates, most people assumed that it was the new normal. When Randy and Officer Watkins headed back to the station, Hank and I returned to his bungalow.

I decided to take Jeanne Cruz up on her offer and go out to Malibu to write my adaptation of *Edendale*. Except, I had one problem. Well, actually, two. I'd committed to taking care of Beryl's two cats, so I needed a huge favor from Hank. I asked him if he would take care of Beryl's cats while I was gone. I told him if he did this for me, I'd buy all the hot dogs and beer at our Olympic baseball game. Fortunately, Hank had a soft spot for animals, as well as for hot dogs and beer. He agreed to take care of Beryl's cats for me until I returned. I told him where he could find the key and everything else he needed to know.

"Don't worry," he assured me, "just go write your play, and try not to fuck it up."

Monday
July 23

❧ The next morning, I loaded up my Firebird for my stay in Malibu. I made sure I had my swim trunks. Hell, I wasn't going to be writing 24 hours a day, and how often do I get to stay at a place called "Paradise Cove?"

I'd only been to Malibu a few times, so I didn't know the place that well. I was much more familiar with the South Bay area beaches: Redondo, Hermosa, and Manhattan. That was where I'd squandered away my youth: body surfing, playing volleyball, or just riding my bike along the strand. I'd always thought of Malibu as "Beverly Hills by the sea," an enclave for the rich and pretentious, Ferrari convertibles and little Chihuahua dogs yipping and yapping. For the next few days, I would have to learn to fit in. Somehow, I knew I would survive this harrowing ordeal.

Paradise Cove, or "The Cove," as Jeanne had called it, was first developed back in the 1940's as a place for sport fishing. There'd been a bait and tackle shop, a fishing barge, and a boat rental. The nearby kelp beds were then full of sea bass, yellowtail, and halibut. Divers could easily pull up abalone and lobsters as well. By the 1950s, there was also a small, but enthusiastic surfing community. That all changed in 1959, with the movie, *Gidget,* and the slew of Beach-Party movies that followed. The area was no longer a secret, and its popularity mushroomed. In the early 1970s, land on the bluff above the cove had been graded for a mobile home community. Almost three hundred homes, or double-wide trailers to be exact, were added. These mobile homes managed to coexist with the more palatial homes in the area.

There was one particular home on Pacific Coast Highway that I really wanted to see. I'd recently learned about it from the Los Angeles Conservancy. The Adamson House was built back in 1929, but it had recently opened to the public. Designed in the Spanish Colonial Style, it was supposed to be well worth seeing, with its garden setting, and a picturesque view of Santa Monica Bay.

According to the Conservancy, the original owners had also owned the Malibu Potteries Tile Company, and their home became a showplace for their products. Following the death of the owner in the late 1960s, the home was purchased by the state of California for the purpose of demolishing it and using the land for beach parking. This demolition was only prevented by the hard work of the Malibu Historical Society. Eventually, a foundation was formed to preserve the house as a museum.

I arrived at The Adamson House in time for the 11:00 AM tour. The home was even lovelier than I'd imagined. But it was the Malibu tiles that impressed me the most. In the sun splashed loggia, the sixty-foot-long, simulated Persian carpet was stunning. It was made of 674 tiles, complete with fringe. After seeing the Adamson House, I began to think maybe Malibu wasn't the worst place to visit.

It was late afternoon by the time I finally arrived at Paradise Cove. I found Jeanne's mobile home and quickly unloaded my things. The place was comfortable and cozy, just like a good beach house should be. Once I had everything put away, I sat for a moment on the small outdoor patio, enjoying the ocean view. I could feel the cool afternoon breezes coming up from the shore.

Well, I thought to myself, I could get to work on my writing, or go down to the beach. What kind of writer would I be if I didn't procrastinate just a little? I threw on my swim trunks and headed down toward the ocean. Out in the water, I noticed some swimmers, and a group of surfers trying to catch waves. I found a spot on the sand and laid down on my towel. There was a bevy of attractive young women lying around in their skimpy swimsuits, all working on their tans. The afternoon sun hung just above the horizon. I was glad I was wearing my Ray Bans because the sunglasses also helped to conceal my black eye.

Two male surfers came out of the water carrying their surfboards. It was difficult to see their faces because the sun was directly behind them. I could see that one of the two surfers was tall, with broad shoulders, while the other surfer looked to be about my size.

A pretty blonde girl kicked sand on my towel as she made her way to the water. "Oh my God," I thought. Look how beautiful she is, her bikini only a mere suggestion of a swimsuit. When she reached the water's edge, she turned back and gave me a winsome smile. "Oh, be still my beating heart." Was there anything more lovely in all the world? Where were all the modern day Michelangelos? Why weren't they here painting her?

Just then, one of the two surfers who'd been walking by me suddenly stopped.

"Niko," he barked. "What's up, dude?"

I quickly recognized my old friend, Benny Drew. Benny was a long-time surfer, and a famous shaper, a designer and builder of surfboards. As a kid, I watched him build surfboards in his parents' garage. Since then, he'd made hundreds, if not thousands of boards. He had his own shop, "Surfboards by Drew," in Hermosa Beach.

"Hi, Ben," I said. "Aren't you a long way from Hermosa?"

"I'm selling one of my boards to Oats here," he said, indicating the other surfer. "He loves my boards, man."

The other surfer looked familiar to me but I didn't know from where. He had to be in his mid-fifties, with a full head of blond hair, and the frame of a body builder. He looked like he'd just arrived from Muscle Beach, and carried his surfboard around like a toothpick. In the middle of his board was an oval shaped logo, which read: "Drew Surfboards." He looked over to Benny.

"Why don't you stay and talk to your friend?" he said. "Just come by when you're done, and I'll write you a check. I really like the board." He smiled, then started to walk away.

"Will do, Oats," Said Benny. "Thanks, man." Benny laid his surfboard down and sat cross-legged on the sand beside me. "Another satisfied customer," Benny smiled.

One day back in the old neighborhood, a few of us kids were playing football in the street by Benny's garage. He was inside making a surfboard, like usual. Some older kids showed up, took our football, and started to bully us. When Ben saw what was happening, he stopped his work, and came over and took back our football, then told these older kids to get lost. We all thought Benny was so cool, and he always had the most beautiful surfer chicks at his side. Sometimes he'd bring out his baseball glove and the two of us would just play catch together. It turned out, he'd played all the different sports in high school and was good in every one of them. Benny became the big brother I never had. Unfortunately, I never took up surfing, and it became Ben's whole life. We tried to stay in touch, but it was difficult.

"How long has it been?" I asked. "I haven't seen you forever."

It's been far too long, *mi compadre,*" he smiled. "You should come by the shop."

"Why?" I asked. "Every time I come by, you're always out surfing."

"Dude, that's what I do," he smiled. "But I still want to get together."

Benny taught me most of what I know about surfing. He said surfing began in Polynesia and Hawaii. Then, in 1907, while vacationing on Waikiki Beach, Henry E. Huntington, railroad magnet and real estate developer, noticed a man,

George Freeth, surfing the waves, or "walking on water," as he called it. Freeth's surfing exploits had already been written about by the author, Jack London, who referred to him as the "Brown Mercury." Huntington, knowing a good thing when he saw it, hired Freeth to come to the luxury hotel he'd built on the beach in Redondo to give surfing exhibitions. Huntington hoped to lure visitors there with his Red Cars to sell them parcels of land he owned. Freeth's demonstrations were a sensation and inspired others to take up the sport. When not demonstrating surfing, Freeth worked as a lifeguard, creating the lifeguard procedures that are still used to this day. Sadly, in 1919, George Freeth died at the young age of thirty-five, when he contracted the Spanish Flu during the pandemic.

"So," I asked. "How's business? It sounds like this guy likes your boards."

"Business is awesome," he answered. "And Oats is the best. He's bought like a dozen boards from me. Sometimes he'll call me up and say, "surf's up in Dana Point, do you want to join me?" And I'll say, 'hell yes!' And we'll drive down there together, and we'll surf all day. Oats has tried all of the other board makers: Hap Jacobs, Dewey Webber, Greg Noll, Bing Copeland, but he keeps coming back to me."

Back in the 1960s and 1970s, all of those surfboard makers had their shops on Pacific Coast

Highway in Hermosa Beach. If you were looking to buy a good surfboard, you had to come
to Hermosa. I never figured out how Huntington Beach got the name "Surf City" because I
thought Hermosa deserved that title, especially
back then.

"This guy, Oats, what does he do? I asked.

"Oh, man," Benny smiled. "He used to work
at the *Los Angeles Times*. Oats is just his nick-
name."

"Was he a sports writer? He looks like he could
have been an athlete."

"Dude, he would have been on the 1952 U.S.
Olympic team, but he got hurt. To this day, it still
pisses him off. He's super competitive."

"Well, who is he?"

"That's Otis Chandler, man, the former publisher. His family has owned the *Los Angeles
Times* for like a hundred years."

Of course, I thought; that's Otis Chandler. I'd
seen his picture before, but he'd always been in
a business suit, not in swim trunks. Since he'd
left the *Times*, he'd stayed pretty much out of the
public eye. As a media figure, he'd always been
something of an enigma. Most people didn't know
what to make of him. But if he was friends with
Benny, then I knew he had to be okay.

In 1981, for the *Los Angeles Times* 100-year anniversary, the newspaper opened its building for special tours. Of course, I was one of the very first to get in line. I was treated to an extensive tour of the entire building. I got to see how the newspaper was put together from start to finish.

As a kid, I was a paper boy delivering the *Herald Examiner*. It was a huge ass paper back then. In high school, I was on the staff of our high school newspaper. Later, I even sold a few articles to the *San Pedro News Pilot*. I loved newspapers, and thought journalism was something I might pursue, but I never did.

Benny began to tell me more about his long-time friend, Otis Chandler. He said Otis still had a corporate position at the *Times,* but left the day-to-day operations to others. He wanted the time to surf and pursue different interests. One of those interests was a collection he was putting together of 1960s and 1970s American muscle cars. Otis had also recently taken up auto racing, competing in the Watkins Glen endurance race at the age of fifty, coming in sixth overall. He was even doing some big game hunting in Africa. Too bad Ernest Hemingway wasn't around because Otis seemed like a character right out of a Hemingway novel.

Benny and I eventually made our way back to the Paradise Cove Mobile Home Park, finally stopping at the street directly in front of Otis Chandler's mobile home. I could tell it was Chandler's place because his new surfboard was propped up near the front door. Benny started walking up to Chandler's door.

"Dude, call the shop, and tell them when you're coming by," he said. "I'll make sure to be around. We'll go grab some tacos and a *cerveza.*"

"I'll do that," I said. "Maybe right after the Olympics."

"Sounds bitchin'," he smiled. "See you then."

Ben set his board down by the front steps, then climbed those last few steps up to Chandler's front door. As I was walking away, I heard Chandler open the door and greet Benny. I turned and watched Benny go into Otis Chandler's home.

After I had something to eat, I decided to finally get to work. I found a pen and grabbed my copy of Carlos Cruz's novel *Edendale.* I unwrapped a pack of index cards and opened a box of push-pins. I labelled three cards: "ACT I, ACT II, and ACT III." Beginning at page one of *Edendale,* I made a card out for each scene that I'd previously marked in the book. Every card included the names of the characters, what happened, and the location where the scene took place. After just a few hours, I'd actually plotted out the entire story on my bulletin board.

I understood Cruz's novel, and I could summarize it in just a couple of sentences. But for my needs, I always tried to distill the story down to a one-word theme. For other scripts, I'd used such words as: "Love," "Hate," "Fear," "Regret," and "Desire." For *Edendale,* I finally settled on the word "hope" because Cruz's main character was a young man filled with a burning need to succeed in life. In short, the character had great "hope." I pinned that word at the top of the bulletin board. With that, I was finished for the day. I wanted to leave something in the tank, as they say.

Jeanne had a television in the living room, as well as a small AM/FM radio, but neither interested me. There was also a large bookcase with several shelves of books. I started looking over the various titles. Finally, I found one book that got my attention. The book was: *The Powers That Be,* by David Halberstam. Published in 1979, it was about America's great media institutions. I'd once read Halberstam's *The Best and the Brightest,* about the Kennedy White House and liked it very much. This book's dust jacket mentioned Henry Luce's *Time Magazine,* William S. Paley's CBS Television, Phil and Katharine Graham's *Washington Post,* and finally, the one that sold me, the Chandler family's *Los Angeles Times.*

Since I'd met Otis Chandler on the beach, I thought this book might be give me some insight into Otis and his family. I knew some of the history of the Chandler's newspaper from the writings of Carey McWilliams and Louis Adamic, but that was all written some time ago. This book would be much more up to date. Here was Halberstam's introduction of the Chandler family: *"Its power and reach and role in Southern California are beyond the comprehension of Easterners, no Easterner can understand what it has meant in California to be a Chandler, for no single family dominates any major region of this country as the Chandlers have dominated California."*

That was an interesting and bold statement, so I continued reading: *"They did not so much foster the growth of Southern California as, more simply, invent it. There is water because they went and stole water. The city is horizontal instead of vertical because they were rich in land, and horizontal span was good for them, good for real estate. There is a port because they dreamed of a port."*

These facts weren't exactly new to me because McWilliams wrote all about the Owen's Valley water grab. But it did remind me of how influential the family had been. Halberstam started out with Otis Chandler's great grandfather and namesake, General Harrison Gray Otis: *"General Otis was a zealot, an angry choleric man, who had gone out to California after the Civil War. He wedded his paper to his prejudices and he founded a dynasty... The General was an impet-*

uous swashbuckler, poised for the slightest prov-ocation, ready to punch out with either his fists or his newspaper at all who dared offend him. The newspaper was a strident extension of his prejudices and passions and ignorance."

After reading about the General, I then read Halberstam's writings on Harry Chandler, the General's son-in-law, and Otis Chandler's grand-father: *"Harry Chandler was different, he was an entrepreneur, a businessman first and fore-most. A pirate visionary... He had no time for anger, for petty feuds and squabbles, he was, in the most hardheaded and calculating way imag-inable, a dreamer, and he was always dreaming of the future of Los Angeles, tied as it was to the commercial future of Harry Chandler."*

Halberstam went on to explain how Harry Chandler used the newspaper to promote his own business and real-estate holdings. The newspaper to him was simply a tool to achieve great wealth and power. I then proceeded to his successor and son, Norman Chandler, Otis's father: *"Norman Chandler was, in terms of California history, the transitional man, the man who bridged the era of the pirates and the era of his son, Otis... He was a simple man, Norman Chandler, fear-somely good-looking, the Marlboro man, with a touch more elegance, perhaps a touch of Cary Grant in him... He liked being a publisher very much-since destiny did not permit him to be a rancher-and he was very good at it, or at least he was very good at the business side of it. He had no feeling for the editorial side... It was a world he did not understand; he could not write and he would not know a news story unless he read one... Could the line survive beyond Norman Chandler, mild, gentle, a man who dreamed wistfully of spending his life on the Tejon Ranch, which he really loved?"*

Fortunately, for the sake of the dynasty, Norman seemed to meet, then marry the right woman to shore up any of his weaknesses: *"Dorothy Buffum of Long Beach, a restless, highly energized woman of soaring ambition, ambition for her husband, for herself, above all for her son. She became the Chandler incarnate, more Chandler than the real Chandlers. Buff, who was a favorite of Harry Chandler's... She had a rage, nothing less, to be someone and do something; a rage and a drive as strong as anything that had burned in Harry Chandler."*

I'd forgotten that Dorothy Chandler started out as a Buffum. Her father had been the mayor of Long Beach, and their department store Buffums' was the premier store in that town. My family often made the short trek over to Long Beach to go shopping. Buffums' was usually above our means, but sometimes we splurged.

Not only did Dorothy Chandler raise the money to build the Los Angeles Music Center, but she hired Zubin Meta as the conductor of the L. A. Philharmonic, and also my boss, Gordon Davidson to run the Center Theatre Group. On Gordon's office desk was a prominent photo of Mrs. Chandler.

As much as I was enjoying *The Powers That Be*, it was getting late, and I knew I needed to get some rest. That night, I had a new dream, one I'd never had before.

I recognized the old shopping district in downtown Long Beach from my childhood. Pine Street was filled with 1950s cars, and the sidewalks were bustling with well-dressed shoppers. All the men wore coats and had ties on, and the women wore long skirts or dresses. Everyone seemed to be wearing a hat.

My mom had me by the hand, and she was dragging me along while she shopped. In her other hand, she held a Buffums' shopping bag. Their slogan "I've been to Buffums'," was printed across the bag.

For lunch, we stopped at the Woolworths' lunch counter. I ordered a club sandwich and chips with a chocolate malt. At the other end of the counter there were a group of sailors eating their lunch. Back then, Long Beach always had sailors. The Naval base practically buzzed with activity. The waitress was very nice and asked me how I liked my food. She called me "deary," and smiled.

While I was slurping up the last of my chocolate malt, the entire Woolworths began to shake, slowly at first, then more violently. It felt like I was sitting on my mom's washing machine. The waitress grabbed a hold of the counter to steady herself, and one of the sailors at the other end of the counter shouted: "Earthquake!" Several shoppers made a mad dash for the store's front door. But then miraculously, as quickly as the shaking started, it stopped. People who had left the lunch counter slowly returned to finish their food. It turned out to only be a slight tremor, not a real full-blown earthquake.

"Honey," the waitress said to me. "You're lucky this isn't 1933. Now that was an earthquake."

I knew she wasn't exaggerating, because in 1933, Long Beach did have a major earthquake, a magnitude 6.4, which leveled most of the town and killed over 120 people. It was Southern California's version of the 1906 San Francisco Earthquake, the so called "big one."

Tuesday
July 24

●◆ The marine layer had moved in overnight obscuring my morning view of the ocean. I carried my coffee and *The Powers That Be* out to the patio. Like the cocaine Hank Pilsner was so preoccupied with, I'd become hooked on Halberstam's magnum opus. Fortunately, though, the book didn't dull my appetite or make it difficult for me to sleep at night.

After my coffee, I put Halberstam's book aside and looked at yesterday's story board. I went from scene to scene, trying to remember how each scene fit together. Then, I considered the endings of each act, and then the end of the play. I had to make sure they were all effective and compelling.

I slipped a sheet of paper into Vidor's Smith Corona, and using my copy of *Edendale,* I began to translate Cruz's novel into a play. I didn't worry about typos or miss-spelling. I just wanted to get it all down on paper. Once I finished, I could go back and edit and revise as needed. I'd already decided to take my draft to Charlie Chan's and have it retyped professionally. I wanted to hand Richard a perfect copy.

With Cruz's book as my guide, I typed away for hours, only stopping when I got too tired to work. I had a small stack of pages. It was a good start.

The marine layer had finally burned away, and I could now see the water, blue and inviting. It seemed easier for me to write here than in Koreatown. Maybe someday, I thought, I could have my own place near the ocean, where I could just write and not worry about anything else.

Benny had told me about a small pizza place up near the Mayfair Market on Point Dume. I slid into the Firebird and headed up Pacific Coast Highway until I saw the Mayfair sign. Cousin Guido's Pizzeria was right by the market. Just as I was parking, a helmeted motorcycle rider pulled his bike right into the parking spot next to me. As I walked to the door of the pizzeria, I watched as the rider dropped his kickstand and climbed off of his bike.

While I was ordering my pizza, I heard the door open, and assumed it was the motorcycle guy coming in. After I'd gotten my change, I turned around to find Otis Chandler looming over me, helmet in hand. Even though he looked right at me, I could tell that he didn't recognize me from the other day.

"Hi," I said. "I'm that friend of Benny's from the beach."

"Oh, yes," he smiled. "It's good to see you."

It might have been good to see me, but he was there to order his pizza. I moved aside, allowing him to step up and place his order. I found a table and had a seat. After Chandler placed his order, he came over and sat down at a nearby table. He glanced outside at my car, and then looked over to me.

"Nice Firebird," he said. "Too bad about your damaged right side, ouch."

"That was my fault," I said. "One too many alcoholic beverages."

He chuckled. "It looks like a 1967 Firebird 400?"

"It is," I replied, "and it was in good shape until I crashed it."

"It has a 325 horsepower V-8 engine," he said. "It's the same engine as that year's GTO. I don't have any Firebirds in my collection, but I do have a 1970 GTO convertible, and it's a good one."

"Back in high school," I said, "my friend, Jake, had a wicked 1967 GTO. We still had cruising and street racing back then, it was all pretty cool."

"Ah, yes, high school." Chandler nodded wistfully. "I never got to experience any of that. I was shipped off to an east coast prep school, my parent's idea," he frowned.

It seemed to me he would have been much happier in California with a hot rod and his surfboard.

"How long have you known Benny?" he asked.

"We grew up on the same block in San Pedro. I used to watch him make surfboards in his parent's garage. I was like his annoying little brother."

"Benny is a really good surfer," Otis said, "but I don't think he's competing much anymore."

"No," I said, "he's focusing more on his surfboard business."

Chandler set his helmet down on the table. "Do you surf?" he asked.

"No, but sometimes I do a little body surfing." I answered. "I was once stupid enough to go body surfing at the Wedge in Newport Beach; it almost killed me."

"I'm not surprised. It's a pretty treacherous spot."

On the wall of the pizzeria, there was a huge poster advertising the upcoming Olympic

Games. I remembered what Ben had told me about Chandler.

"Benny said you almost competed in the 1952 Olympics. Shot put, right?"

"That's right," he answered, pausing for a moment. "I held the NCAA record while I was at Stanford, and I was ranked number two in the world. Unfortunately, I injured my wrist the same week they were selecting the U. S. team."

Up until this point, Chandler had shown very little emotion. But I could tell that Benny was right, this Olympics thing still bothered him.

"It must have been devastating," I said. "You prepare your whole life for something, and then not even get a chance to compete."

"Some athletes are fortunate to have several opportunities, but that was my one chance. It was the biggest disappointment of my life." He paused. "I got to know Mal Whitfield while I was in the Air Force. He was able to compete in the 1948 and 1952 Olympics. He won three gold medals, a silver, and a bronze. I would have given anything to be him."

Mal Whitfield, also known as "Marvelous Mal," was one of the greatest middle-distance runners of all time. He grew up in the Watts neighborhood of Los Angeles, and often told the story of how he snuck into the 1932 L. A. Olympics as a kid and watched Eddie Toland beat Ralph Metcalf in the 100-meter sprint. That was the first time, two African American's competed for the title of "world's fastest human." Watching that event inspired Mal Whitfield to set his own Olympic goals.

"You know, Mal Whitfield was an amazing guy," Otis said. "Not only was he a great athlete, but he was also one of the original Tuskegee Airmen, flying combat missions during World War II and the Korean War."

"That is amazing," I said. "What were you doing in the Air Force?"

"After Stanford, I really didn't know what I wanted to do with my life. I even thought about becoming a doctor, if you can believe that," he said with a smile. "Then I got the idea to join the Air Force so I could fly jets, really fast jets, not bombers or cargo planes. I had no interest in that."

"Did you attend flight school?"

"I did. But that's where I found out I was too big to fit in the cockpit. I even lost weight and stopped eating for a while. But even with that, my shoulders and everything wouldn't allow me to fit in the pilot's seat. I served my commitment, then asked for a discharge. At that point, I had a wife and family, and I had no idea what I was going to do with the rest of my life."

"I think you did okay for yourself." I smiled, knowing he had been the publisher of the *Los Angeles Times* for twenty years.

"Yes," he nodded, "in the family business."

Chandler said "family business" in a way to diminish his accomplishments, as if he'd taken the easy road and not forged ahead on his own. The guy at the counter called out to us, letting us know that both our pizzas were ready. As we were getting up from our chairs, Chandler stopped me. He extended his right hand.

"I'm sorry, I didn't get your name."

"Niko Petrovich," I answered, shaking his big mitt of a hand.

"Niko, what do you do for a living?"

"I work as stage manager, sometimes at the Mark Taper Forum."

"Oh, really," he replied. "Then you must know Gordon Davidson?"

"I do. He's our artistic director and my boss."

"I remember when "Mrs. C" hired Gordon," Otis smiled. "His first play caused quite a stir."

When Otis said "Mrs. C," I knew he was referring to Dorothy Chandler, his mother. After she'd built the Music Center, she picked Gordon to lead the Taper. During the black-tie, opening night gala for his premiere show, *The Devils,* some in the conservative crowd bolted for the door. They wanted Gordon fired immediately, but Mrs. Chandler stuck with him."

The guy at the counter handed us our pizza boxes. Mine was a small box, while Chandler had ordered a family-sized one. As we were walking out to our vehicles, I turned to Otis.

"Gordon thinks the world of your mom," I said. "Her photograph sits right in the middle of his desk."

"There are many people who love my mother," he smiled. "But there are probably an equal number who can't stand her. She never worried much about ruffling a few feathers. For her, it was all about getting the job done."

Otis continued his conversation as we walked to our vehicles. When Otis got to his motorcycle, he had the pizza box in one hand and his helmet in the other. I noticed that the motorcycle didn't have any place to carry the pizza.

"How are you planning to carry your pizza?" I asked, standing there by my Firebird.

"I was just wondering the same thing," he smiled. "I guess I can just balance it on my gas tank."

"That's not a very good idea. We're going to the same place; I can carry it for you in my car."

"That's very kind of you. As long as it's not a problem."

"No problem at all," I assured him, taking his pizza, and putting both boxes in my car's trunk. I then followed Chandler back to Paradise Cove. As I drove, I thought about the car collection he mentioned and wondered what cars were in it. We drove into the mobile home park and stopped directly in front of his house. While he was removing his helmet, I got his pizza out of the trunk and brought it over to him.

"Thanks," he said. "I appreciate it."

"You're welcome. I'm curious. You mentioned that you were putting together a car collection. What cars have you collected so far?"

Evidently, I'd asked the right question because his eyes lit up and he grinned from ear to ear. I could see this was a topic close to his heart.

"I'm putting together a collection of the finest American muscle cars of the 1960s and 1970s. When I'm done, I hope to have at least thirty cars."

Chandler went on to name a list of cars he'd already acquired. It was quite a list, and he took pride in each car that he mentioned.

"You should open a museum," I suggested.

"That's a good idea," he smiled. "I might just do that."

☙ ☙ ☙

That day, I finished typing the first draft of my play, and then began to revise and edit what I typed. I worked obsessively, sometimes going over the same scene a dozen times until I felt it was okay. When I felt burned out, I would walk down to the beach and go for a swim. The water always rejuvenated me. I never ran into Otis Chandler, even though I'd always pass by his home on the way.

Reading *The Powers That Be* made me a little in awe of all that he'd accomplished. While

I was growing up, the *Los Angeles Times* was one of the top newspapers in the country. That, I learned, wasn't always the case. Because Southern California was prosperous, the newspaper's advertising revenues were always profitable, but the quality of the paper never matched its financial health. In fact, the paper was long considered one of the very worst newspapers in the country. Otis Chandler changed all that.

After Otis's time in the Air Force, he drove back to Southern California with his young family. When they arrived at his parents' home, he was greeted with a detailed seven-year executive training plan to learn the family business. Otis would start at the very bottom of the newspaper, doing every job, and learning every department. At the end of that seven years, he would know the newspaper inside and out. Not really having any other options for employment, Otis agreed to give it a try. During those seven years, he filled a dozen notebooks with ideas and ways to improve the paper. Then finally, on April 11, 1960, at age thirty-two, he was named the publisher of the *Los Angeles Times*. When his promotion was announced at a public gathering, Otis simply replied with one word: "Wow." There were many who were expecting him to fail. He was too young, too liberal, a jock, a surfer, not serious enough. Newspaper publishers were supposed to look like bankers, not Mr. Universe.

The decisions Otis Chandler made elevated the newspaper from one of the very worst, to one of the very best in an incredibly short amount of time. Otis Chandler had taken the focus and tenacity of an Olympic athlete and translated it to the publisher's suite.

I closed Halberstam's book, then using Jeanne's phone, I gave Hank Pilsner a call to see how he was doing with Beryl's two cats.

"Hey," Hank said. "What's up?"

"I've already finished typing the first draft. Now I'm editing and revising. How are Beryl's cats?"

"They're fine. In fact, I've got them right here."

"What are they doing at your place?" I asked, surprised he brought them home.

"That old house was empty and depressing. They deserved better than that."

Hank was a tough guy dealing with people, but a big softy when it came to animals.

"You really didn't have to go to all that trouble," I said.

"No trouble. It was more trouble having to visit that sad old house every day."

I thanked Hank again, and told him I'd see him soon.

ᜣ ᜣ ᜣ

Just as the sun was about to set, I finished the last of my editing and revising. I just hoped

Charlie Chan's could make sense of all my editing marks and notations. I'd finished reading the chapters on the *Los Angeles Times* in *The Powers That Be,* but I wanted to read the rest of the book as well, so I packed it in my bag. I left Jeanne a note, telling her I borrowed it.

Before leaving Malibu, I headed to the beach for one last visit. On my way down, I noticed Otis Chandler's surfboard was missing from his front porch. When I got to the beach, I laid down my towel and looked out at the surfers in the water. It was easy to pick Otis Chandler out from the other surfers. I watched as he rode his last wave all the way into shore. He then tucked the surfboard under his arm and carried it onto the beach. I was going to try to get his attention, but he noticed me first and came right over. He was still trying to catch his breath.

"How were the waves?" I asked.

"They were okay, nothing special," he smiled. "But even a bad day surfing, is better than any good day at work."

He set his board down on the sand, then sat down beside it.

"I just bought another car," he smiled. "A 1970 Dodge Challenger R/T convertible with a 426 Hemi engine. Only nine of them were ever built."

"It just might earn you a few speeding tickets," I said.

"Just a few," he smiled.

"The house where I'm staying has a copy of the book *The Powers That Be.* I've been reading it."

Chandler's mood suddenly turned sullen.

"I didn't like the way Halberstam portrayed me," he said. "He made me sound emotionless and cold."

"Maybe a little, but I thought he was complimentary about your accomplishments."

Chandler was silent as he stared out to the horizon.

"Why did you leave the newspaper the way you did?" I asked. "After you'd worked so hard to make the *Times* an elite newspaper."

He looked at me with surprise, as if asking, "Who died and made you a reporter?" But then he answered my question.

"Most observers ranked our paper right there with the *Washington Post,* some ranked us even higher. Our focus had always been to go after number one, the *New York Times,* that was our goal, to be the best newspaper in the country. If we couldn't be number one, then what was the point?"

What was Chandler telling me? That being number two or three was meaningless? That if his newspaper couldn't be number one, then nothing else mattered? This revealed just how competitive he was. To him, finishing second was like being the first loser.

"Also," he added, "I had other interests, and I just wanted to have some fun in my life. I had done everything expected of me. Now it was time to do a few things for myself."

No one could fault Otis Chandler for slowing down the pace of his life, and maybe never having fulfilled his Olympic dreams left a void that he was still trying to fill.

"Are you planning to attend the Olympics?" I asked.

"I wouldn't miss them for anything. Right after I'd been named publisher, I took my wife to Rome for the 1960 Olympics. We were so glad we went. And also, my grandfather, Harry Chandler, played a major role in bringing the 1932 Olympics to Los Angeles. So, we Chandlers have the Olympics in our blood, for better or for worse."

∞ ∞ ∞

It was early evening when I finally pulled into the Villa Serrano. I planned to quickly unload my things, then head over to Hank's to retrieve Beryl's two cats. But as I was pulling things from my Firebird's trunk, I noticed someone approaching me from the darkness. I quickly realized that it was just my friend, Jake Polanski.

"Jake," I said. "What are you doing here?"

"I left you several phone messages, but you never called me back."

"Sorry. But I've been out in Malibu writing a play. Why, what's up?"

Jake noticed the large dent on my Firebird.

"What the hell happened to your car?" he asked, touching the large dent with his hand.

I gave him a summary of the events. Then, he told me the reason for his visit.

"You're not going to believe this," he smiled. "I finally found my old GTO. This guy out in the valley has it, and he's willing to sell it back to me."

Just after high school, Jake blew out his GTO's rear end during a street race. The guy who beat him offered to buy his "Goat," damaged rear end and all. Jake was so pissed off about losing the race, he took the cash and signed over his pink slip right there. Within a week, the guy had fixed the GTO and was out on the streets taking on all challengers. Everyone was surprised Jake's famous "Goat" was no longer his. He tried to buy the car back, but was told it wasn't for sale. Every time Jake saw his old car, he kicked himself.

That was ten years ago, and he had long ago lost track of the GTO. Like a poor man's Otis Chandler, Jake always had a thing about cars, buying them, and selling them. After the GTO, Jake never again formed a real attachment to any car; they were all just transportation, or a commodity to be bought and sold.

"If I get the Goat back," Jake said, "I promise, I'll never sell it again."

"Never is a long time," I smiled. "What kind of shape is it in?"

"The guy told me it's in perfect shape. He said it looks good, and it runs like a champ."

"So, you haven't actually seen it yet?"

"No, but if it's like he said, then I'm buying it on the spot. I was hoping you could take me out there tonight so I can pick it up."

"Sure. Just let me take this stuff up to my apartment."

Jake helped me carry a few things up to my place, and then we hopped in my Firebird. We took the Cahuenga Pass out to the valley. The address Jake showed me was in the City of San Fernando, just south of Sylmar, where that earthquake occurred back in 1971. San Fernando was a working class, Latino community, made up of modest homes and small apartment buildings.

The house we were looking for was just off San Fernando Road, near the railroad tracks. In fact, we had to stop to allow a freight train to go by. Most of the homes on the street needed painting, and several had beat-up, old cars on their front lawns. We eventually found the correct address, then parked across the street from the house. Right on the curb, in front of that house was a 1967 Pontiac GTO.

"I think that's my old car," Jake said, somewhat confused. "But it looks different."

The paint on this GTO appeared to be the same Mariner Turquoise color as Jake's car, but it was now so badly faded that we couldn't tell. The car also had a few gray primer spots where several dents had been repaired. One of the wheels didn't even match the other. The car also needed a wash.

"It doesn't look like it's been well cared for," I said.

"Most of that is just dirt," Jake said, optimistically. "It just needs a little soap and water."

We walked up to the car and stopped to give it a once over. To me, the car looked tired, like it led a difficult life after Jake sold it. There were even more primer spots on the passenger's side. Inside the car, the seats were covered with trash.

"It'll need a little work," Jake said.

Jake didn't seem to be referring to the same car I was looking at. This car would need weeks in a body shop, and that would cost real money. We walked up the driveway to the small house, and Jake knocked on the front door. There was a porchlight on, which illuminated the front of the house.

A fair skinned Latino man named Joaquin came to the screen door. He looked to be about our age. He didn't seem very friendly. I wasn't getting a good feeling about any of this. He and Jake talked for a while about the GTO.

Jake asked the usual questions: Where did he buy it? How long did he have it? What kind of work did he have done? Jake also asked him if he had any repair records, which Joaquin said he did not. Then Jake asked if he could look under the hood and also take it for a test drive. After an awkward pause, Joaquin finally said: "Okay." Joaquin turned and said something to his wife, Juana, who was wearing a loose-fitting house dress: her attempt at staying cool in the always warm San Fernando Valley.

When Joaquin came out of his home with a set of car keys, Juana followed him out carrying a black garbage bag. Juana was a large "big-boned" woman, more physically imposing than her slender husband. For some strange reason, Juana's face reminded me of the football player, Norm Bulaich, the 220-pound fullback for the old Baltimore Colts. Norm was known as a bruiser, an absolute beast. Juana, for some strange reason, reminded me of him.

After Joaquin popped the hood, Juana proceeded to clean all of the trash from the inside of the car. The old fast-food bags, soft drink cups, and food wrappers filled the entire trash bag, which Juana then tied and placed near her home's garbage cans. The engine compartment didn't look much better than the rest of the car. It was greasy and dirty, and some parts seemed to be missing. Nothing about this car looked good, and for the price Joaquin was asking, it wasn't a very good deal.

"Could I take it for a test drive?" Jake asked. "I'd like to get it out on the road."

Joaquin thought for a moment before he slammed down the hood.

"No," he said. "But you can both come along with me while I drive the car. That's the only way we can do it."

Jake wasn't too happy about Joaquin driving the car and not him. He wanted to drive his old car, but he reluctantly accepted Joaquin's decision. I got in the backseat while Jake got in the front passenger seat with Joaquin behind the wheel.

No sooner did the car start, then Joaquin hit the gas pedal hard. It felt like we were speeding around the track at Ascot Raceway. At the first corner, he turned right, keeping the car's RPMs high as we slid around the turn. Joaquin did the same thing around the next three corners as well. It reminded me of a taxi ride I once survived in Tijuana. Joaquin made it around the entire block in what seemed like only seconds. As soon as the car was back in front of his home, he killed the engine and we came to a screeching halt.

As we stumbled out of the car, Joaquin looked over to Jake.

"Well," he asked. "Do you want it?"

Jake mentioned a few of the car's issues to him, trying to bring the price down, but Joaquin wouldn't budge. He knew Jake had once owned the car, and for him, this was an emotional purchase. I had to intervene and try to talk some sense into Jake.

"Excuse me," I said to Joaquin, "but I need to talk to my friend for a moment."

I pulled Jake aside while Joaquin went over to speak to his wife.

"What the hell are you doing?" I asked. "This isn't your old GTO anymore; this thing is now just a piece of Detroit iron."

"It does have a few flaws. I'll admit that."

"A few flaws?" I asked, exasperated. "I'll bet you the car can't even idle. That's why he kept the RPMs so high."

"Niko, I really want the car. Ever since I sold it, I've wanted it back. This is a chance for me to reclaim some of my youth."

Last year, Jake and I had gone to our ten-year high school reunion. People there had asked him whatever happened to his old car. Back in school, Jake was king of the streets, a notorious lady's man, and a track star. Who wouldn't want to wallow in those memories? It was like that Bruce Springsteen song that Hank's neighbor Gabe was always playing, "Glory Days." There was nothing I could say that would convince him not to buy this car.

I watched Jake hand over a stack of crisp one-hundred-dollar bills, which Joaquin counted. Then Joaquin handed Jake his signed pink slip, giving him the title to the Goat. They shook hands, and then Joaquin handed Jake the car keys. With that, Jake finally got behind the wheel of his old GTO, the car he had dreamed of for ten long years. I pulled my car behind Jake to follow him home.

We only managed to get back to San Fernando Road before the Goat stalled for the first time. Jake got it started, but then it quickly stalled again. Jake opened the hood, did something, then managed to get it started once again. When we got to a stop light, the car finally died for good. Jake worked on it for over an hour but with no luck. We hadn't even made it a mile from Joaquin's house, much less onto the freeway. Jake looked beaten and dejected. The dream he long hoped for had now turned into a nightmare.

"What are you going to do?" I asked, frustrated with the whole situation.

Jake thought for a moment before finally speaking.

"I'm going to get my fucking money back," he said, steely eyed. "This is bullshit."

Jake got into my Firebird, and I drove us back to Joaquin's house. Jake was no longer despondent; he was now pissed off. He knew he'd made an impulsive and irrational purchase, and it had come back to bite him on the ass. I was hoping Joaquin would be reasonable, and just give Jake back his money. I certainly didn't want any trouble with these people.

"Niko," Jake said. "I should have listened to you. I wasn't thinking."

"You wanted your 'glory days' back," I said, "but those days are over, and that car is done."

After Jake knocked, Joaquin came to the screen door. His arms were folded, and he had a smirk on his face.

"Sorry, man," he laughed. "A deal is a deal. You bought it; now you own it, problems and all."

"You sold me a car that doesn't even run," Jake protested. "You said it was in great shape but it's not."

"The car died on San Fernando Road," I added. "We didn't even get a mile away."

With that, Joaquin flung open the screen door and charged out of his house.

"I guess I just need to kick both of your asses," he announced, motioning for us to approach him. "Come, on, who's first?"

Goddamn it. This was just like being back in high school. Jake's old GTO, and some guy who thinks he's going to kick Jake's ass. Sure, he's bigger than Jake, and maybe he's won a few fist fights in his day, but the poor bastard has no idea what he's in for. Jake eats guys like him for lunch. Maybe I should tell him about the three guys who Jake sent to the hospital. No, some guys just need to learn the hard way.

Joaquin's wife, Juana, had now stepped outside, joining us. Jake started to prepare himself, assuming he was going to have to fight this guy.

"Look," I said, "we don't want any trouble. Just give us our money back, and we'll leave."

"Fuck you, pussy!" he yelled. "I'm going to kick your friend's ass, then I'm going to take care of you."

I stepped over to Juana holding my arms up in a peaceful gesture.

"I won't interfere if you don't interfere," I said. "Let them settle it in a fair fight, just the two of them."

She didn't look very convinced, but she nodded anyway.

Joaquin swung at Jake with a left and a right combination, missing with both swings. Then Jake hit Joaquin with a solid right cross. Boom! Right on the jaw. This stunned Joaquin, who managed to fall forward grabbing a hold of Jake in a clench.

Just then, while I wasn't looking, Juana punched me hard across the side of my head. "Ow!" My ear rang, and it stunned me for a moment.

"Hey," I said, blocking another punch. "What are you doing?

"Tell your friend to stop fighting," she shouted, holding up both fists.

"I'm not going to hit you," I assured her. "So, you don't need to hit me."

She and I watched as Jake broke free of Joaquin's hold. Jake then hit Joaquin hard with a flurry of punches. These staggered Joaquin and he fell backwards. Before I could stop her, Juana had gone over to Jake and punched him across the back of his head, the same way she'd hit me. I managed to somehow get between her and Jake, shouting for her to back off.

As she watched helplessly, Jake proceeded to beat the crap out of her husband. Every punch Jake threw landed, and now Joaquin's face was a bloody mess, and his nose looked broken.

Unable to help her husband, she turned and ran back into the house. Oh crap, I thought, is she going to get a knife or something? Jake finally knocked Joaquin to the ground where he laid battered and bleeding. Suddenly, from the other end of the driveway, an older man appeared. He must have been a neighbor. He was pointing a handgun at Jake, then at me, then back at Jake, then again at me.

"Stop, goddamn it!" the neighbor shouted. "Leave him the fuck alone!"

Jake and I both put our hands up in the air. The man looked nervous and jittery, like he might shoot us at any second. I figured I'd better say something quick.

"This guy came out of his house swinging at my friend," I said. "He tried to cheat us and sell us a car that didn't run. All we want is our money back."

"I didn't want to fight this guy," Jake said. "He came out and attacked us."

Suddenly, Juana came out of her house holding the stack of one-hundred-dollar bills in her hands. She handed the money to Jake, then slapped him hard across the face. I could tell it hurt because it was a loud slap. Joaquin hadn't landed a single punch on Jake, but his wife landed two. Not to mention, the one she landed on me. Like I said, Norm Bulaich.

Juana then dropped to her knees, and with tears in her eyes, she tended to her battered and beaten husband.

"Get the fuck out of here!" she shouted. "And don't you ever come back!"

Reaching into his pocket, Jake took out the pink slip and the GTO's car keys and dropped them both on the driveway. We then carefully negotiated our way past the neighbor, who was still nervously pointing his gun at us. We got into the Firebird, and I drove us away. Jake counted the money Juana had handed him. It was all there.

Wednesday
July 25

●◆ The next day, I rode my bike over to Charlie Chan's Printing to have my script retyped. I was glad Jake and I survived our insane evening, but I was disgusted because none of it really had to happen. Jake was foolish for making such an emotional purchase, and Joaquin was foolish for thinking he was going to kick Jake's ass. Jake and I were also lucky we didn't get shot. The title for the evening could have very easily been *Shot Dead in San Fernando*. I thought that sounded like some cheap Mickey Spillane crime novel, right alongside *One Lonely Night,* and *Kiss me, Deadly.* Fortunately for us, we hadn't needed Mike Hammer.

After I handed Charlie Chan's my manuscript, I rode around the corner to Beryl's studio. Beryl's cats were at Hank's, so I knew there was no need to go inside. On the lawn, there was a "For Sale" sign with Nina's name and her real estate company. Tacked onto that sign was a smaller sign, which read: "Sold." Oh, crap, I thought. While I was out in Malibu, Nina sold Beryl's house. Since Beryl's photographs were still inside, I wanted to know who'd bought the house and what plans they had for it. I rode right over to Sidney and Nina's. When I got there, Sid answered the door.

"Niko, hello," Sid said, holding a coffee mug.

"Hi, Sid," I replied. "May I come in?"

"Sure." He let me inside. "Would you like some coffee?"

"That would be nice. Is Nina around?"

"No, she's out showing houses, but I expect her back any time." He grabbed a coffee mug and poured me some coffee. "Oh, by the way, Nina sold that photographer's house."

"I know. I just saw her sign."

We carried our coffee out to the backyard patio and sat down at a small table. A tall ivy-covered wall surrounded the yard, and his large lawn looked freshly mowed.

"Do you have any idea who bought the house?" I asked.

"I believe Nina said that it was a Korean man named Lee. He also owns some other properties in the area."

"That must be my landlord," I said. "He's been looking for other houses to buy."

"Small world," said Sid, sipping his coffee.

Sitting here with Sidney felt like old times. He'd been my acting coach for years, and the first director I worked with as a stage manager. Sid taught me most of what I knew about theater. Whenever I told actors around town I studied with Sid, they all shared their admiration and respect. They remembered Sid as a rising Broadway star and one of the best young actors in New York. This was during the 1950s, and it was about the same time Marlon Brando and James Dean were starting out. It was difficult to imagine Sid competing with those two, but he gave it his best shot.

Sidney made a big splash in his Broadway debut. The play was a good one, and for a while, Sid was the toast of the town, the rising young star. But after that first success, things just didn't go the way he hoped. He was never able to build on that initial triumph. Sidney had the good looks and the talent, but it just never happened for him. I'd always wanted to ask him why he didn't become a big star like those others.

"An older actor I met told me, that back in the day, you were one of the best young actors in New York. He said your Broadway debut was electric, no performance that year even came close. He compared your debut with Marlon Brando in *A Streetcar Named Desire*. What happened, Sid? Why didn't your career take off?"

Sidney let out a chuckle. "That was a long time ago." He thought for a moment before speaking. "Most people assume all you need is that first big break. Then everything just falls into place, like pieces on a puzzle. Maybe that's the way it happens for some, but it doesn't always work that way. My next play closed after four performances, and the play after that closed after a week. After those two failures, nobody remembered my initial success. Then, all the good roles just disappeared."

Sidney told me that's when he transitioned into directing and teaching. He still acted on occasion, but less and less over time. He never again got another meaty role, one in which his talent could shine, and soon his initial success was long forgotten.

Somewhere inside, this middle-aged acting coach was still that gifted young actor, highly praised for his early work. In Europe, they have a different attitude toward artists. There, artists are judged by the best work they produced in their lifetime. While in this country, artists are judged by their most recent work. In other words, "What have you done for me lately?"

"I guess things don't always turn out the way they're supposed to?" I asked.

"Things just turn out the way they do," Sid said. "Who's to say how they're supposed to."

∽ ∽ ∽

Nina never did show up, so I thanked Sid for the coffee and rode back to Koreatown. Later, I grabbed my car and drove over to Hank's to pick up Beryl's cats. Hank informed me Maggie and Dottie had been excellent house guests, and they could return anytime. He also reminded me of the beer and hotdogs I owed him. I assured him it wouldn't be a problem. The two cats looked quite comfortable, like they didn't want to leave. Hank lent me a duffel bag, which I could use as a cat carrier.

"How was Malibu?" he asked. "Did you get your writing done?"

"I did, and my manuscript is now being retyped at Charlie Chan's."

I told Hank about seeing Benny Drew, and meeting Otis Chandler. I thought that might impress Hank, but of course I was wrong.

"Next time you see Otis, ask him why my newspaper is always late. Maybe he can do something about it."

"Yeah," I smirked. "I'll get right on it."

I also told Hank about my adventures out in the San Fernando Valley with Jake. Hank just shook his head.

"Another one bites the dust. It would be news if Jake didn't kick somebody's ass."

I thanked Hank again, then loaded the duffel bag into my Firebird. The two cats were surprisingly calm during their ride over to Cedar-Sinai.

Beryl was watching the local TV news when I came into her room carrying the duffel bag. They were doing a story on the USA Olympic gymnastics teams, and they were reporting from Pauley Pavilion at UCLA.

"Niko," Beryl smiled, "I was hoping you'd come by."

I closed Beryl's door so we could have a little privacy.

"They sold your old house," I said. "And I'm afraid it's probably going to be torn down."

"Yes. I heard. But it might turn out to be a blessing in disguise. What's in the bag?"

I set the duffel bag down on her bed. "Open it."

Beryl unzipped the bag and Maggie and Dottie's heads popped up.

"My cats," Beryl shouted, pulling them both into her arms.

"I thought you could use a little reunion," I said, watching them get reacquainted.

Beryl kissed Maggie and Dottie and stroked their fur. "Speaking of reunions," she said. "I'm going to need your help with one reunion I can't make."

"What are you talking about?"

"First, before I get into it, did you make the phone call regarding my photographs?"

"I did, and things are looking good," I smiled. "My friend is willing to help."

"That's wonderful," Beryl nodded. "Tell me all about it."

I told Beryl all about the conversation I had, and she seemed pleased. I also said she should expect a phone call and probably a visit sometime soon.

"They know where to find me," Beryl said. "Now, about that reunion I mentioned. Do you remember those pictures of the women swimmers from the 1932 Olympics?"

"Yeah. They were athletes and not bathing beauties."

"That's right, and I stayed in touch with one of those ladies. We became good friends, and we still exchange cards and letters."

"Really?"

"Yes. Back then she was very artistic and interested in photography. So, I explained to her about the different cameras and lenses I used, and about the way I developed the photos. It all fascinated her. She ended up marrying a professional football player. Eventually they both settled in the San Francisco area. She's been invited to these Olympics as a past Olympian, and they're having special ceremonies. We made plans to have lunch together before I wound up in here. Obviously, I can't make it now."

"When were you supposed to meet?"

"Tomorrow, at the Ambassador Hotel. She's staying there. I need you to meet her for lunch and give her this."

Beryl reached over to her nightstand and picked up a large, well-stuffed folder. Newspaper clippings and black and white photographs were poking out. She handed me the folder.

"What's all this?" I asked.

"These are the newspaper clippings I saved and some of the old photos I took.

"These women must have been very special to you?"

"They were, they saved women's sports. Can you imagine having an Olympics without women competing? It's inconceivable now, but it certainly wasn't back then."

I stuffed the folder into the bottom of my duffel bag, leaving just enough room for the two cats.

"Now that my house has sold," Beryl said, "we don't need to sell the photographs to pay my bills."

"That's right," I smiled. "Now we just need to wait for everything to come together."

"Oh, and you'll need this," Beryl said, handing me a folded scrap of paper. "It's the combination to the vault. All of my photographs and negatives are inside."

I unfolded the paper and looked at the numbers: "7–30–32." It took me just a moment to realize that the numbers represented the opening date of the 1932 Los Angeles Olympics: July 30, 1932.

"You could have been a little more original with your combination," I said. "Anybody could figure that out."

"Maybe. But nobody has yet."

I folded the paper and put it in my pocket.

"So, who is this woman I'm meeting for lunch?"

"Her name is Jane Fauntz, but she now goes by Manske, her married name. She grew up in Chicago and was in the same swim club there as Johnny Weissmuller. She competed in two Olympic Games, Amsterdam in 1928, and Los Angeles in 1932. Also, while her brother was stationed here in the Navy, she attended your old high school."

"San Pedro High?" I asked.

"Yes, I believe so."

Beryl said her goodbyes to Maggie and Dottie before I placed them back into the duffel bag. She offered me some money for cat food and litter, which I gladly accepted. I told her I was taking them to my place, but I had to be careful because my landlord didn't allow us to have pets.

"Goodbye girls," Beryl said, blowing the cats a kiss just before I zipped up the bag.

⟀ ⟀ ⟀

Mrs. Trask, the building's manager, was just getting out of her 1970 Chevy Nova as I pulled my car into my parking spot. Long retired from her days as an accountant, Trask came out once a day to start up her old Nova. Because the car was in perfect shape, people were always trying to buy it from her.

I hoisted the heavy duffel bag off the passenger seat and closed the car's door.

"Hello Mr. Petrovich," she said, noticing my heavy bag. "Are you planning a trip?"

"No. A friend asked me to hold onto some old pictures and newspaper clippings for her."

"Oh. Anything interesting?"

"No, not really."

Just then, one of the cats meowed.

"Did you just hear a cat?" Trask asked, looking around by the cars.

"It must be that stray I see around here. I think it lives in the neighborhood."

As I walked away, Trask was looking around for the cat she'd heard.

Inside my apartment, I put out some bowls with food and water bend set up their litter box in my bathroom. After Maggie and Dottie explored their new digs, they curled up on my bed for a much needed nap. I opened the folder and spread the photographs and newspaper clippings out on my kitchen table. Everything there had to do with the U. S. women's swimming and diving teams of the 1932 Olympics.

Even in their antiquated swimsuits, they all looked lovely, and there was an innocence about them. They were all young, slender, and fit. Oh, and those legs. Standing there on the pool deck of the old Olympic Swim Stadium, they seemed so confident, so ready to take on the world.

I started reading some of the yellowed clippings and examining more of Beryl's photos. Fortunately, she'd written everyone's names on the backs, so I could easily identify everyone. I also found an article on Jane Fauntz, who I was meeting tomorrow, and a photograph of her as well. In the photo, Jane appeared tall and lean with dark hair and eyes. Her hair formed a widow's peak on her forehead and her arched eyebrows gave her face a slightly mischievous expression. The article stated, at the age of seventeen Jane represented the USA at the 1928 Summer Olympics in Amsterdam as a swimmer, but in 1932 in Los Angeles, she won a bronze metal as a diver. It also mentioned those 1928 Olympics were the last Games in which Johnny Weissmuller had competed. Weissmuller won five freestyle gold medals over two Olympic Games before leaving competitive swimming to play Tarzan in the movies. There were several publicity photos of Weissmuller in a swimsuit posing with the 1932 swimmers. A number of other Hollywood stars were also in Beryl's photos, including Douglas Fairbanks, Mary Pickford, Will Rodgers, and the Marx Brothers. Amelia Earhart, fresh from one of her record setting flights, was another celebrity captured in Beryl's photographs.

I found pictures of the U. S. women's diving team's medal winners. They were posed by height, with Jane, the tallest, on the left, then Marion Dale Roper, Georgia Coleman, Dorothy Poynton, and the petite Katherine Rawls on the end.

Another group picture was of the gold medal winning women's 400-meter, freestyle relay team. Posed left to right were: Josephine McKim, Helen Johns, Elenore Garatti Saville, and Helene Madison. There were quite a few articles about Helene Madison, who won gold medals in all three of her freestyle events. Evidently, in the months leading up to the Games, Madison broke sixteen freestyle world records at various distances. The article labeled her as the most dominant female swimmer of her era. There was one photo of her with gold medal winner, Clarence (Buster) Crabbe, the only U. S. male swimmer to have earned a medal during those Games. Buster Crabbe would later join Weissmuller in the movies, playing Flash Gordon among others.

I hadn't planned to, but I ended up losing myself in Beryl's stuff, spending a couple of hours just reading the articles and looking over the pictures. By the time I was finished, I actually knew something about the 1932 Olympics.

I finally put everything back in the folder and grabbed the telephone to make some calls. First, I called Jeanne Cruz to let her know I'd finished my adaptation of *Edendale.* I also thanked her for lending me her place in Malibu.

"I'm glad you enjoyed Paradise Cove," Jeanne said. And I'm impressed you got so much work done."

"It's all finished, and your beach house was the perfect place to work."

"Carlos never liked working there," she said. "He just wanted to sit out on the patio with a strong drink and a good book."

"Speaking of good books, I borrowed *The Powers that Be.* I'll return it to you when I'm finished, if that's okay?"

"Keep it as long as you'd like."

She let me know her place at Paradise Cove was available anytime I needed it. I told her I might take her up on her offer, especially since I never did find that nude beach Isabella mentioned. Jeanne laughed at my comment, not knowing Isabella and I had our own nude swim. I didn't think it was a good idea to mention it.

Next, I called Richard to tell him I'd finished my adaptation of *Edendale.*

"Good," he said. "If you drop it off tomorrow, I'll read it ASAP."

"You'll have it by then," I assured him.

Then, I asked him if I could speak to Cynthia Aldrich, since I knew they shared the same office. He transferred me to her phone.

"Hi," I said. "Are you busy?"

"Always," she answered.

"I know it's not much notice, but I have a friend who owns a little French restaurant where they sing opera. How would you like to join me there tonight for dinner?"

"Sure," she said. "That sounds like fun."

Cynthia wanted to meet me there, so I gave her the restaurant's address and suggested a time for dinner. She agreed on the time and took down the information. I was excited about seeing Cynthia again and hoped that I could finally get her over to my place."

Then, I called Jules to make a reservation for dinner. He seemed to be in good spirits.

"I'll put you down for two," he said. "In fact, I'll give you our best table."

"How's everything with you and Betty?"

"Everything's been great," he answered. "I think we're finally getting past this whole mess."

❦ ❦ ❦

Just as I was getting ready to meet Cynthia

for dinner, Sung-ho, my neighbor, knocked on my door, and I opened it.

"Hyun-sook and I are leaving soon," he said. "I finish school, go back to Korea."

"That was quick," I said. "It seems like you guys just got here."

"I'm here on student visa. School over, now we go home."

"I'll miss you all," I said. "You've been great neighbors."

"Hyun-sook wants you to come to dinner."

"I'd be honored. When?"

"Tomorrow night, okay?" he asked.

"Tomorrow night would be perfect. Can I bring something?"

"No," he smiled faintly. "You come hungry."

"I can do that," I smiled. "I'll see you tomorrow night."

We'd never socialized much, but I was truly sad to see them go. With the Cho family gone, Vidor would be the only person I even talked to in the building.

∽ ∽ ∽

Since I arrived at Larchmont Village early, I walked over to Chevalier's Bookshop. I went straight to the fiction section and immediately found the book I was looking for. I bought it, and the clerk slid it into a paper bag.

Minutes later, Cynthia met me on the sidewalk in front of the Le Petite Mustache. She looked great and greeted me with a kiss. I noticed she'd gotten her hair cut. It looked good, but it looked a little trendy for me. She also had on a new outfit, which made her look stylish and contemporary. Her look was so different than what it had been when she first got here. I actually missed the old Cynthia. Of course, none of this was a deal killer because I still wanted to peel off whatever clothes she was wearing and get her into bed. Not that I wanted a one-night fling. Cynthia was the kind of woman I could have a real relationship with.

In anticipation, I washed my sheets and cleaned my apartment. I even banished Beryl's cats from my bedroom, since the two had made it their own. I also made sure I had a fresh supply of condoms. Isabella taught me that lesson.

I handed Cynthia the bag from Chevalier's Bookshop.

"This is for you," I said. "I hope you like it."

She opened the bag and pulled out a copy of *What Makes Sammy Run*, by Budd Schulberg.

"I've heard about this book," she said, looking it over. "And I've always wanted to read it."

"Believe it or not, but I just met the author, and I'll tell you about it after you've read the book."

She gave me a quick hug. "Thanks so much. I'll probably finish it in a couple of days. I'm a fast reader."

She placed the book back into its bag and then slid the bag into her purse. As we entered the restaurant, Jules was there to greet us.

"Bienvenue, mademoiselle." Jules said, welcoming Cynthia to his bistro.

"Merci, monsieur," Cynthia replied.

As Jules was leading us to our table, he asked Cynthia if she spoke French. When she said she did, the two broke into an entire conversation, which of course left me out. When we got to our table, Jules finally reverted back to dull old English.

"Betty will be your waitress," he said, smiling. He then returned to the front door to greet some new arrivals.

"Betty is Jules' wife," I said. "She's an actress, but sometimes she helps out in the restaurant. Jules is also an opera singer, and we might hear him sing tonight."

"Wonderful," Cynthia replied. "I love opera."

"That makes one of us," I joked. "But he's my friend, and he's pretty good."

The busboy brought us some water, and we began to look over our menus.

"I didn't know you spoke French," I said.

"There are a lot of things you don't know about me," she smiled.

Something told me Cynthia was going to be a bit of a challenge. Fortunately, I like challenges, as long as they're not too challenging. Nobody likes beating their head against a wall.

"I assume you're going to Richard's bash?" she asked.

"Of course. Especially since *Sonora Town* was the hit of the season and we'll be celebrating that."

"Jeanne Cruz might be there," she said. "I know we're not exactly her crowd."

Richard always threw a party at the end of every Literary Cabaret season. This year's party was going to be at the Yee Mee Loo Chinese restaurant in Chinatown. It wouldn't surprise me if Richard used the opportunity to announce my new play, *Edendale* as the first play for next season.

Betty arrived at our table and I immediately introduced her to Cynthia. We all spoke for a bit before Betty took our dinner order. While I was giving Betty my order, Cynthia seemed to stare at Betty for some reason.

Cynthia ordered the *coq au vin*, chicken in wine, and I ordered a *steak au poivre*, the peppercorn steak. After Betty left, Cynthia leaned over to whisper something to me.

"You said Betty is an actress?" she asked.

"Yeah. Why? Do you know her?"

"No. But we were having auditions yesterday at the Annex, and I recognize her from that."

"So, what happened?" I asked. "She must have done something to stand out."

"She was there with a young male actor. The two were all over each other. It was practically foreplay. She was on his lap, and nibbling on his earlobe."

Cynthia's description of the young male actor, matched Matteo. I then told Cynthia the issues between Betty, Jules, and Matteo.

"Well," Cynthia said. "It sounds like Jules still has a problem."

"I'll tell him at the end of the evening," I said. "If I tell him now, they'll just have a big fight right in front of everybody."

"It's probably a good idea to wait."

While we were talking, Betty brought out our salads, wine, and some bread. She smiled her phony smile, but now I knew it was just a façade. Jules loved her, and he was doing everything he could to make their marriage work. I guess she wasn't really interested in any of that.

Fortunately, this drama didn't ruin Cynthia's and my evening. Just as we were finishing our meal, a musician took his seat at the piano, and the lights dimmed. Jules stepped into a waiting spotlight and introduced himself. He then announced that he would be singing "La donna e mobile," from the opera *Rigoletto,* and then he began to sing. His voice filled the room. As I looked around at the tables, I noticed everyone was glued to Jules. Cynthia looked over at me and nodded, acknowledging how well she thought Jules was singing. I wanted to lean over and tell her: "Wait till I make love to you tonight. You'll hit that high

"C" note yourself." But of course, I didn't say anything because I wanted it all to be a surprise.
When Jules finished, he received a loud ovation.

After I paid the bill, I asked the busboy to tell
Jules I needed to speak with him. It was almost
closing time, and most of the other diners were
now leaving. I didn't see Betty around and thought
maybe she was in the kitchen. Jules approached
our table, and Cynthia said something to him in
French, praising his performance. This made Jules
smile, and he then responded back to her in French.

I finally told him what Cynthia had seen at the
audition downtown. Jules' expression changed
from joyful to dour, and for a moment, he was
speechless. He finally asked Cynthia if she was
sure of what she saw, and Cynthia told him
she was. Jules thanked us for coming and then
returned to the kitchen.

It was dark and cool out on the sidewalk. I
held Cynthia's hand as we walked. When we
reached our cars, she turned toward me, looked
me in the eyes, and gave me the most sensuous
kiss I'd gotten in a long time. She even placed my
hand on her breast. It felt so good that I thought I
should feel the other one, just to make sure they
were balanced. I'm happy to report, they were
like twins.

"How would you like to come over to my
place?" I asked. "I have some wine, and we can
get to know each other better."

"Sure," she smiled. "I was hoping you'd ask."

"You'll meet my two house guests," I smiled.

"Your house guests?" she asked, with a glare.

"I'm cat sitting for a friend. They're good cats. You'll like them."

"I don't think so," Cynthia frowned. "I'm deathly allergic to cats. I can't go anywhere near them because I get really sick."

It was obviously too late to drag the two cats back to Hank's place. But because of them, my plans with Cynthia were dead in the water. How was I to know she had a cat allergy? According to her, it could be quite severe, and even caused problems breathing. On the positive side, Cynthia seemed genuinely disappointed with the evening's abrupt ending. I knew I was going to see her tomorrow at Richard's party, so all was not lost. Hopefully, by then I could get rid of my furry house guests for the night. Cynthia and I kissed once more, then said our reluctant goodbyes.

When I walked into my apartment, Maggie and Dottie both rubbed against my leg and meowed. They were glad to see me, but I wasn't glad to see them. These little monsters had ruined my night with Cynthia. But it was impossible to stay angry for long. When I finally got into bed, they both climbed on top of me, curled up, and went to sleep. Their weight felt comforting. Soon, I joined them in a deep slumber.

Thursday
July 26

●◆ After I loaded Beryl's file folder into a back-pack, I flung it over my shoulders and rode over to Charlie Chan's Printing. Besides my newly retyped manuscript, I'd also asked them to make me one extra copy. Somehow, I managed to squeeze everything into my now full backpack.

Since I was nearby, I rode around the corner to Beryl's house. On the front lawn, Mr. Lee was there conferring with two men. Parked in the driveway, there was a pick-up truck with "A-1 Demolition" on the door. Mr. Lee refused to answer any of my questions about his plans, but he did confess that Beryl's photo vault was still locked up tight. I then got back on my bike and rode east on Eighth Street.

The Ambassador was one of Los Angeles' historic grand hotels. Built in 1921, the hotel was primarily known for two things. The first, its famous Coconut Grove Nightclub, where in its heyday, was frequented by a galaxy of Hollywood stars. The second, it was where Senator Robert Kennedy was assassinated, something the hotel could never really live down.

Even in its present state, the hotel remained charming and comfortable. Not long ago, a guest could have looked across Wilshire Boulevard at the original Brown Derby, and the gardens of the Chapman Park Hotel, where the female athletes had stayed during the 1932 Olympics. In Beryl's clippings, there were articles about the parties held at the Ambassador during those Games.

In 1949, famed Los Angeles architect, Paul Williams, led a renovation of the building. But now, it was definitely due for another remodel. As I stepped into the hotel's coffee shop, I saw distinctive design elements of William' s style. He had previously remodeled the Beverly Hills Hotel, and this coffee shop shared the same banana leaf wallpaper that covered the walls of the Beverly Hills Hotel's famous Polo Lounge.

I looked around, trying to find Jane Fauntz. The only pictures I had of her were from 1932, which was fifty-two years ago. Just then, a group of people entered the restaurant. Among them was an older woman who looked like what Jane might look like now. The woman was wearing a dark blue blazer with a shield logo of the 1932 Los Angeles Olympics over her breast pocket. I walked over to her, figuring I had the right person.

"San Pedro High School?" I asked, smiling.

"Why, yes," she smiled back at me. "A fellow Pirate?"

"Niko Petrovich," I said, extending my right hand. "Beryl Hartgrove asked me to meet you here."

"Where's Beryl?" she smiled. "Did she get a better offer for lunch?"

"No. She's sorry she couldn't make it, but she's in the hospital."

"Oh, dear," Fauntz frowned. "I'm so sorry to hear that."

"I have some things for you. Do you mind if I get us a table?"

"No. But only if you'll tell me how Beryl is doing."

"Of course."

As we waited for a table, I told her all about Beryl's current condition. Jane was sorry to hear that she wasn't well, and wanted me to pass along her best wishes. Jane also told me she'd enjoyed living in San Pedro back in the day, but she only attended high school there for one semester. She finished high school back in Illinois.

After we were seated at one of the half-round booths, I pulled out the thick folder I'd brought with me.

"What's all that?" she asked.

I handed the folder to Jane and she opened it. Her eyes grew large as she saw the contents. A range of emotions flashed across her face. She finally stopped at a photo of a group of women standing poolside in their swimsuits.

"We all looked pretty good, didn't we?"

"They called you the 'glamour girls' for a reason."

"It didn't hurt that Hollywood offered us all movie roles."

"You too?" I asked.

"Buster Crabbe tried to interest me in a film he was making. I foolishly turned him down. Eleanor Holm couldn't shake her Brooklyn accent, but she was gorgeous. Jo McKim was seeing the actor, Joel McCrea, during the Games. She eventually became a pretty good actress herself, eventually doing Broadway. Even Helene Madison tried making a movie, but she really didn't have the personality for it, sadly."

"I didn't know you were all such celebrities."

"That's not why we came to Los Angeles in 1932; we were here to compete and win Olympic medals. All of that celebrity business came afterwards.

It couldn't have been easy for the female athletes during that time. Many people still believed women didn't belong in athletics. Most high schools wouldn't even allow women to compete in swimming and diving. While finishing high school in Illinois, Jane wasn't even allowed to use the school's swimming pool, even though she'd been an Olympic swimmer. Men competed in high school, and then in college athletic programs. Women were rarely given that opportunity. They were treated as second-class citizens and expected to accept their fate quietly. Whatever obstacles male athletes endured; women athletes faced even more.

"You also participated in the 1928 Olympics in Amsterdam," I said. "How was that?

"That was so much fun," she beamed. "I was seventeen, and here I was crossing the Atlantic Ocean on the S.S. President Roosevelt with the entire U. S. Olympic Team."

"You didn't fly there?" I asked.

"This was 1928," she frowned. "Lindbergh had only made his solo flight one year earlier."

"Oh, right," I replied, embarrassed at my lack of history.

"Once we got to Amsterdam, after two weeks at sea, the ship was our accommodations during the Games."

"Then, in 1932, all of the women athletes stayed across the street at the Chapman Park Hotel," I said. "While all the men were up in Baldwin Hills at the Olympic Village."

"It was much more fun when we were all in the same boat, so to speak," she smiled. "But the 1932 Games were so much better organized."

Jane then told me about Beryl, and what she was like as a young woman. Evidently, she was well liked and had many friends among the athletes.

"She just loved photographing the Olympic events, and we adored her because she was one of us."

As we talked, I learned Jane studied art in college and eventually became an artist and educator. She had recently been asked to design awards for FINA, the international swimming organization. Greg Louganis, the great American diver, was to receive one of the awards at these upcoming Olympics.

We then returned to the subject of the 1932 Olympics, and Jane went on to tell me how the American women had swept the diving competition.

"In the 10-meter platform, Dorothy Poynton won the gold. Georgia Coleman won silver, and Marion Roper took the bronze. Dorothy was only thirteen when she first won a silver back in Amsterdam. To this day, she's still the youngest American to ever win a medal. She was still only seventeen in Los Angeles."

"I thought Dorothy was very pretty, judging from her photos, blonde and cute," I said. "And I read something about her father working here at the Ambassador at that time."

"Yes. As a girl, Dorothy started doing diving exhibitions right here at the Ambassador Hotel's swimming pool."

Jane also described some of the parties they all attended here at the hotel. They were star studded events, and the female athletes only had to cross Wilshire Boulevard to attend.

"We were all dancing with our partners when Helene Madison danced right by me with Clark Gable. Now, Helene is six-feet tall, and Clark looks like he's a full head shorter. I never quite watched his movies the same way after that."

She hadn't mentioned her diving competition, or her own Olympic medal, so I brought it up.

"I believe you won your bronze medal in the 3-meter springboard?" I asked.

"I was in first place, leading everyone, when I performed the worst dive of my career. I went from first to third, just like that. Georgia Coleman took the gold, and young Katherine Rawls won the silver."

"It's too bad one bad dive cost you a gold medal," I said.

"Georgia and I had been competing since Amsterdam, we had quite a rivalry."

"You mentioned Helene Madison," I said. "Evidently, she was an excellent swimmer."

Jane paused for a moment, collecting her thoughts.

"Helene and I were never really friends; she was a little standoffish. When the other girls went shopping, or out to any number of parties, Helene would just stay at the hotel and do her nails, she loved bright red."

"So, she kept to herself?"

"Yes. She wasn't as outgoing as some of the others. But every time she got into the pool; Helene won a gold medal. No one on the planet could beat her. I swam with Johnny Weissmuller for years; we were on the same Illinois swim club. Helene Madison was every bit the star of the 1932 Los Angeles Olympics that Weissmuller had been in prior Olympic Games. Why is it Johnny Weissmuller became world famous, and hardly anyone has ever heard of Helene Madison?"

"What happened to her after the games?" I asked.

"She returned to her hometown of Seattle, Washington, to a parade and banquet in her honor. She was given the key to the city and feted by all of the local dignitaries. But this was during the worst of the depression, and her family was broke. They expected her to start carrying her weight. She reluctantly gave up competitive swimming and applied for a job as a swim instructor at one of the city's municipal pools. But she was told that she didn't qualify because she was a woman. They only hired men. Can you believe that; the greatest swimmer of her generation didn't qualify to teach swimming because she was a woman?"

This reminded me of Janice Romary's experience in 1968. Was it possible not much had changed between 1932 and 1968? Jane continued telling me more about Helene Madison.

"She struggled for years before things finally improved a bit. But I don't think she ever really recovered from that indignity."

Jane and I looked over some of the many photographs Beryl had sent. It was almost like her pictures were there representing her.

Jane told me all about her husband and their children, and all she's been doing since she competed in the 1932 Los Angeles Olympics. She'd lived a full life, and she was here in 1984 as a special guest. She was looking forward to the opening ceremonies, which were only a few days away.

We finished our lunch, and she asked me to please give Beryl her very best wishes. Then she shared one last story. It was about her final day in Amsterdam during those 1928 Olympics.

"Josephine McKim and I still had some Dutch currency to spend, so we went shopping, I was looking to buy a trench coat, which was very stylish back then. So, we're out on the town, shopping, and we sort of lost track of time. Then we hear the sounds of our ship leaving the port. We raced to the docks and found the ship had pulled away, but it stopped in the middle of the harbor. They sent a tender from the ship to pick us up. Someone evidently told them we missed the boat. Now, Jo and I finally get to the ship, and General MacArthur, the head of the American Olympic Committee, is waiting for us."

"General Douglas MacArthur?" I asked.

"The very same," she replied. "And he proceeded to give us a serious dressing down. Let's just say he was very unhappy with us."

"I can imagine."

"We were so afraid to show our faces that we stayed in our stateroom for hours. Little did we know how famous he would someday become."

◌ ◌ ◌

From Figueroa, I climbed the steep access road up to Bunker Hill. In the early 1960s, after the Victorian homes, boarding houses, and small hotels had been cleared away, the Music Center's theaters were some of the first new buildings to be erected on the hill. One of the last surviving structures from old Bunker Hill still stands on Temple Street, right across from the Music Center. It's a two-story utilitarian building now known as the

Music Center Annex. In its previous state, it once served as the Los Angeles County Morgue. In fact, this was where Marilyn Monroe's body had been brought after her untimely death. Strangely enough, for the Olympic Arts Festival, the play *American Clock,* written by her ex-husband, Arthur Miller, rehearsed in the building's main rehearsal hall. I wondered if Miller was aware of the strange coincidence.

I locked my Rayleigh to a pole and went inside. Tom Williams, the production manager, had his office just to the right, and Richard DeVries, the literary manager, had his office just to the left. That main rehearsal hall was straight ahead. It looked like someone was doing some casting, because a group of actors stood around practicing their lines. Just past Richard's office was a staircase that led up to Gordon Davidson's office and to the large suite of offices for the Blue Ribbon 400.

When I entered Richard's office, he was busy reading a play. Cynthia was working at her small desk over in the corner. She smiled when she saw me. I then pulled my adaptation of *Edendale* from my backpack and set it on the corner of Richard's desk.

"It's my first draft," I said. "Let me know what you think."

"Thanks," he muttered, taking my script and laying it on top of a small stack of scripts already on his desk. "I'll have it read by tomorrow."

I was grateful he hadn't slipped my script on the bottom of that stack. I then went over to speak to Cynthia.

"I had a great time last night," she smiled.

"Me too," I said. "I just wish it hadn't ended so abruptly."

"I've started reading *What Makes Sammy Run,* and I really like it, all that great 1930s Hollywood stuff."

"I'll tell you all about my meeting Budd Schulberg when you're done."

"It won't take me long, I promise."

Richard cleared his throat, politely letting me know I should let Cynthia get back to her work.

"I'll see you both tomorrow night in Chinatown," I said. I walked out and headed straight to Tom William's office.

Tom's door was open, so I walked right in. He was seated at his desk looking over some papers. His assistant wasn't there today, so the other desk in the room sat empty. Tom asked me to have a seat. I grabbed a chair by his desk. I could see he'd been looking over a Taper's basketball team roster. For some reason, several names appeared to be crossed out, but I couldn't make out which names they were.

"I really liked Wanda," Tom said. "Do you have any more like her?"

"There aren't any more like her," I smiled.

"Do you think she and Hank might want to play next season?"

"Hank might be interested, but Wanda will probably be back in Europe. I'll let you know what they say."

Tom nodded, then slid the team roster off to the side. He then grabbed some other papers.

"It's finally been decided," he said. "We will be doing a mainstage production of Len Sebastian's play."

"That's great news. When Sebastian meets with the designers, I'll need to be included. I want to make sure everything is done correctly."

"You won't need to concern yourself, Niko, because I've already hired another stage manager for the show."

I was a bit confused. Was Tom telling me because it was a main stage production, he was bringing in a more experienced stage manager for me to work under as an assistant?

"Are you saying I'm being demoted?"

"No, you're being replaced. The new stage manager will select his own assistants."

"I don't understand? I helped to create that show. I took Sebastian's wild ideas and made them all work."

"But you neglected to stroke his ego, and that was a large part of the job. He said you actually disagreed with him in front of the cast and crew."

"Tom, nobody in the production could even stand the guy. I had to stop the cast from trying to kill him."

"I'm aware of how difficult Sebastian can be, but he's still the director, and it was your job to support him."

I felt like I'd just been punched in the face once again. I didn't want to work with Sebastian any more than he wanted to work with me. But I couldn't even imagine how they were going to do the show without my help. There were just so many little things I did behind the scenes to make everything function. But then I remembered Tom was also staffing other shows for the new season.

"What about working on one of your other shows?" I asked. "I've already worked with several of those directors before."

"Sebastian doesn't want you around here in any capacity. I'm sorry, but he made that very clear."

It was difficult accepting my stage-managing career could be over, and I had no idea what I would do for a living. Tom grabbed the basketball roster from his desk.

"Don't forget to ask Hank and Wanda if they want to play basketball next season. We're going to need a few new players."

"I'll get right on it," I frowned.

co co co

As I rode up to the Villa Serrano, I noticed several police cars crowding the curb in front of the apartment. Yellow police tape cordoned off the area and a group of police officers milled about. The apartment's front door was propped open, and cops entered and exited the building. I went right up to a uniformed officer who was standing near the yellow tape.

"What's going on?" I asked. "I live here."

Before the officer could answer, another officer came out from the crowd. It was Randy Ferlinghetti.

"I'll handle this," he said. "I know this guy."

Randy approached me as the other officer stepped away. I then noticed Officer Watkins standing nearby with some of the other officers.

"What's going on?" I asked Randy.

"Man, when I heard your address on the radio, I just about shit. I thought it might be you."

"Was it another burglary?"

"Yeah, a burglary was part of it," he answered. "But evidently somebody died."

"What?"

"They say it looks like a suicide."

"A suicide?"

"It was a black guy who lived downstairs in the back."

"Vidor," I mumbled. "He's the only black man in the building."

"He came home and found the burglars had dismantled his piano and carted it off. He left a note saying there was no reason to live anymore, then he hung himself in the shower."

Just then, the coroner's van pulled up by the front door. Two men got out, grabbed a stretcher, and walked with it into the building.

"I need to get to my apartment," I said. "Can you help?"

"Sure, follow me." He walked me right into the building, up the stairs, and right to my apartment's door. "Hey, I'm working security at the L. A. Coliseum tomorrow for the Olympic track and field practices. You should come down; I've got two security passes."

Same old Randy, I thought. I remember when he forged student activity cards back in high school. Those phony cards got us into all the football and basketball games. He's certainly moved up in the world. Randy told me where I could find him at the Coliseum and what time to be there.

"Okay," I said. "You mind if I bring Jake? He's not working tomorrow."

"No. Bring Jake, it'll be good to see him," he grinned. "Believe me, you'll be happy you came."

As Randy headed back toward the front of the building, I glanced down the stairs at Vidor's open door. I could see camera flashes coming from inside and police personnel entering and exiting. It was hard to believe that I'd never see my friend, Vidor, ever again.

☙ ☙ ☙

Since I wasn't a big fan of either kimchi or tofu, I was surprised how good Hyun-sook's kimchi tofu soup tasted. By combining the ingredients so perfectly, she created a truly delicious soup. I gladly spooned the delectable concoction into my mouth, trying not to spill a single drop. Sung-ho and their two children, Min-ho and Eun-ju, slurped it up as well.

Sung-ho confessed they were flying home tomorrow to South Korea, so this was their final opportunity to have me over. I could see they'd already packed up most of their belongings, there were boxes stacked everywhere.

Because they'd only been in this country for a short time, they admitted they didn't know much about Los Angeles' Korean community and wanted to know more. Sung-ho mentioned several cousins who'd lived here for some time, including Mr. Lee, our landlord. Hyun-sook asked me what I knew about the Koreans who first came to this city.

"I believe the first Koreans lived up on old Bunker Hill, in some of the Victorian homes that had been turned into boarding houses.

"Bunker Hill?" Sung-ho asked, confused because Bunker Hill is now new high-rises.

"It was once a charming old residential neighborhood," I said, "Everything was removed in the name of community redevelopment."

Sung-ho nodded, trying to imagine how that area might have once looked.

"Years ago," Sung-ho said, "my cousins lived near Jefferson Boulevard, by USC."

"I had family there too," said Hyun-sook. "This was many years ago."

"That area was the city's first Koreatown" I said. "It thrived from the 1930s through the 1950s."

"One cousin told me they were forced to live in a very small area," Sung-ho said. "And they couldn't live anywhere else. How can that be?"

It felt awkward trying to explain the city's restrictive racial covenants of that era, which forced people of color to only live in designated areas of the city. Sung-ho looked at me in disbelief, amazed a country that boasts about freedom and liberty had such awful laws in place.

"So, this Koreatown here is new?" he asked.

"It started sometime in the 1960s," I said. "It's now a very diverse community."

Earlier, we discussed the death of our neighbor and friend, Vidor. Sung-ho said he would always cherish the memory of Vidor's music, how beautiful it sounded. Hyun-sook said it would be one of her favorite memories of their stay here. America, to her, would always sound like Chopin.

Neither Sung-ho or Hyun-sook could understand the senseless violence that seemed to happen so regularly in this country. They couldn't understand the gang activity that plagued large parts of the city, or the crack cocaine epidemic that fueled much of it. They saw many economic opportunities here but were glad to be headed back home. Hyun-sook had a question for me.

"Have you heard of Dr. Sammy Lee?" she asked.

"Of course," I answered. "He was a doctor, an Olympic athlete, and a coach."

"Yes," Hyun-sook beamed. "He was born here, and he's a Korean man."

She was right. Sammy Lee was born in Fresno, California, to parents of Korean descent, and moved to Los Angeles as a child. He was twelve years old when the city hosted the 1932 Olympics Games. Watching the diving events inspired him to become an Olympic Diver. He became the first Asian American man to win an Olympic gold medal. He eventually won two, along with a silver, and two bronze medals. When he became a doctor, he served in the U.S. Army Medical Corp during the Korean War. In 1976, he coached a sixteen-year-old Greg Louganis to a gold medal at the Montreal Olympics. Hyun-sook said she was proud of Sammy Lee's many accomplishments.

As we enjoyed the spicy Bulgogi, marinated ribeye steak, I told them how delicious the food was, and how sad I was they were leaving.

After the meal, I thanked them for having me over to dinner, and even offered to drive them to the airport the next day. Sung-ho said they had already made arrangements, but thanked me for my offer. I realized they would probably be seeing many people at the airport arriving for the Olympics Games.

"You're going to miss the Olympics," I said. "That's too bad."

"It's okay," Sung-ho said. "In four years, Summer Olympics in Seoul, our home."

I'd forgotten the 1988 Summer Olympics were scheduled for Seoul, South Korea. It made me happy knowing my new friends would be there.

Friday
July 27

❦ The next morning, I was awakened by the telephone ringing on my nightstand. Besides a morning earthquake, a ringing phone was my least favorite way to be awakened. I reached over and grabbed the phone before the answering machine could pick it up. There was a weight on my legs, which made it difficult for me to reach the phone, and I noticed Maggie and Dottie lying there on top of me.

"Hello," I groaned into the phone.

"Stop sleeping the day away," said the gruff female voice. "You have things to do."

"Is this Beryl?" I asked, recognizing her voice.

"Yes, it is," she replied. "Consider this your free wake-up call."

The weight of the two cats made it difficult for me to sit up. "I'm trying to get comfortable here, but the bed's crowded these days."

"Oh," she chuckled. "Do you have a female there in bed with you?"

"Not only do I have one female in bed with me, Beryl, but I have two. Do you know what the French call that?"

"My goodness," she sighed. "This is too much information for me."

"Relax. It's only Maggie and Dottie."

"Oh, what a disappointment," she sighed. "How did everything go with Jane Fauntz?"

"It went well. She loved seeing all the clippings and photographs. But she really would have preferred to see you."

"Of course. My sunny disposition brightens up any room."

I told Beryl about seeing Mr. Lee looking over her old house with demolition people, and asked her if she'd heard anything new regarding her photographs.

"That's why I'm calling," she said. "Your old professor squared everything away for us, and the curator of special collections at the Doheny

Library was here yesterday so I could sign the necessary paperwork."

"That's the best news I've heard in awhile," I said, smiling.

Just the other day, I managed to contact my old professor, Michael Lafayette, and he was happy to hear from me. After we caught up on what we'd both been doing, I told him all about Beryl's situation with her historic photographs. I mentioned the Doheny Library as a possible home and asked if he would help facilitate a donation. Lafayette already knew all about Beryl and her photo archive and said he would be glad to help. I gave him Beryl's information and told him there was some urgency. Lafayette said not to worry, this would all happen very quickly. Evidently, he was right.

"I still need you to help the university with the exchange," Beryl said.

"Of course," I said. "I'm ready and waiting."

"Excellent. You have the combination to the safe, and you know where the key is. They'll call you when they're ready to pick everything up and you can meet them there."

"Perfect," I said. "I'll be waiting for their call."

ᖆ ᖆ ᖆ

My fencing class I had to reschedule was for that morning, so I drove over to the Falcon Studio. Even though I'd been taking fencing for several years, I hadn't really made much progress. I'd always been competitive, and it frustrated me I was barely in the intermediate level.

Faulkner's assistants led us through a warm-up routine and then some fencing drills. When it came time to actually fence against an opponent, we were paired off into groups of two. That's when Maestro Faulkner finally made his appearance. I didn't like the opponent they'd chosen for me because I'd had mixed results against him. He'd already beaten me several times, so I knew it wouldn't be easy to beat him.

Faulkner watched us as we fenced. I would get a touch and win, and then my opponent would get a touch and win. Neither of us was dominating our duel. Between bouts, Faulkner would give us tips on how to improve our technique. I listened, and unfortunately, so did my opponent.

At the very end, my opponent got me one last time, giving him the win and the match. We removed our masks and shook hands. He said I'd been a worthy competitor, which is always what you tell the loser. I really hated to lose at anything, and I never took the loss well.

After everyone had gone, I sat down on a bench, sullen and disappointed with myself. Maestro Faulkner came over and sat beside me.

"You could have easily won that match," he said.

"I know. It just wasn't my day."

I didn't need Faulkner telling me all I'd done wrong because I already knew what those things were. I just wasn't able to fix them at that moment. The more flaws he pointed out in my technique, the more I just tuned him out. He finally realized he wasn't getting through to me.

"You really don't want to hear this, do you?" he asked.

"Sorry, Maestro, but no. When I first started out with fencing, I wanted to become a great fencer. Now, I'd be happy just to be a good one." I suddenly realized I didn't even know who the standard was for greatness. If someone asked me who the greatest baseball player was, I could answer, "Babe Ruth." But I had no idea who the greatest fencer was.

"Maestro," I said. "Who would you say was the greatest fencer of all time?"

"Why do you want to know?"

"I'm just curious I guess."

Faulkner pondered the question. "I would probably say Aladar Gerevich of Hungary. Hungary was once a great fencing power, and Gerevich won seven gold medals, one silver, and two bronze. He competed from 1932 all the way to 1960." Faulkner chuckled at something he'd just remembered.

"What's so funny?" I asked.

"During the Hungarian Olympic trials in 1960, their Olympic committee told Gerevich that he was too old to compete anymore and he should step aside for a younger fencer. So, Gerevich challenged the entire Hungarian sabre team to individual matches. He ended up winning every single match. So much for being too old."

It just occurred to me Faulkner had also fenced sabre in the 1932 Olympics.

"You were both there in 1932," I said. "Did you ever compete against Gerevich?"

"Yes," he smiled. "And I beat him."

I knew Faulkner had been an excellent fencer in his day, but I also knew he was never able to earn a single Olympic medal.

"No offense, Maestro, but If he was as good as you say, how did you ever beat him?"

"1932 was Gerevich's first Olympics. He was just twenty-two years old. I was forty at the time. I was the crafty veteran, and he was the novice. Fencing is not all athleticism. So much of it is technique and strategy. Years later, I would have never beaten him. It was just my day, not his."

Faulkner then told me about two other fencers on that same 1932 Hungarian team, Attila Petschauer and Endre Kabos.

"I never faced Petschaer, but Kabos beat me badly," he said. "Both of them were Jewish, and later lived in Nazi-occupied Europe; it was all very sad."

"What happened?" I asked.

"Petschauer was arrested by the Nazis in 1943 and never survived the camps, and Kabos was put in a forced labor camp and died in 1944."

"How awful."

"It was," said Faulkner. "But their time at the 1932 Los Angeles Olympics had been golden, and not even the Nazis could take that away from them." Faulkner paused. "After the war, when the Olympics finally resumed in 1948, London was the host city. Aladar Gerevich returned with his new Hungarian fencing team, and just like Los Angeles in 1932, they won a gold medal in team competition. Gerevich, of course, won the individual gold medal in his event."

"And you beat him once," I said.

"Yes," Faulkner smiled. "I did."

∞ ∞ ∞

Jake met me at my place, and we drove to the Coliseum together. We were both excited to see what the inside of the freshly decorated Coliseum looked like, and to see the Olympic athletes preparing for their big moment.

Exposition Park was a whirlwind of activity, with tourists mingling and the various track and field teams arriving in yellow school buses. Using the school buses, while school was out for the summer, was another cost cutting measure the L. A. Organizing Committee had come up with.

Jake and I found a parking spot and then walked over to the small Los Angeles Police Department's substation at the closed end of the Coliseum. A group of LAPD bigwigs had arrived in front of the substation for some sort of gathering. I recognized Randy's brother-in-law, Matt Barbarri, who was now a commander in the department. I also saw Police Chief Daryl Gates there. I never thought much of Gates. I thought he was arrogant and pompous, and never seemed to learn from his own mistakes.

Jake and I continued walking toward the tunnel entrance to the stadium. We found Randy Ferlinghetti right where he said he'd be.

"You guys made it," Randy smiled. "You'll be glad you did."

Randy hadn't seen Jake in years, so the two quickly got caught up on things. I listened to their conversation but also watched as groups of athletes arrived in their buses. After they exited their buses, the athletes then made their way down the ramp and into the Coliseum's main tunnel. I knew on the other end, the tunnel emptied right onto the Olympic track.

"I have two security passes here," Jake said, handing us each a laminated badge attached to its lanyard."

The Stars in Motion logo and the Olympic rings made the passes look official.

"These passes look real," I said, examining mine.

"That's because they are, man," Randy smiled. "They're the real deal."

Randy had certainly progressed from supplying fake high school activity cards. He was now in the big leagues.

"When you guys are ready to leave," Randy said. "Just make sure you exit back up the tunnel, and check in with me. Okay?"

"Sure, but why?" I asked.

"You'll see," he smiled. "Now, go have some fun."

Jake and I hung our lanyards around our necks and proceeded down the ramp with the athletes and coaches. At the security check, they looked at our passes and let us go right by. In the tunnel, we met up with a couple of USA coaches who actually recognized Jake from his track days. Back in high school, Jake was the fastest hurdler in the city. One year, at the L. A. City Track Finals, Jake won his event and Bobby Jefferson, took second. We were hoping to run into Bobby today knowing his sprinters might be practicing there.

Even without the spectators, walking out of the Coliseum's tunnel and onto the track was a breathtaking experience. The old gray lady never looked lovelier. We did notice quite a few subtle improvements.

A brand-new running track had been installed, and the grass had all been freshly re-sodded. Each of the spectator tunnels were painted in a different pastel color, making them look like a collection of Easter eggs. Jake and I both noticed the newly expanded press box and the two new video displays above the Peristyle.

The most obvious enhancement was also at the Peristyle end, and it was temporary. Just like on a movie studio backlot, Hollywood had wrapped the entire granite Peristyle in an enormous facade. The facade was white, with pastel-colored accents. The Stars in Motion logo appeared on either end, and the Olympic rings were just below where the Olympic flame would soon burn. Written in large block letters, from one end of the Peristyle to the other, it read: "Games of the XXIII rd Olympiad - Los Angeles California 1984."

I don't know about Jake, but I got a lump in my throat. I remembered the photographs Beryl had taken at the opening ceremonies back in 1932. I could only imagine what these upcoming ceremonies would look like in comparison. For one thing, 1984's ceremonies would be preserved in color, while Beryl's images were in black and white. But other than that, I imagined they would be surprisingly similar.

We looked around for our friend, Bobby, but learned we just missed him. He'd been there earlier practicing with his sprinters. We wandered around the floor of the Coliseum for a while before we finally decided to leave. As Randy had instructed, we exited the same way we'd come in, right back up the tunnel.

We found Randy still there at his post. As the yellow school buses were arriving to drop off athletes, we also noticed some of the police dignitaries from earlier. They were now huddled with a group of reporters and TV camera crews. It looked like a press conference of some kind was about to begin.

Randy pointed out his brother-in-law, Matt, in the group, and also Daryl Gates, the police Chief.

"All of the department's brass are here," Randy said, grinning. "And they have no idea what's about to happen."

I didn't know what Randy was referring to, but I now realized Jake and I had been brought here to be part of the audience, along with the police dignitaries and the news media. We thanked Randy again for the chance to see the inside of the Olympic Stadium and then handed him back his two security passes.

"Don't leave just yet," Randy smiled, shoving the two passes into his pocket. "You'll want to see what happens next; I promise you."

While everyone was focused on the news conference, Randy reached deep inside a nearby trash barrel and pulled out a brown paper bag. He then took the bag and circled around behind one of the yellow buses. From the bag, Randy pulled out an object that looked like a pipe with wires. Then, for some reason, he attached that object inside one of the bus's wheel wells. Randy then crumpled the paper bag and just tossed it aside. Jake and I both wondered what the hell our friend was doing. If we didn't know better, we would have thought Randy was planting a bomb. Just then, Randy came out from behind the bus, shouting and waving his arms.

"Get back, everybody get back!" He shouted. "There's a bomb!"

Randy continued shouting until he had everyone's attention. This included the police bigwigs and the news media. Some people in the crowd started slowly moving back, while others started running away. Randy then circled behind the bus. He grabbed the object and brought it out to show everyone. It was the same object he'd placed there only moments earlier. He held the object up high for everyone to see. The television news cameras were now filming this entire spectacle.

Randy brought the object out to the large empty grass area, pulled the wires out, then hurled it as far as he could. It landed with a thud out in the middle of the field. When he returned to us, he was swarmed by the reporters and TV cameras. Randy started giving interviews like he was a celebrity, and for the moment, he was.

Chief Gates then made a speech proclaiming Randy as a true hero. Gates went on to say Officer Ferlinghetti was exactly the type of police officer the LAPD was looking for: someone with initiative and courage. Randy's brother-in-law, who was standing near Chief Gates, knew better. He had known Randy for years and immediately appeared skeptical of his actions.

It only took a few minutes for the LAPD bomb squad to arrive. They carefully checked the device, and then proclaimed there was no danger. They said even though the lead pipe was filled with what appeared to be gun powder, the igniting mechanism was never functional.

Other police officers, who'd been inspecting vehicles at the park's perimeter, stated they'd inspected that bus just minutes earlier and they found no such device. They had a bomb sniffing dog, and a full team went over it. The bomb, they claimed, had to have been attached to the bus right at the spot where it was discovered.

It's amazing how quickly Randy went from a hero to a suspect. He started to realize he'd made a huge mistake, but by then it was too late. His story was filled with holes, and everyone knew it. Jake and I watched as some high-ranking officials questioned Randy. Finally, his brother-in-law, Matt, got him to confess he'd staged the whole thing. Randy admitted to everyone he'd wanted to be a hero, and he thought this would bring him some attention. He certainly received the attention.

❧ ❧ ❧

Jake and I couldn't believe Randy had done something so stupid, and for what reason, just so people would consider him a hero. Chief Gates, who, moments earlier, was singing his praises was now calling for his head. Randy probably shouldn't have admitted he'd done anything wrong and just asked for a lawyer. But the police had him dead to rights and he knew it. So much for his career in law enforcement.

When we got to my apartment, Jake took off for home, and I went inside. There was a new message on my answering machine. It was from a curator at USC's Doheny Library. He was about to head over to Beryl's house with a team of people, and they would wait there for me to let them in. Fortunately, the message was less than thirty minutes old.

I quickly got into my car and drove over to Beryl's place. There, I found a large truck backed into the driveway and a small group of people standing by the front steps. Among that group, I recognized my old professor, Michael Lafayette. He greeted me with a big smile on his face.

"Hello, Niko," he said, shaking my hand. "I'm glad we're getting this done."

Lafayette then introduced me to the curator of special collections. We spoke for just a moment. I then found the key and led the group inside to the sealed vault. Using the combination that Beryl had given me, 7 - 30 - 32, I opened the door. Inside were all of Beryl's photographs and original negatives. I felt like I just opened King Tutt's tomb. The boxes were stacked neatly, and everything was well labeled. With everybody working together, we had the truck loaded and the vault emptied in less than a half-hour. When we were finished, the curator told me Beryl's photos would be the university's largest single collection of historic photographs, and once everything was properly catalogued, anyone could visit the Doheny Library and explore the Beryl Hargrove Photographic Archive. The collection would be preserved there forever.

I wanted to give Beryl the good news, So I headed right over to the Cedar-Sinai. As I drove there, I thought about some of the photographs Beryl had shared with me. There were images of long-gone buildings, streets that were now unrecognizable, and whole neighborhoods that had vanished over time. Whenever Beryl compared two photographs, an old photo, with a current photo of that same view, I always preferred the older picture. I don't know why, but for some reason, everything always looked better back then.

In the hospital's lobby, I entered the first elevator that opened. Inside were two young nurses standing over a wheeled gurney. On the gurney was a figure covered from head to toe with a sheet. The two nurses apologized to me and tried to explain how they thought they were using the service elevator. They began to argue amongst themselves and blame each other for their mistake. One of them finally pushed the button for the basement.

I glanced down at the covered figure on the gurney and noticed one wrinkled hand was sticking out from under the sheet. There was a large emerald ring on one of the fingers. I immediately recognized the ring.

When the elevator doors opened, the two nurses wheeled the gurney out into the basement's hallway.

"We're so sorry," the tall nurse said, as they wheeled Beryl's body away.

I just stood there, stunned, and unable to move. Finally, the doors closed on their own.

Richard's party was that night, and we were planning to celebrate the success of my play *Sonora Town*. Even though I wasn't in the mood for a celebration, as the playwright, my absence would be glaring. Especially, since I was hoping to hear some good news about my *Edendale* adaptation. I also knew Cynthia would be there, and if anyone could make me feel better, she could.

When I got home from Cedars, I called Hank and asked if he would take Maggie and Dottie for the night. I told him I was hoping to get Cynthia over to my place. He said if I was going to get laid, he'd take them for a week. Now, that's a true friend. I brought him the cats, then came home and cleaned my apartment better than I'd ever cleaned it before.

Just when I was about to leave for Chinatown, the phone rang. It was Jules. He sounded like he'd been crying.

"I've asked Betty for a divorce. We're done. I never want to see her again."

"Jules, I'm so sorry."

"I spoke to my attorney, and he said Betty should do okay in the settlement, but I had the house and business before we met, so she's not entitled to any of that. Maybe you could come by the restaurant tonight?" he asked. "I'll even buy you dinner."

"I'm sorry Jules, but I already have plans. I'm hoping to finally get Cynthia over to my apartment. I could come by your place tomorrow morning, if that's okay?"

"That's fine. But you could always bring Cynthia by for a night cap. You know what time we close."

"Maybe we will. But most likely, I'll see you in the morning, I promise."

❦ ❦ ❦

The Yee Mee Loo Café was a wonderfully preserved 1940's era Chinese restaurant in the heart of Chinatown. An autographed photo of actress Anna May Wong, a one-time café regular, was proudly displayed on one wall. Next to that photo was a black rotary pay phone with "MAdison 4-4539" on its dial. I could easily imagine Humphrey Bogart and Mary Astor seated at a booth, enjoying the roast duck and pork egg foo young.

The Restaurant, along with its adjoining Kwan Yin Temple bar, occupied a two-story, brick building on the corner of Spring Street and Ord. A beaded curtain was all that separated the two establishments. During the course of an evening, it was common to move freely from one place to the other.

While the restaurant was bright and airy, the Kwan Yin Temple bar was dark and foreboding. There was always a sense of danger, real or imagined. When I entered this time, a Billie Holiday song was playing on the jukebox, and the brawny Chinese bartender stood behind the bar, a half-chewed cigar in his mouth. Behind him was a hand carved altar and Buddha, surrounded by candles and burning incense. The place was known for its mysterious blue drink. The regulars called it a "Tidy Bowl" because it resembles the bluish colored toilet bowl cleaner advertised on TV.

Instead of the bar's usual clientele, that night, everyone here had some connection with the Taper. Richard was in the middle of it, holding court with several of his playwrights. There seemed to be an awful lot of ass kissing going on; the playwrights all trying to get their plays produced. Me, I didn't need to kiss any ass. I'd written last season's most successful play, and I'd already handed Richard the new play he requested. I was in the catbird's seat.

I noticed Jeanne Cruz was there and seated at a booth beside Cynthia Reich. Isabella Cruz was seated on the other side of the table with my friend, Danny Sanchez. Despite their age difference, Danny and Isabella looked like they belonged together. Fortunately, Danny didn't seem to have any issues with me over my time with Isabella, and I was relieved.

Just then, Richard came up and tapped me on the shoulder and said he wanted to talk. He invited me over to the bar area and ordered us a couple of beers. The bartender poured two beers from the tap.

"I read your play last night," Richard said.

"Great," I said, sipping the suds off the top of my beer. "What did you think?"

"I liked it. It's even better than your *Sonora Town* play, and that's saying a lot."

This was wonderful news. He liked my script. Now, all he had to tell me was when they were going to produce my play.

"It's still a first draft," I said, "so I know there'll be things you'll want changed."

"That's funny," he said, giving me a curious look. "If only you'd been willing to make changes the last time I asked you to."

"Excuse me?"

"Never mind," he muttered, shaking his head and then sipping his beer.

I hadn't realized there was still bad blood between us. I'd assumed that since *Sonora Town* did so well, all was forgiven.

"I made several changes you asked for. I just didn't make that last one."

"Whatever," he said. "That's old news."

I decided to let that comment drop. "Anyway, I'm happy you like the *Edendale* script.

"I do like it, and you did some really good work." He paused. "But unfortunately, we're not going to produce it."

"I don't understand. Why?"

"It's just too much like your first play, and that's not exactly what I wanted."

Richard knew what was in *Edendale* before he asked me to write an adaptation, so this didn't make any sense.

"You asked me to write an adaptation of Cruz's novel, *Edendale,* and that's exactly what I gave you."

"I guess maybe I just forgot what was in the book," he smiled, "my mistake."

This was bullshit. He couldn't have just forgotten everything in the book he'd assigned me to adapt.

"So, all of that work I did was for nothing?"

"I guess so," he smiled. "Better luck next time."

I finally realized what was going on here. Richard was teaching me a lesson. He had no plans to produce my play. He just wanted me to waste my time writing it. He wanted to show me who was boss.

"Let me give you some advice," he said, glaring at me. "Next time a producer asks you to make changes to a script, make the fucking changes."

Isabella and Danny had gone over to the café for some food, so I sat down where they'd been sitting. It was difficult for me to tell Jeanne and Cynthia the *Edendale* play was now dead. But after I told them, neither of the two appeared surprised by the news. Jeanne was the first one to speak.

"Niko, it would have been wonderful if the play had been produced, but fortunately, other opportunities have presented themselves."

Jeanne looked over to Cynthia as if she expected her to explain. After a moment, Cynthia did.

"Jeanne and I formed a partnership," she announced. "And we now have a deal with a movie company to turn Carlos Cruz's novel *Sonora Town* into a film."

"When did all this happen?" I asked, taken aback by the news.

"Cynthia has been working on this deal for some time," Jeanne said. "Practically since your play opened. In fact, she brought producers to see the play to sell them on the idea of a movie. They all loved your play, by the way."

I remembered Cynthia bringing people to the play, but I never questioned her because I figured if they were important, she would have told me.

"You're going to need a screenwriter," I said. "And nobody knows the material like I do."

Cynthia frowned. "Unfortunately, the director we hired also has a screenwriter he wants to use."

"When were you going to tell me about all this?" I asked. "We could have all been partners. I could have helped you."

"Niko," Cynthia smiled. "Once I had Jeanne on board, I didn't need your help."

I looked at both of them for a long moment, then I got up and headed for the door.

"Niko," she said, "let me explain."

I didn't reply. Instead, I just opened the door and stepped out onto the sidewalk. Cynthia followed me out.

"Niko," she shouted. "Wait, please."

I stopped, then turned toward her. "For some reason I didn't expect this from you."

"I'm sorry, Niko. But this is my career we're talking about."

"I guess that's all that matters."

Cynthia thought for a moment. "You know, I wasn't completely convinced I was doing the right thing by cutting you out of our plans. But then last night, I finished that novel that you gave me: *What Makes Sammy Run.*"

"What are you talking about?"

"After I'd finished reading it, I saw exactly what I needed to do. Now I had a role model. Sammy Glick was everything I wanted to be."

є є є

"Well, that could have gone better," I thought to myself as I drove home. How did everything in my life suddenly turn to shit? All of the hours I'd put in on *Edendale,* and all for nothing. And Cynthia, whom I thought was so wonderful, somehow turned out to be the second coming of Sammy Glick.

When I got home, I called Jules at his restaurant and told him what I'd just been through. He suggested we go out and have a drink to commiserate. He asked me to meet him at his restaurant at closing time. I told him I would see him then.

After I got off the phone, I sat there going over everything that happened to me these last few days, all the decisions I'd made, all of the choices

I'd selected. I then began to seriously question my own judgment. I realized this was a pivotal day in my life, and a day of reckoning. I knew I couldn't go on like this. I had to make some changes, and everything was on the table.

A few hours later, I drove over to Larchmont Village and parked directly across the street from Le Petite Mustache. All the other businesses in Larchmont Village had already closed for the night. It was quiet with almost no traffic. I noticed Jules' car parked out in front of his restaurant and watched as his staff came out, one by one. Jules was usually the last one to leave because he had to balance the night's receipts and then close everything up. I'd been here before at closing time, and watched him carry the restaurant's cash deposits to the bank next door. He would place the cash into the bank's night drop for safe keeping.

After just a few minutes, the front door of the restaurant opened and Jules came out carrying a leather pouch. He noticed my car across the street and waved. After he locked the restaurant's door, he walked over to the bank. I got out of my Firebird and started to walk across Larchmont Boulevard to meet him.

When Jules reached the bank, a tall figure suddenly appeared wearing a ski mask and holding a handgun. I hollered to Jules to warn him, but it was too late. Without saying a word, the man shot Jules three times, dropping him to the ground. Then the man pointed his gun at me. I had nowhere to hide, so I dropped to the asphalt. He fired three shots. One bullet ricocheted off the pavement while the two others hit my Firebird. I then heard the gun click several times. He reached down, picked up Jules' leather pouch and started running. He turned the corner on First Street and disappeared into the residential neighborhood.

Even though my heart was pounding, I got up and hurried over to Jules. When I got to him, I saw blood everywhere. I looked him over. He wasn't breathing, and he had no pulse. I shook him and shouted his name, but there was no response.

When I realized the gunman was getting away, I got up and ran after him with no idea what I would do if I ever caught him. I just hoped he hadn't stopped to reload. I raced past several homes. They were only illuminated with porch lights. Fortunately, there also a few street lamps that lit up the street and sidewalk. I tried to scan the yards for anyone who might be hiding, but I couldn't see a thing because it was so dark.

When I saw the headlights of an approaching car coming toward me, I hid behind a van. As the car got closer, I recognized that it was a red BMW 1600. The man in the passenger seat was removing a ski mask, and I saw it was a woman behind the wheel. "Oh my God!" I said to myself, realizing Betty was the woman driving, and the man removing his mask was Matteo. As the car passed me, I managed to get its license number, repeating it several times to myself so I wouldn't forget it. This was no random robbery, I realized. These two planned it, and Matteo had carried it out. They wanted Jules dead.

I hurried back to the bank, and found several people standing over Jules. An LAPD patrol car had already arrived, and the two officers were asking the crowd to back away. That's when I spotted Randy's partner, Officer Watkins, and he also spotted me. Watkins had a new partner, another black officer. I went over to Watkins, and told him exactly what I'd witnessed.

I was there for hours answering questions and telling the police everything I knew. Eventually, I heard one of the officers say they'd apprehended the two suspects and they were in custody. This was the only good news I'd heard all night.

Before I could leave, the police informed me they would have to impound my Firebird because the two bullets lodged in it were now evidence. Finally, when the detectives were finished with me, they had Watkins and his partner give me a ride home.

Saturday
July 28

●◆ I opened my eyes to the morning sun and realized the aroma I was smelling was coming from my Korean neighbors downstairs. When I got up, I called Hank and told him about Jules and everything else that had happened. Hank was surprisingly sympathetic, and he mostly just let me talk.

"That's some crazy shit," he said. "Sorry about your friend."

I then told him about Beryl, and Vidor, and what happened in Chinatown.

"I didn't know Richard was such a dick," he said. "And Cynthia, you don't need those headaches. Let her go ruin somebody else's life."

Since I didn't have a car, Hank offered to bring the two cats over to me. When he arrived, he had the cats, but he'd also stopped to get tacos from Yucca's. Hank knew exactly how to brighten up my day. We also finalized our plans for the Olympic Baseball game we were attending in a few days. The USA team had some good young players whom we both wanted to see, including Will Clark, Barry Larkin, and Mark McGwire. Before Hank left, I thanked him again for being such a good friend.

"Don't get too used to it," he smirked. "And also, don't forget, you're buying the beer and hot-dogs at the game."

Since I didn't know when I would get my Firebird back, I knocked on Mrs. Trask's door and offered to buy her 1970 Chevrolet Nova. I must have offered her the right price because she accepted my offer. I walked right to the bank and withdrew all the money I had.

At 4:30 PM, I sat down in front of my television to watch the opening ceremonies of the 1984 Summer Olympics. As I got comfortable, Maggie and Dottie curled up beside me. I already had decided to adopt them and become a pet owner. I think Beryl would have approved.

ABC Television was covering these Olympics. So, Peter Jennings, from their news division, and

Jim McKay from The Wide World of Sports were hosting the opening ceremonies. An audience of almost 90,000 people were packed into the Los Angeles Memorial Coliseum, with an audience of about two and a half billion viewers watching from home.

Before President Reagan officially opened The Games of the 23rd Olympiad, composer John Williams led the Olympic orchestra in the playing of his 1984 Los Angeles Olympic Fanfare, which he'd just written.

For me, the ceremonies' highlights were the flying man, floating in on his jet pack, and the eighty-four grand pianos that appeared when "Rapsody in Blue" was played. This reminded me of my neighbor, Vidor, who could have easily been one of those players.

By tradition, Greece led the parade of athletes. The host country, in this case the United States, was always last. In between those two, the countries enter in alphabetical order. The larger teams seemed to get the loudest ovations. Yugoslavia received an enthusiastic ovation because they had just hosted the 1984 Winter Olympics in Sarajevo.

Ed Burke, a hammer thrower, carried the United States flag and led the USA Olympic Team to the sound of John Phillip Sousa's "Stars and Stripes Forever." Everyone in the Coliseum stood and cheered. The cheers continued as the

U. S. athletes made their way around the Olympic track.

Then, to represent the many nationalities that reside in the City of Los Angeles, a parade of the city's residents, dressed in ethnic costumes represented their heritage, entered the stadium. It was amazing to see how many different cultures lived in our city. Native Americans, dressed in their traditional American Indian costumes represented the American nationality.

I found one of the photographs that Beryl had given me from the 1932 Olympics opening ceremonies. It was a wide-angle photo of all of the world's athletes standing exactly where they were now. I compared the old black and white photo to the color image on my television. Despite the fifty-two years that had passed, the two images were strikingly similar.

Epilogue

In almost every way, the 1984 Los Angeles Summer Olympics proved to be a success. Impressive athletic performances were displayed by Carl Lewis, winning four gold medals in track, and Mary Lou Retton, winning the USA's first women's all-around gold medal in gymnastics. The very first women's Olympic Marathon was won by USA's Joan Benoit. I knew my new friend, Wilfred, was pleased when West German swimmer, Michael Gross, "The Albatross," scored two gold and two silver medals in swimming.

Even though baseball was only a demonstration sport at these Olympics, Hank and I had fun. We watched the USA Team beat Chinese Taipei, Italy, and the Dominican Republic, only to lose to Japan, which finished in first place overall. As I expected, Hank took advantage of me regarding the beer and hotdogs, but I didn't mind.

Even though she'd missed out with being an Olympian herself, Wanda Jefferson was overjoyed when this year's women's USA basketball team won its first ever Olympic gold medal. Wanda was also happy for the USA's female sprinters, including Evelyn Ashford and Valerie Brisco-Hooks, who both won gold medals. Maybe Wanda's brother Bobby couldn't beat her in basketball, but he now had other bragging rights.

Sabre fencer, Peter Westbrook from Newark, New Jersey, won the first Olympic medal by a U. S. fencer in 24 years. The son of a black U. S. GI father and a Japanese mother, Peter's earliest childhood fencing inspiration was watching his hero Zorro wield a sabre on television. I wondered if Ralph Faulkner had staged any of those sword fights.

Speaking of television, the TV ratings for these Olympics went through the roof. About 90 percent of U. S. homes tuned in. Almost 200 million Americans watched, making these 1984 Summer Games the most viewed television event in history.

Ticket sales also set another record, with 5,797,823 tickets sold, almost doubling the old record set in Montreal.

Led by L. A. Olympic Organizing Committee President Peter Ueberroth, the 1984 Los Angeles Summer Olympics were the most financially profitable Olympics of all time, with a final profit of $250 million. Almost $100 million of that would stay in the city and create the LA84 Foundation, dedicated to youth sports and sports education. Coincidently or not, the only other Olympics to ever turn a profit, was the 1932 Los Angeles Olympic Games. It appears the city knows how to throw an Olympics.

Jules's murder trial became a media event and received much publicity. It was a staple on the nightly news. I was a key witness and had to testify over many days. The whole trial lasted a couple of years in all. During the trial, it came out that Betty had planned the whole thing and had convinced Matteo to help her carry it out. At the end, they were both convicted of first-degree murder and sentenced to life in prison. I was glad when it was finally over.

I wasn't surprised when Tom Williams called me regarding Len Sebastian's play when it was in rehearsals. Evidently, Sebastian's production team was at a loss at how to solve certain technical issues. Tom asked me if I would be willing to meet with the new stage manager and explain to him exactly how I made everything work. I said: "Sure. Hire me as an assistant, and I'll be glad to help." When Tom told me that wasn't going to happen, I simply said: "Good luck."

In 1985, my ex-girlfriend, Carol invited me to tour the newly renovated Wiltern Theatre. As she showed me around, I saw how beautiful the old building was once again. She was right, it looked just as good as it did back in 1931. Carol told me she and her husband, Douglas, were expecting their first baby. I was happy for them, but the news was still bittersweet.

Cynthia Aldrich did produce her movie version of Carlos Cruz's *Sonora Town*. The film garnered mostly negative reviews and disappeared quickly without a whimper. But with that film, Cynthia had now established herself as genuine Hollywood producer, doing lunch and making deals all around town. It saddened me to see how well she fit in with that crowd.

Just after the Olympics, my friend, Marvin Grossman, recommended me for a stage-managing job. It was for the 1985 Datsun Automobile's new car unveiling at the Shrine Auditorium. Datsun had gotten the entire 1984 USA men's gold medal winning gymnastics team, and the entire 1984 women's silver medal winning gymnastics team to make a public appearance. Just before they were to go on stage, I accidentally backed right into little Mary Lou Retton. It was like backing into a concrete post. I couldn't believe how strong she was. I apologized immediately, and she smiled that great smile of hers. It made my day.

After that event, I quit stage managing. I also put Vidor's typewriter away. To get by financially, Jake threw me work every now and then, having me deliver picture vehicles to various shoots around town. It was okay, but I eventually realized I needed to get a real job.

I found a small apartment in Long Beach, just three blocks from the ocean, and signed up for classes at Cal State Dominguez Hills, with the goal of getting my teaching credential. I knew I could work as a substitute teacher during the day, while I took classes at night. I actually enjoyed being back in college, and I started dating some cute young teachers. Life was pretty damn good at the beach.

Just days before I left Koreatown, I was having coffee and watching the morning news. Suddenly, my apartment began to shake. For a moment, I was confused, but then I realized it was an actual earthquake. The newsman on the TV excused himself, and then ducked right under his desk. Maggie and Dottie also went scurrying into the bedroom and under the bed. As I was supposed to, I stood in a nearby doorway. On the TV, they showed a view of the two cameramen just standing there doing their jobs, while the newsman was still hiding under his desk. Finally, after what seemed like forever, the earthquake stopped. It had been a strong quake. The newsman then sheepishly got out from under his desk and resumed his duties.

This earthquake became known as the Whittier-Narrows Earthquake, and it had registered a 5.9 on the Richter Scale. The shaking had been felt as far as San Diego to the south, and San Luis Obispo to the north. This was the strongest Southern California earthquake since that Sylmar Earthquake in 1971. I took this as a sign that it was a good time to leave town.

ABOUT THE AUTHOR

Peter Adum studied theater at The University of Southern California. After graduation, he worked on the staff at the Mark Taper Forum in Los Angeles. During this time, he wrote screenplays and plays. At the Taper, he adapted John Fante's novel *Dreams From Bunker Hill* for their literary cabaret. He also collaborated with Joyce Fante on the play *The Boys in the Backroom*, about the group of 1930s writers who gathered at the Stanley Rose Bookshop in Hollywood. For the past 25 years, Peter has been a teacher living in the Seattle area with his wife, Elizabeth, and their overly demanding cat, Ellie. In 2018 Amazon and Kindle books published his first novel, *A New Day Yesterday*, set in his hometown of San Pedro, California.

ACKNOWLEDGMENTS

I'd like to thank my good friends, Shelley Keeler and Tim Hannon, for proofreading early drafts of this novel, and giving me their suggestions for improvements. Also, my sincerest appreciation to John Budz and Vee Sawyer at Ward Street Press, for their skill, advice, and creativity. Without their help, you simply would not be reading this.

COLOPHON

A typeface can recall an era in memory. For that task Clarendon was chosen as the face of *Shaky City Welcomes the World*. Originally created in London in 1845, this wide slab-serif font was designed by Robert Besley and engraved by Benjamin Fox. Though always popular with designers, in the late 1960s and 1970s Clarendon was ubiquitous: on posters, logos, movie title sequences, magazine spreads, headlines, and book text. A new digital version was created in 2007 by Ray Larabie, the Super Clarendon family. It is this face with the distinctive Clarendon round ends (called ball terminals) on the lower case a, c, f, g, r & y.